Other Books by Niobia Bryant

Admission of Love

Three Times a Lady

Heavenly Match

Can't Get Next to You

Let's Do It Again

Count on This

Heated

Live and Learn

"Could It Be?" in
You Never Know

LIVE and LEARN

NIOBIA BRYANT

KENSINGTON PUBLISHING CORP.
http://www.kensingtonbooks.com

DAFINA BOOKS are published by

Kensington Publishing Corp.
119 West 40th Street
New York, NY 10018

All Kensington Titles, Imprints, and Distributed Lines
are available at special quantity discounts for bulk pur-
chases for sales promotions, premiums, fund-raising,
and educational or institutional use. Special book ex-
cerpts or customized printings can also be created to fit
specific needs. For details, write or phone the office of
the Kensington special sales manager: Kensington Publishing Corp., 119 West 40th Street, New York, NY 10018,
attn: Special Sales Department, Phone: 1-800-221-2647.

Dafina and the Dafina logo Reg. U.S. Pat. & TM Off.

ISBN-13: 978-0-7582-1721-9
ISBN-10: 0-7582-1721-8

First trade paperback printing: March 2007
First mass market printing: February 2010

10 9 8 7 6 5 4 3 2

Printed in the United States of America

After eight books, I'm going to be selfish and dedicate this one to my damn self. Hats off to me for my hard work in getting here and going even further.

(Yup, I went there. LOL)

Acknowledgments

To my family, friends, and loved ones—thank you for your love and support.

Big shouts to everyone at Compliments Hair Studio on North Maple Avenue in Irvington, New Jersey—yes, that was a shameless plug. LOL!

To the readers, this is different from my romance. It is the next level in my writing career. I thank y'all for having an open mind, heart, and wallet. Love y'all.

To Claudia Menza, thank you for your ear.

To Karen Thomas, thank you for the belief in my words.

To Gloria Naylor and Tina McElroy Ansa—my two favorite writers—thank you for putting pen to paper. You both inspire me.

To the haters—thank you for pushing me to step up my game every chance I get.

Prologue

Ladies

"Check *this* bitch out."

Three more pairs of eyes varying in shades of brown immediately darted like bullets to the feet of their unknowing victim. The woman sashayed by their table in the crowded nightclub with her head held high, unaware of their catty criticism and disdainful looks.

"Pay-*less*," the four friends sang in mocking uni son, distaste obvious on their faces as they thought of the national shoe store specializing in low-end footwear. It was one chain of stores they wouldn't dare frequent.

When it came to fashion, they searched for only the best labels: Gucci, Prada, Roberto Cavalli, Armani, and Dolce & Gabbana—just to name drop a few. Fresh hairdos and nails were weekly necessities. And when it came to the men who flittered in and out of their lives with the longevity of a lit match, only those who could afford their taste got a second look:

celebrities, athletes, and wealthy warriors of the streets who had blown up like a keg of TNT. *Unless* he had that "turn your straight roots nappy" kind of sex that the women enjoyed. But those sex-you-down brothas didn't get any of their real time—just late night calls to supply them with a nut, if their more financially set man at the moment couldn't do the job.

Alizé, Moët, "Dom" Perignon and Cristal—a.k.a. Monica Winters, Latoya James, Keesha Lands, and Danielle Johnson, respectively—were four childhood friends. They were sisters without the blood lineage with plenty of lessons to learn.

PART ONE

"Friends . . . how many of us have them?"
—Whodini

1

"Whassup y'all? I'm Alizé."

I'm anything but a morning person, especially *this* particular morning. Rah's king-sized water bed felt too damn good, and my body felt hella bad. A late night of drinking, partying, and then having sex until three in the morning will do that to you.

Last night my girls and I all met up at Lex's apartment—that's Dom's boyfriend—to celebrate his twenty-fifth birthday. Whoo! We got so tore up off Henny—ahem, Hennessey—that I didn't want to see any more liquor for a minute. I could feel the effects of it all up and through my body. Trust.

There was no way I was ready to face the world yet, but I had a ten o'clock class.

Trying like hell not to wake my man up, I eased up the arm he had over my waist. I couldn't do nothing but roll my eyes when he stirred in his sleep and tried to hold me tighter. Rah and I were cool. We were basically happy with each other, but when I wasn't in the mood to fuck, I just wasn't—in—the—

mood—to—fuck. Too bad I couldn't get *his* ass to understand that.

"Rah, I gotta get up. Move."

He shifted closer to me and pressed what I hoped was a piss hard against my bare ass. "Where you goin'?" he asked, his voice full of sleep and his morning breath reaching me like a slap in the face. His hand rose to tease my nipple as he started kissing my shoulder.

Now I was wishing like hell that I'd gone home to my mom's and not spent the night at his apartment. My own mother wasn't *this* aggravating, and she was Mrs. Persistence with an extra large, extra tall, big and bold-ass capital *P*. My daddy swears it's one of the main reasons they got divorced. I couldn't front on my father; my mother could be hell to reckon with.

But let me repeat, when I wasn't in the mood to fuck, there wasn't shit *anybody* could do to get me in the mood.

I shifted his hand from my breast, but he just moved it down to lift my leg up to play in my moistness. "Rah, I gotta go to class. Let me up."

I was a senior at Seton Hall University in South Orange, NJ, majoring in business finance. I loved money and all of the nice things it bought, so my major was an easy choice for me. Oh, trust, I'm a sistah with a plan when it comes to my career. I will graduate this May and then take full benefit of my two-month summer internship at one of the top investment firms in the country. Then in the fall it will be back to the grind at ole SHU to work on the all-important MBA—Master of Business Administration to some and More Banking of Assets to me.

I'm headed to the top of the corporate ladder with my MBA in one hand and my Gucci briefcase in the other as I take no prisoners and accept no shorts. I'm *going* to be part of the next wave of African-American women bursting through the glass ceiling. My name *will* be on *Fortune* magazine's Fifty Most Powerful Black Executives. *Black Enterprise* magazine will do a spotlight on me and my rise to the top. I ain't playing.

One thing I know about myself: if I set a goal I will reach it. Anyone not with my program can either ride with me or get run the fuck over. Period.

"Skip class."

See, *that* ain't a part of my program.

"Roll over, baby," he moaned against my neck as his hand rose again to claim my breast. Neither my body, mind, nor spirit was in the mood.

See, money is power, and right now Rah was thinking—whether he said it or not—that he was the money man in the relationship, so he could get this pussy whenever he wanted.

He thought wrong.

I turned on my back and looked up into his fine face with "the look"—a mix of faked sadness and regret that gets 'em every time. Trust. "Baby, I wish I had time, but I'm running late and I have a big test today that I can't miss," I lied with ease. "You know I get sleepy after sex."

Rah pulled me atop him and slapped my ass with a quick kiss to my cheek. "Get goin' 'fore I change my mind."

I felt like a prisoner who got a "get out of jail free" card. I didn't hesitate to roll out of bed and dash into the bathroom.

I literally jumped back at my reflection in the mirror. I looked like a cross between Don King and a raccoon with my thick shoulder-length hair all tangled and sticking up over my head. There were telling circles under my red-rimmed eyes that didn't look good at all against my bronzed cinnamon complexion. Drool was dried on my face.

Too much partying. Too much drinking. Too much damn fun. And it showed big-time.

After a long hot shower, a facial, a few eye drops, and getting rid of the tangles in my hair with a ventilated brush, I felt a *little* better. I could only shake my head at the condition of my hair. Even though I'd just been for my weekly appointment to the hairdresser yesterday, I would be on my cell at nine sharp making an appointment for later today. There's no way I'm sporting a dang-on ponytail all weekend.

Looking and dressing my best was important to me. See, my girls and I always made sure we stepped out of the house with our shit together from our hairdos to our Jimmy Choo shoes. This was a must.

All through high school and our entrance into early adulthood we were the popular ones. Other girls either hated us or wanted to be one of us. We kept our hair in the latest styles, and our gear was always the trend. We wore nothing but designer fashions: from the stonewashed Guess jeans and Timberlands of the nineties to Prada and Manolos in the new millennium.

Ever since our freshman year at University High there were always just the four of us. We looked out for one another. We had each other's back. There's an unbreakable trust between us built on ten years of friendship and sisterhood.

There's Latoya, Keesha, and Danielle, a.k.a. Moët, "Dom" Perignon, and Cristal. Dom came up with the nicknames one day back in 2000 while we were eating lunch in the caf. She got the idea from the late and great rapper Biggie Smalls' 1994 classic "Juicy." Those nicknames made us even more popular, and they've stuck ever since.

Six years later, although no one was really popping Dom as much, and Jay-Z had called for a boycott of Cristal because some bigwig had dissed hip-hop, we kept those names.

Oh, me? I'm Monica, but everyone *except* my parents calls me Alizé. No, I don't have a fancy champagne name like everyone else, but that's cool. Just like the drink, I'm the sweetest of the bunch anyway.

I didn't leave his bathroom until I wrapped a towel around my body because there was no need to tempt fate. I was too happy to open the door and find the bedroom empty. I heard him in the kitchen.

Good. He loved to catch me fresh from the shower or a bath and eat me out.

I grabbed my overnight bag and pulled out some fresh undergarments to hurry into. My cell phone rang. As I sprayed on the only perfume I wear— Happy, by Clinique—I picked my phone up and flipped it open, forgetting the mandatory check of my caller ID.

"Hey," I said in a little singsong fashion—my usual greeting.

"Whaddup, baby girl."

I felt my face wrinkle into a nasty frown as I recognized my ex's voice. I couldn't stand the sight, smell, or sound of Malik's sorry ass. This knucklehead tried to holler at Cristal behind my back.

That was a definite no-no.

Being the home girl Cristal was, she told me all about it . . . *after* she slapped the hell out of him.

But that wasn't the first time Cris and I didn't let a boy cause drama between us.

It was 1999. Freshman year of high school. New school. New faces. New rules. New cliques.

And since I was the only one from my elementary school to get accepted into University High, that meant new friends, but I had no worries.

I was looking good in the latest Parasuco gear. My bob was laid out, and my gold jewelry was in place. My pocketbook and bookbag were Gucci. My parents were *real* good to me. Being the only child had its benefits.

All eyes were on me as soon as I walked into my homeroom. The various conversations buzzing around the room lulled. A few of the boys whistled or shot me their "let me holla at you" smile. I went right into spin control and threw on a smile like I had the world in the palm of my hand. A few people smiled in return. A couple of girls immediately bent together, and I felt like they were talking about me.

There was an empty seat next to a tall, slender girl with skin the color of shortbread cookies. She was busy flirting back with a slender dark-skinned kid with long, asymmetrical braids and a big Kool–Aid smile. I made my way past the rows of students in chairs with attached desks, speaking to every last person I made eye contact with.

"Whassup," I said to Shortbread and Braids as I set my things on the long bookshelf behind us.

Braids looked at me from the tip of my fresh white Nikes to my eyes, not missing anything in between. There was no denying the interested look in his deep-set hazel eyes as he turned in his chair to face me and turned his back to Shortbread. "Better yet, shorty, how *you* doin'?"

I saw the disappointment on Shortbread's face, and even though he was as fine as Tyrese, I wasn't looking for drama this early in the school year. "I'll be doin' even better when you go back in her face and out of mine."

His pretty-boy face fell, and I knew lover boy was shocked that all his deliciousness rolled off my back like water.

Shortbread laughed, holding her hand over her mouth. "No need him turning this way again," she said with attitude.

"Oh, so both y'all gone play me?" he asked, straight white and even teeth flashing.

We both looked at him like "Negro, please."

He sucked his teeth, waved his hand, and turned to a dark-skinned cutie sitting in front of him.

Shortbread and I looked at each other, gave each other some dap, and then laughed at how we shut down his wanna-be playa ass.

"I'm Monica."

"Danielle."

We've been inseparable ever since, and we've always been loyal to each other.

Too bad Malik's dumb ass didn't know that.

"What you want?" I snapped, my eyes flashing as I focused my attention back on him. "No! As a matter of fact, who gives a shit?"

I slammed the phone closed, immediately dismissing that clown. True, his money had been good and he had been free-giving with it, but bump that, I don't need a no-good Negro trying to play me with one of my girls. When it comes to shit like that, I'm like Aretha: give me my R-E-S-P-E-C-T, understand?

Besides, I've moved on to bigger and better things. Malik didn't have nothing on Rah.

Once a big-time drug dealer, Rah had pooled his money and bought businesses that let him get out of the game before the game got him.

Okay, Malik can throw down a thousand times better in bed, but R-E-S-P-E-C-T, remember?

It's not like I ever loved Malik or even Rah for that matter. Shit, I've never been in love and that's fine by me. Love's nothing but a bunch of bullshit. What I wanted from men, I got: money, nights out on the town, shopping sprees, and companionship when I wanted it.

True, Cristal was always hounding me about my need for "thug love," but I liked me a roughneck. Timbs and "wifebeaters" turned me on more than suits and ties. A hard brotha with that swagger and an "I don't give a fuck" attitude made me wet while those whitewashed brothas (from the same corporate world I yearned to be a part of) made me laugh.

I can't explain it. I just liked what I liked.

Rah walked into the bedroom naked as the day he was born and smoking a blunt as thick as three fingers. I was glad my ass was already dressed.

A little shopping excursion would be good, but putting up with him and his minute-man sex wasn't on my agenda for the day.

He held the blunt between his straight and even teeth as he climbed back into bed. "What time you get out of class?"

"I have classes all day and my dance class tonight. Did you need something?"

"Naw, I'm straight. I'll be at the new store all day," he said, reaching for the remote to turn on the sixty-one-inch flat screen on the wall.

"Wish me luck on my test," I said, moving to the bedroom door.

"Good luck." He exhaled a thick silver cloud from his pursed lips. "Love you, baby girl."

"And I love you, too," I said without pause.

Another lie. Maybe the biggest of them all.

2

"Hello, how are you doing? I am Cristal."

"**G**ood morning, Platinum Records, please hold."

I used a clear coated half-inch fingernail to push down the small button marked hold on the multi-line phone system. I slanted my hazel cat-shaped eyes up to the brotha who stood before my desk with a cocky "you know you want me" pose.

He was Bones. The label's newest rap artist whose self-titled debut album just went platinum. The fool actually looked like one of those guys in a prison photo still trying to be down like they were in a club and not in jail. Hands on hips, legs apart, chin tilted up like "What?"

Oh, he was nice looking in a roughneck, corner thug sort of way, but unlike my less discriminating best friends, I do not go for the allure of a thug. Baggy blue jeans, untied Timbs, and a white T-shirt (which I refuse to call a wifebeater) do not make my panties moist. Now, do not get me wrong, I appreci-

ate a man with an urban attitude, but I want it mixed
with a little of the sophistication I read about in
magazines and see in those old black-and-white
movies I love so much. Tailored suits and ties.
Culture-filled dates. Legal income. Stability.

So this man/child standing before me trying to
look and dress like he was mad at the world was
definitely not my type.

"Can I help you?" I asked in a friendly manner,
forcing a smile to my round, pretty face.

"Damn, lovely, how *you* doin'?" he asked, his grave
voice full of that unmistakable East Coast accent.

"Fine, and yourself?" I answered.

Working as the sole receptionist for one of the
hottest Black-owned record companies—and looking as good as I do with redbone appeal—I was
pushed up on by many of the male artists and members of their entourages. Thus, looking up at Bones
as he gave me a toothy grin did not send my senses
reeling like he obviously thought it would.

Back when I first started working here, I got a
little star struck at times, but now . . . humph, now
I make them feel they should be just as honored to
meet *me* as I am supposed to be about meeting
them. Okay? All right.

I learned early and often in the game not to out-
right offend these thugs. They were quicker than a
fly to shit to call you a bitch or a whore, and then
turn around and tell you, "You ain't all that anyway."

Now, my girl Dom does not give a damn. If she
does not want to speak, there is not a soul alive
that can make her. Alizé is like me and just plays it
nicely. And Moët? Well, she has the kind of innate
sweet charm that can soothe a savage beast. Men

want to care for her, when in fact she has the smarts and the strengths to take care of herself if she wants.

Yes, I loved my friends, but I was woman enough to admit that I envied them. They all had families. Even Dom had Diane, who was not much of a mother, but she beat a blank. And Alizé and Moët had futures ahead of them. Both were graduating college this year, and I could only wish I could have afforded to go.

I grew up an orphan. I had no family. I have never been in love. I could not afford college. I was barely making ends meet to pay the rent on my one-bedroom apartment in The Top, a luxury apartment complex just outside of the Livingston suburbs.

Struggle as I might, I was not downgrading. My next step out of The Top would be into even more luxurious surroundings.

I outgrew the ghetto. Newark was no longer my home. I did not even claim it. In my opinion, why should I? Sure the girls always gave me a hard time about my feelings, or rather lack of them, for my hometown. It had not been good to me, so why should I be good to it. Okay? All right.

"Go right on up. Mr. Linx is on his way into the office," I told Bones, finally directing my attention back to the man/child standing before me. I quickly but smoothly moved my hand as he reached for it.

Bones just smiled. "Later, shorty," he hollered over his shoulder as he walked toward the elevator with his entourage in tow.

I waved and ducked my head, not wanting to make any contact that suggested that I was eager for that later. I did not release the breath I was holding until he and his associates gathered noisily onto the elevator. The chrome doors closed, and they were gone from my view.

More of the phone lines lighted up. I put three on hold and answered the earlier call. "Platinum Rec—"

The rest of the words froze in my slender throat as *he* walked through the rotating chrome doors. I inhaled *and* exhaled, trying to cool my reaction. In my eyes there was a glow around him. He seemed to move in slow motion. Harps played a tributary tone in my head.

He was Sahad Linx, CEO and founder of Platinum Records. The producer turned record executive shaped the multiplatinum success of all of his artists and built one of the most financially successful hip-hop labels in a very short amount of time.

Sahad, the CEO, the producer, the entrepreneur, the sexiest man alive, the porn star of my wet dreams; but most importantly, one of the wealthiest African-American men around.

Lawdy. Lawdy. Lawdy.

A diamond-encrusted Chris Aire watch winked from his wrist. His suit was so obviously hand tailored as it flowed on his tall frame. Rimless aviator Gucci shades were in place on his handsome, angular face. Italian shoes softly cushioned his feet. Classy diamond jewelry glistened from his neck, wrists, and hand. The scent of his Ralph Lauren cologne blended in the air with my own Ralph Lauren Glamorous perfume.

He was the new era of the Black elite. Urban. Hip. Smart. Wealthy.

And I was going to have him. Okay? All right.

3

"Hey. I'm Moët."

"Let us pray."

My parents, my two preteen sisters, Reverend Luke DeMark, and I—Latoya Shavonne James—all clasped hands and bowed our heads around the dinner table. My father said grace.

The Reverend DeMark was the minister of our family church, The Greater Temple of Jesus Christ. He ate dinner with my family every single Thursday night after prayer meeting. He wasn't married, and my mama, a doting soul, felt it was her Christian duty to make sure he got a good home-cooked meal at least once a week.

Not that Reverend DeMark was starving. The rest of the days he either ate with another family, or one of the single-and-looking ladies from the congregation fixed a meal to take to the one-family house where he lived alone. The fact that these women considered the thirty-four-year-old minister an eligible bachelor was quite obvious.

My parents were his most devout and loyal members. Sister Lou Mae and Deacon Saint James (he tried hard to live up to his name) never missed worship services, prayer meetings, church conventions, or Bible studies. They tithed *both* their incomes, participated in fund-raising, and lived for the Word of the Almighty. They crossed the *t*'s and dotted the *i*'s when it came to being good Christian soldiers for the Lord.

And they expected nothing less from their children.

"Sister James, this roasted turkey is *di*-vine," the Reverend exclaimed. The gold and diamonds from his pinky ring sparkled under the glare of the ceiling light. He wiped his lips with a linen napkin. "You are truly blessed with your cooking skills."

"Why, thank you, Reverend DeMark," my mother answered, her southern Alabama accent still prominent even after living in Jersey for thirty years.

My mother looked the role of a good Christian wife in her prim white button-up blouse and knee-length navy skirt. Her hair, which she refused to cut, flowed to the middle of her back when she let it down. Even though she tried to hide how pretty she was, she couldn't. At sixty, without one drop of make-up on, she was naturally beautiful. And so she demanded the same of us, telling her daughters to remain unpretentious as well . . . just the way God meant us to be.

Tonight my chin-length hair was pulled back into a severe ponytail—Cristal swore my edges were going to fall out. My unflattering spectacles were in place on my slender face. My ears aren't pierced. No make-up. No jewelry. Nothing.

God must have also meant for women not to wear pants, skirts above the knee, or anything remotely fitted. My closet at home was filled with plenty of my respectful garments. Not a pair of jeans or slacks. No shorts to save my life.

At twenty and a senior at Seton Hall U., I had a curfew of ten o'clock because my father thought "no decent woman would be caught on the street alone that time of night." The only reason it was even ten o'clock was because of a mandatory class I had to take that didn't end until 9:15 P.M. I couldn't wait to graduate with my degree in Elementary and Special Education this May. I was going to get me a full-time teaching J-O-B so that I could be O-U-T my parents' house.

With the strict rules we lived by, I felt like a sect of Black Quakers living in the city. Any deviations from the rule meant a thorough guilt trip on the sins of the Lord, a three-hour prayer session, and fasting so that the Lord could forgive his wayward child. I learned that lesson when I was twelve and got caught wearing strawberry-tinted lip balm from Avon that a classmate had given me.

To my parents I am the perfect child. Demure. Loyal. Respectful. Trustworthy.

If only they knew.

Dinner continued in silence until the shrill and alarming ring of the lone telephone in the house jarred us from our serenity. We all jumped at the sound of it and then laughed nervously.

"I'll get it," I said, keeping neutrality in my tone as I set my fork down on my plate slowly. Sudden movements made my father suspicious. The last thing I wanted was to draw his attention to me, because that would only mean being judged or scolded. That was all the attention I ever got from him.

The look on his stern face was immediately disapproving. "Latoya, you know we don't take calls during dinner."

Yes, I knew that, but it was worth a try.

The shrill ringing continued, persistent just like a hungry baby seeking a bottle.

I watched as Reverend DeMark eyed the phone in the next room. "Deacon James, perhaps Sister Latoya should answer it. I don't think whoever it is will quit until someone does."

As soon as he spoke I pushed my chair. I knew before my father even uttered the words that I could *now* answer the phone.

"James residence." I stepped out of my father's line of piercing vision.

"Whaddup, girl? What the hell took so long answering the phone. Y'all praying or sum'n?"

I smiled at the sound of Dom's raspy voice. My parents would clutch their hearts at her use of slang and profanity. "We're eating supper, so I can't talk long."

"Supper!" Dom shrieked. "Girl, y'all cracks me the fuck up."

"Dom."

"A'ight. I'll holla at you real quick," she said around a piece of gum that she was popping like firecrackers on the Fourth of July. "I got your perfume for you."

"The Freedom by Hilfiger?"

Dom sighed heavily into the phone. "No, the

Timeless from Avon," she said sarcastically. "Of course the Freedom. That's all your ass wear, ain't it?"

It's all I wore, and it was all I wanted. "Thanks, Dom."

"Guess who's diggin' you?"

I edged around the corner some more, lowering my voice to a whisper. "Who?"

"Lex's partner Rayvaun's cousin's baby father—"

"Dom," I whispered shortly. "Get to the point."

She sighed again. "A'ight. 'Member Tsari?"

Oh, I remembered Tsari all right. The man put Morris Chestnut to shame with his deep chocolate appeal, but he had more women than a dirty dog had fleas. "Please," I whispered, rolling my eyes in dismissal.

"He wanted your number."

My eyes widened like saucers. "To my house?" I whispered in horror, my heart nearly jumping out of my chest. "You didn't give it to him, did you?"

"Hell no. I know your wardens be trippin' and shit."

"Thank you, Jesus." Relief filled me in waves

"How you live in a house and can't even have men call you?"

"I got my cell phone, Dom."

"Your Mama ain't snooped up on it yet?" Dom asked, completely aware of my parents' strict ways.

"No. It's in my book bag. She doesn't go in it."

"Yet," Dom snapped. "Look, your ass better be careful. If they knew about the second set of clothes you keep to Cristal's, they'd lock you in your room and douse you with holy water."

I forced a laugh at her teasing, although part of

me was ashamed of it all. At Cristal's I was able to change into the tight jeans, stilettos, makeup, and fly gear that I loved.

A double life.

Latoya the Christian at home; Moët everywhere else.

"Girl, I got to go—"

"Latoya?"

I jumped at my father's stern voice so suddenly behind me. "No, we're not interested in vinyl siding at this time, but thank you," I improvised quickly.

"And they say people in the projects is crazy." Dom laughed before hanging up.

I replaced the receiver on the base and turned to face my father. His small, thin face was frowning, and I wondered if I'd ever seen him smile. Shit, I can't remember the last time he hugged me or said he loved me. But that's the hypocrisy of church folks preaching love and can't even show love in their own home. "Telemarketer," I said weakly with a nervous giggle, before walking past him quickly to reclaim my seat.

He followed me back into the dining room, and dinner resumed.

My mind was steady on getting up to my room, or rather my haven, when I felt a warm, masculine hand squeeze the top of my thigh. Heat infused my body, and my cheeks warmed as I looked over at the good and honorable reverend.

No one else at the table was aware of him inching my skirt up around my thighs under the table with his right hand. Nor were they aware when one of his long fingers slid under the band of my prim white cotton briefs.

Wanting him to get just what he was seeking, I opened my legs, letting his probing hand play in the warm hairs and moist flesh. I had to bite down on my fork to keep from moaning in sweet pleasure.

No one knew that the good and honorable Reverend Luke DeMark and I had been lovers since I was seventeen.

That was why I was not as devout a Christian as my parents thought. My beliefs definitely were not as strong as theirs. It was hard to believe in God when one of His own disciples was sexing the hell out of you in between sermons.

4

"I'm Dom. What?"

"**P**layers . . . ballers . . . shot callers. Welcome . . . to Club XXXcite!"

I squinted my eyes against the silver haze of smoke I exhaled and looked through the stank-ass curtain at Vic, the club owner, out on the stage.

Damn, Mookie got the best weed ever. Three tokes and I was already feelin' it. I was gettin' seriously f'ed up.

Ain't no shame in my game. Besides, I wasn't the only one gettin' blunted. Streams of thick smoke drifted up from different corners of the crowded club. There was no mistakin' the scent in the air.

I checked out the crowd. The spot was live tonight. Good. The *ching-ching* of money was ringin' all up in my ears. I was gonna drain these m'fers for all I could. I was here to get paid. Straight up.

Maybe even enough to buy those bad-ass Cole Haan boots I saw in Nordstroms last week.

"Give it up for a club favorite. Her name says it all. Here's . . . Juicy!!"

I took one last drag from the blunt, lettin' it fill my lungs as Vic finished my introductions. "Here, Candy," I called over to another dancer waitin' backstage. I handed her the blunt. "Go 'head and kill that."

She took it with the tips of her four-inch acrylic nails. How she washed her ass, I don't know.

"Is it laced?" Candy asked, her eyes already glassy.

"Hell, no," I snapped.

Candy stepped back from the pissed-off look on my face. "Chill out, Dom."

"What a blunt and some damn Henny don't do for me, I don't need," I spat, angry as hell that she thought I'd lace my weed with cocaine or pedope.

"Whatever," she sighed, before she walked away on five-inch heels in her pink sheer baby doll.

"Dumb ass," I muttered, forgettin' about her as I stepped through the break in the curtain to take my spot on the T-shaped stage.

The lights lowered, and the spotlight fell on me. I felt like Mary J., Alicia Keys, Beyonce, or some shit. A star. All eyes on me. Wantin' *me*.

But I can't sing.

I don't act.

I ain't rich.

I'm a stripper. So?

"I'm N Luv (Wit a Stripper)" by T-Pain started playin' loud as hell, drainin' out that ying-yang them fellas was hollerin' at me from the floor. I'm glad 'cause I just wanna shake a little ass, flash a little titty, get my loot, and head to the crib.

A bunch of regulars from Hawthorne Avenue started singin' along with the song, their champagne bottles and Heinekens swayin' in the air as I gave them m'fers a reason to fall in love.

Dressed in nothing but my red plastic thong and thigh-high boots, I danced to the music, slow and sexy, just the way these hardheads wanted. I could dance my ass off, and when it came to performin', I could work my body like a snake and make my ass tremble more than a saltshaker.

Being a stripper you can't have hang-ups and shit. When I was on stage I was willing to do whatever to make my money. It was my job to turn these cats on. That's why I was the best at Club XXXcite.

Squattin', I knew they didn't have to imagine a damn thang as all my business pushed forward like a fist. Bam!

Them fellas went wild, and the paper money fell down around me like rain.

That's what the hell I'm talkin' about. Makin' that loot. Dollar dollar bills, y'all.

I finished my set, grabbed my cash, and hauled ass off stage.

Sweat was pourin' off me as I walked that walk in my stilettos and counted my cash. One hundred and ten, thirty, fifty, seventy-five, two hundred dollars. That was cool. We made the real money durin' the club's showdown. That was when all of the dancers either mingled with the crowd givin' lap dances or took customers into one of the special rooms for some freak-a-deak private dances and who knows what the hell else.

I danced. I gave hellified lap dances. I might even let a dude suck a tittie or two, but no fuckin', no suckin', and no dykin'. Period.

I went downstairs to the dressing room. Man, it smelt like old fish and feet up in this piece. Damn.

I grabbed my Coach leather sac from my locker just as my cell phone rang. Flippin' it open, I answered it. "What?"

"Kimani wants to talk to you, if you ain't too busy shakin' that *little* ass of yours."

Oh, Lord, here we go. I hated to hear the sound of Diane's—she's my mother—voice when she was in her "I'm a bitch" mode. She was trippin' again 'cause I stuck her with baby-sittin' my four-year-old daughter, Kimani. Okay, it *was* foul for me to lie and tell her I was going to the store when I knew I was really headed to Lex's for me a good dickin' down before I went to work.

Ain't like I never did it before. Dang, she should be used to it.

"Diane, you wasn't complainin' about me strippin' last week when I bought that big screen TV for your bedroom," I snapped back.

"You want that sorry m'fer back, because you can *have* that sorry m'fer back," she yelled at me through the phone line.

See where I get my nasty mouth? Diane's a straight wacko. Either she boostin' me up to do this shit—talkin' 'bout make that money—*or* she wreckin' my nerves tellin' me I'm wrong. Her praise or criticism depended on her moods, which depended on whether she was f'ed up or not.

Ready to get off the phone, I promised to bring her some goodies so she would calm her ass down: a six-pack of Smirnoff Ice—which she drinks like water—and a couple of Philly blunts. You know she wanted a little sum'n sum'n to go *in* the blunts.

To get ready for the showdown I wiped the sweat from my body with a towel and did a couple of spritzes of my favorite perfume, Beautiful by Estee Lauder. I threw on a two-piece sheer bathing suit and headed upstairs before all the free-givin' customers were taken.

Funny-colored lights flashed around me as I danced around in the dark until I chose my first mark. I didn't feel nervous. Ain't had no shame. I just wanna make my money. These men don't mean shit to me. Most of the time I'm thinkin' 'bout anything but the m'fers while I'm grindin' on 'em.

I saw a big buff brotha still in his work uniform with a wad of money in his hand tryin' to catch my eye. I saw the glint of his wedding ring on that left hand, too, but that ain't my damn problem, ya heard me? I headed straight in his direction.

He was a new face in the crowd. Another lost soul lookin' for a damn fantasy. As I gave him a lap dance—grinding against his hardness—I had to hold my breath to keep from swallowin' down the stank of his breath *and* his crotch.

Damn.

What people do for money.

Girl Talk

Dom, Cristal, Alizé, and Moët walked up Fifth Avenue together. Their shopping bags were swinging from their hands, their hair blowing freely in the slight winds. The energetic sounds of New York were their background music: the blaring horns, squeal of tires on pavement, and the music pumping from passing vehicles that whizzed past.

"What's better than shopping on a nice Saturday afternoon with your friends?" Cristal asked, using a hand to shift her Morgenthal Frederics shades up farther on her pretty round face.

Dom just shrugged and lit another Newport cigarette.

"Lunch at Justin's after shopping on a nice Saturday afternoon with your friends," Moët chimed in, sweetly smiling at a sexy police officer on horseback who winked at her.

"Aw, hell no. I know what's better." Three sets of eyes turned on Alizé. "Having great sex all night *long, after shopping with your friends and having lunch at Justin's on a nice Saturday afternoon,"* Alizé answered, lightly knocking her shoulder against Moët's as they came to a stop on the corner.

"Now that sounds like a f'ing plan," Dom drawled.

The four friends all burst out with laughter.

5

Alizé

I never been in love before, but I'm not sad about it because I wanted it that way. To me, love is a weakness. Love, or at least *thinking* you're in love, will fool you into doing some dumb shit. Like letting a man beat up on you. Or cheat on you. Or not support you. Or wait for him to come back to you after he leaves you.

Love shouldn't be a reason to settle for less. I learned that lesson a long time ago when I was fifteen and I let my boyfriend, Marquee, convince me that my first time making love should be in this dingy little sewing room in his best friend's house. See love—or *thinking* I was in love—had me carry my hot ass right up in that room that was no bigger than a walk-in closet and give up my innocence like it was nothing. Later on I found out all of the neighborhood boys used that same little room, with that same little twin bed, as their same little ho central.

Nice memory, right?

That was many years and numerous male "friends" ago, and my love life isn't faring any better now. Everlasting love just isn't in the cards for me. I'm fine with that because I will never fool myself into believing I am in love again.

I'm sick and tired of taking chances with my heart, colliding with liars, cheaters, and beaters until my fairy-tale prince finally comes into my life and proclaims himself "the one."

Hell, as much as I loved my daddy, my mama's love didn't keep his black ass home working on the "happily ever after" and "until death do us part." But that same love had her putting her own life on pause while she waited for him to "realize" that he wanted his family back. How many times did I listen to my mother speak of my father as if they were still married? As if he were gone for the day to work and not gone for good living in his own apartment across town. She called on him to do any repairs around the house. She fixed his favorite meals just hoping he would stop by to see me on his way home from work.

All the while I watched as Daddy blocked her advances, missed the dinners, called repairmen instead of coming himself, and did everything short of hurting her more to let her know it was over.

Love? Oh, love is a stupid fat nothing.

I don't need or want to be in love with *someone*. No, not when I'm in love with *something*.

All the love I had in me—that love I refused to share—I poured into my dancing. As much as I loved my mom and dad, and as tight as I was with my girls, none of them really understood the thang I had for dancing.

They didn't know that when I danced I was in a world all alone. I would put on an R & B or jazz CD and turn up the volume so loud that the music seemed to press and beat upon my body. I would close my eyes and take my position in front of the mirrored wall, shaping and molding my body with the freedom of a silk scarf blowing in a gentle wind. My heart would feel light in my chest, and I would become out of breath but never tired, not with the energy that filled my body as I easily moved through the dance steps. And sometimes, as the music wound down, I would end with a swaying of my hips and find that I was crying.

I never missed a dance class. No parties, no classes, no fellas, and not even a mad clearance sale at Saks could keep me away from that dance studio.

I *loved* dancing. I was in love with it. It was my passion. No man would ever compete.

Yet unlike the twenty or so other dancers in my class, I had no interest in dancing professionally. I'm not a member of the Screen Actors Guild. I don't have an agent mailing me scripts or sending me and my head shots on auditions and casting calls.

Hell, I don't even have a head shot.

When some of the kids read off their resumes and sounded like the Who's Who of the Great White Way, I had no envy. Dancing was in my soul, in the air I breathed, and in the blood that pumped through my veins. I didn't want it to become my means of financial support because that would dim the love and passion.

The owner of Dance with Dana Studios, Dana Shanes, was a Dance Theatre of Harlem alum. She allowed me free usage of one of the twelve studios in her converted warehouse. Usually once a week after classes ended, I patiently waited for the kids to empty out of the dance studio. And it was during that hour that the dance steps in my dreams came to life.

Although no one would ever see it—I did it just for me—I still wanted it to be tight. So tonight after class, I started the CD player and walked to the center of the hardwood floor. It didn't matter that my hair was pulled up into a bun or that I didn't have on makeup. My favorite leotards were well worn, and when I danced in my bare feet I sometimes chipped the perfect polish on my pedicured toes. But see, none of that mattered in *here*.

The music began to play. I closed my eyes and let myself get lost in the notes playing around me. Every spin, every split, every lift of my legs and arms made me feel like I was soaring. My heart pounded from the exertion. Sweat trailed down the crevices of my body.

With one last touch of my fingers to the sky, I slid down into a frontward split before curling my slender frame into a ball.

Sudden applause pushed me back into the real world with a jolt. I opened my eyes and looked up to find Rah leaning against the ebony baby grand piano, his hands still clasped together.

He's my man, true enough, but I don't like anyone messing with my time to dance.

Nobody.

"Hey, Rah, whassup?" I swallowed back my irritation.

"Nothing. I was in Manhattan handling some business, so I dropped by to give you a ride home."

"Thanks, baby," I said, turning my back to him as I rolled my eyes heavenward. I turned off the CD player and removed my disc.

Inside I was pissed the hell off, but this man was my bread and butter right now. I put on this fake smile, pretending I'm happy to see his intruding ass.

Rah was only twenty-seven, and he already owned several thriving businesses in Newark. There was the beauty supply store on Springfield Ave., the upscale clothing store on Broad Street downtown, and Sweet Things, the shoe store on Halsey Street. He took the money he had made slinging dope across the Tri-State area for the last ten and put it into profitable businesses.

And I had to admit that the brotha was fine.

He was six feet of solid muscle, and looking so good in a Sean John velour jogging suit. His platinum and diamond jewelry was sparkling like crazy. His "I don't give a fuck" attitude, with that tilt to his chin and the hooded lids of his eyes, was what first drew me to him.

I saw it in his eyes now that he was getting turned on looking at me in my tight-fitting leotards, but sex in the studio was a definite no-no. This was my private place. Mine alone.

"Let me get my stuff." I walked over to the corner where my purse and duffel bag sat. I pulled my pale blue JLo sweat suit over my dance clothes and pushed my feet into my newest pair of sneakers.

"I got a surprise for you," his deep voice echoed over to me.

I looked up from my cell phone as I turned it

back on. The smile on his handsome face—think Morris Chestnut—was teasing. I wondered if my surprise was the tropical strapless dress I showed him in BCBG last week. Or the ABS wrap dress at Saks. Or was it that cute Gucci camel hobo bag we saw at Short Hills Mall?

"What is it?" I finally asked as we left the brick warehouse building together.

"Patience," was all he said.

His silver Mercedes sat at the curb still as clean as the day he drove it off the lot. Our reflections shone in the polished chrome of his twenty-four-inch rims.

As I climbed in, I peeped out the backseat for any signs of shopping bags, but I didn't see a blessed thing except the usual CDs and Philly blunt cigars scattered about.

"Come on, Rah. What's my surprise?" I asked again, unable to fight my curiosity.

Rah just smiled as he pulled into the busy New York traffic with a soft purr of the motor. He reached down on the side of his seat and tossed a bag of weed onto my lap. "Roll one for me, baby."

I did a double take. True, back in high school I smoked weed like that shit was my lifesaver, but I slowed up on it big-time once I started college. I smoked it only twice with Rah back when we first got together, but no more since. My plan for success, remember?

Hell, back when I *was* smoking Dom under the table, I still wasn't the type of chick to get excited over a man giving me weed.

Was this fool for real or just stupid?

Even as I busted the cigar down the middle with

my thumbnail and emptied the leaves out the window to scatter in the wind behind us, I was steady thinking, *This better not be my surprise 'cause he know I don't play this dumb shit.*

Our relationship worked so well for me because he liked to give and I *loved* to receive. We were a perfect match on that point, right?

"*This* is my surprise?" I asked.

"Hell no. Patience, remember?"

Rah drove his whip smoothly through the New York traffic and into New Jersey, smoking the entire blunt by himself like it was a cigarette. He was steady profiling for any onlookers with his tinted window down, leaning back in the seat with his arm straight as he steered the wheel *and* showed off his new diamond-encrusted Jacob & Co. Five Time Zone watch.

Of course, I was showing off, too. My window was down so that all the females on the cramped buses and walking the streets could see me. They were all hating on me; I knew it and *loved* it.

"You staying with me?" he asked, already pulling into the parking garage of the high-rise Harlequin Apartment building in downtown Newark.

"I guess so, since we're already here." I laughed as I got out of the car.

He climbed out as well and went to the trunk. My heart raced. Disappointment slowed the rate as I watched him pull out his massive CD case.

I didn't say a word as we rode the elevator upstairs.

Cristal failed to understand why a man with his own businesses wouldn't want to own his own home or at least move into a higher end apartment building. She said, "Why do people care more about what they are driving than where they are living? Just ghetto."

She acted like the man lived in the projects or something, but that was just Cris being her usual bougie self. She liked to pretend her ass wasn't from Newark like the rest of us. Always talking proper. Hell, I haven't heard her use a contraction since high school. I still love her stuck-up butt, though.

Rah and I walked into his apartment. It's decked out and you could tell it's a man's space with the ebony furnishings, glass and chrome tables, and the mirrored walls. I dropped my duffel bag on the floor by the door, before I followed his sculptured physique into his master bedroom—or what he liked to call the *master's* bedroom.

"I'm going to shower," I told him, removing my clothes as I strode to the adjoining bathroom with the grace only a dancer could possess. Don't hate.

I preferred to take a hot bath after dance class to help relax my muscles, but I sure didn't feel up to fighting a dirt ring before I could sit down in his tub. A shower it was.

I left the bathroom ten minutes later smelling like soap, with a plush, oversized gray towel wrapped securely around my damp body.

"Damn, I'm tired," I sighed, drawing the words out as I lay down beside Rah on his king-sized water bed.

He was lying back smoking yet another blunt as he watched the ten o'clock news on WWOR-TV. Probably trying to see if any of his friends were arrested today or getting a heads-up on the latest police technology. He offered me the blunt, but I declined. Still, that didn't stop me from catching a contact. Second-hand smoke is second-hand smoke.

Soon my lids felt heavy, and I watched through half-closed eyes as Rah rolled off the bed and left the bedroom. I heard when he came back, but I still jumped in surprise at the sudden feel of something cold and metal against my neck.

My eyes flew open, and I shot up in bed. A delicate gold and diamond chain with a matching cross pendant dropped into my lap.

Bling.

Now see, *that's* what I'm talking about.

I loved it. This was so much classier than all the other ghetto jewelry he gave me—which I also loved, but there was a time and place for everything. I could actually wear this one to my internship.

I removed the Bismarck chain I was wearing and clasped my new one around my slender neck, already picturing all the new V-neck shirts I would buy to wear with my new trinket. Every wall in Rah's bedroom was covered in mirrors, so any way I turned I saw my reflection. That chain and diamond pendant looked good as hell against my smooth caramel skin.

"Ooh, Rah, this is just too delicious. Thank you, baby."

When he didn't respond, I turned to see him busy rolling another blunt over by his black marble dresser.

I lay back sprawled in the middle of the bed, licking my lips as my hand rubbed a trail from my thighs up to my small but firm round breasts.

"That's what I'm talkin' 'bout, baby girl. Do you," Rah said eagerly, clamping down on the blunt with his teeth as he grabbed a chair and pulled it close to the bed to take a seat.

Rah was a big-time freak, and he loved to get off on watching me play with myself. Well, tonight was his lucky night.

As he leaned back in his chair, watching me with his eyes squinted against the heavy silver haze of his weed, my new chain had me feeling pretty damn freaky myself.

I licked my lips as I spread my legs as wide as I could and then spread my *other* lips with my fingers. I purred like a kitten at the feel of my cool fingers against my wet bud, squirming as I massaged it deeply in circles.

Rah shook his head and smiled, standing to drop his sweatpants and boxers to his ankles before he sat down again. He massaged his hardness with one hand and smoked his blunt with the other. "You love playin' in that kitty, don't you?"

Shit, I forgot all about his ass because I was busy going for mine. I licked my lips and closed my eyes as my fingers worked my G-spot. "Uhmmm," I moaned in pleasure, arching my back and spreading my legs even more.

I looked up at the feel of Rah's warm hands on my breasts. He was kneeling between my legs on the bed. I gasped as his fingers played with my aching nipples while he deeply massaged the chocolate globes.

I stroked my wetness with my other hand as we stared into each other's eyes. With a wicked smile I slid those moist fingers into his open mouth and purred as he sucked the juices. "Good?" I asked.

"Mmm hmm."

The energy in the room switched, and for the first time in a long time I *wanted* to have sex with Rah. I wanted to feel his hands on me. I wanted to feel him inside me.

The first time in a long damn time.

I pulled him down atop me and wrapped my legs around his waist as my hands clasped his head, bringing it down to mine so that I could suck his lips whole. I opened my lips at his tongue's probe and enjoyed the taste of it as he suckled my own tongue deeply, like he drew life from it. The hairs of his chest tickled my breasts, and he shifted his hands down to massage my buttocks.

I could feel my vagina jumping to life. It throbbed. It got wetter. The lips swelled and my clit ached.

I sighed as he shifted his weight to take one of my breasts into his mouth. His tongue circled the nipple before he lightly nipped it with his teeth.

"Yes, yes. Suck 'em," I moaned, putting my hands between us to lightly tease my pulsating bud again.

His sucking of my nipples deepened, and I shivered.

With my hand I groped for his dick and enjoyed the feel of the hard heat in my hand as I stroked it 'til the tip dripped with his own juices.

I didn't even stop him as he put gentle hickies on the flesh of my breasts and neck. It made me want him more.

Ready to feel the sweet waves of my release, I pushed him onto his back and straddled his hips like a pro.

"You gone ride that dick?" he asked, his eyes half closed as he looked up at me with a fine sheen of sweat coating his muscled body.

"Damn right." I held his hardness straight as I positioned my open core right on the throbbing tip.

His hands squeezed my breasts and teased my nipples the way he knew I loved as I dropped down onto his heated penis.

His mouth formed a circle. "Damn, girl. Damn."

I was so excited that I was more wet than I liked, so I bent down to where the hard base of his penis rubbed against my clit as I grinded my hips like I was on a mission.

He arched his back and I rode him harder.

He slapped my ass and I rode him faster.

"I want to come," I whispered against his open mouth before I suckled his tongue as deeply as I drew his shaft inside my gripping walls.

"Come for me," he said huskily, his eyes watching me.

Then I felt his release fill me just as the rhythmic spasms of my inner walls coated every inch of him. "Yes," I sighed. "Yes, yes, yes."

Slow and deliberate, I continued to ride him, working my hips as I clutched him tightly with my arms and thighs. "I'm coming," I whispered over and over as my nipples tingled and my entire body quivered.

Even after the waves subsided and my pounding heart slowed to a normal beat, I lay on Rah's chest with his dick planted inside of me. Soon his snores rumbled beneath my ear on his chest, but I lay there long into the night feeling unsettled, unhappy, and unsatisfied.

And I didn't have a clue why.

6

Cristal

"Welcome, ladies. I'm glad to see you all, but you know the deal," I told my friends straight from the door *at* the door.

Alizé, Dom, and Moët all grumbled but removed their shoes before entering, just the way I wanted. I collected their winter coats and hung them up in the closet in the foyer.

My entire living room area was decorated in cream with pale gold accents, and I was not going to let them inadvertently track in dirt. If I could walk around barefoot, so could they.

"Is it a'ight if we sit down, or should we get butt naked first?" Dom asked mockingly, plopping down on the cream leather sectional. "Cristal, you know you full of shit."

I ignored her. Is there anything wrong with wanting *and getting*, the finer things in life? I want things beyond designer clothes and a nice car to ride in. This is a lesson my friends have yet to learn.

Look at Dom. She made good money—even if it was from stripping—and still lived in those nasty projects. I know for a fact the shoes she was wearing cost $225.00, more than her rent for several months. Now, what was *that* all about?

I walked over to the small rolltop desk in the corner. In one brief glance my life was chronicled: my biweekly paycheck from Platinum Records for $700.00, lying next to my bills for the month totaling $3,000.00. Twelve hundred for my lease, four-hundred-dollar car note, high car and property insurance, even higher furniture note, credit card bills, utilities, food, and oh, Lord, clothing. . . .

Aaahhh!

Gwen Guthrie's hit "Ain't Nothing Going on but the Rent" was my anthem. Destiny's Child's old jam "Bills, Bills, Bills" was my theme song. I was definitely looking for a brother to help ease my financial tension.

My male friends brought up whatever slack my paycheck left, and I could rob Peter to pay Paul with the best of them. If that did not work, I could do a lot of creative juggling with what bills got paid when, which was not always good for my credit, but oh, well.

I do not live beyond my means because I *mean* to live the way I live, and nothing is going to change that.

I scooped up my bills from my friends' prying eyes. My eyes fell on Sahad Linx's signature on my paycheck. The bold slashing spoke of his wealth, prominence, and power.

I let my perfectly manicured finger trace the letters of his name slowly with the same sensuality with which I would one day stroke his ebony penis. Stroke it. Taste it. Kiss it. Suck it. Ride it.

"Cristal! Bring your saddidy ass over here, girl."

Dom's voice broke into my erotic thoughts. I slid my bills and paycheck into the drawer, crossing the room to take a seat on the couch next to Alizé. "What are you all talking about over here?"

"We tryin' to decide on a road trip for spring break next month," Alizé answered me, looking too cute in a form-fitting hot pink top with NASTY GIRL blazed across the front in rhinestones and a pair of Apple Bottoms jeans that were killer on her slender figure. Hot pink high-heeled boots, belt, and oversized shades—definitely Gucci—completed her look.

I would bet my paycheck that she had on pink underwear as well.

We each had our own unique look and fashion style.

Alizé was a variation of hip-hop glitterati-queen for her casual wear and tailored business for anything career oriented.

Dom was straight in-your-face sex appeal, especially with the deep V-neck shirt she was wearing with a pair of House of Dereon jeans cut so low on her hips that you could see the very split of her . . . eh, derriere.

I was more of the sophisticate with a Park Avenue socialite sense of fashion, preferring tailored slacks and classic dresses.

And Moët? Well, God bless her soul but the poor child was so confused by her double life that she did not have time to develop her own style. She was a mix of all three of us, depending on whomever she went shopping with that week.

I looked at each of my friends again. We were so different now. Our style. Our jobs. Our goals in life. Our dreams. But back in high school we were all four girls from Newark just trying to make it through high school. Our friendship helped the years pass by quickly. Thank God we found each other.

It was the first party of the school year. Monica and I were excited even before we hopped out of the back of her father's car, threw him a quick wave as he pulled off, and made our way inside. The gym was already packed. The lights were dimmer than they were during school. "Can I Get A . . . " by Jay-Z was blaring, and the dance floor was full.

"What's going on over there?" Monica asked as a crowd gathered to the left of the gym floor.

I just shrugged because we were heading our nosy behinds in that direction.

We wormed our way through the cheering people until we stood together near the edge of the inner circle. A slender dark-skinned girl was in the middle, dancing her behind off like she was working a 9 to 5.

University High was a small school, so no one was a complete stranger whether you ever spoke to them or not. I knew her name was Keesha Lands. I had to admit that she impressed me because she was always cracking jokes in class and her gear was almost top-notch. She had on a gold herringbone chain that had to be three inches wide. And her fingernails were long and brightly airbrushed.

I thought I was a pretty good dresser, but I could not compete with Monica or Keesha. I had to baby-sit after school just to make extra money to buy a few designer pieces to mix with the Wal-Mart clothes my latest foster parents bought for me.

"She keep shaking like that, she gone send that chain flying, and then I know all hell gone break loose in here," Monica joked.

"I know that's right."

Eventually the crowd dispersed and the party carried on. Monica and I had fun at our first high school party, laughing it up with our friends, flirting with the boys (especially the upperclassmen), and dancing just enough to be cute but not wild enough to get funky.

"Girl, I have to pee," Monica told me, grabbing my hand to pull me behind her out the gym and down the empty hall to the girl's bathroom.

Monica scooted into the one near the door as I checked my hair in the mirror over the sink. I started to sing "My Life" by Mary J. Blige. As Monica came out the stall and washed her hands, she started to sing along with me.

We were off-key and not doing Ms. Mary any justice.

Suddenly a third voice chimed in. We stopped singing. Startled, we both looked up to find Keesha's slim face over the side of the stall beside the sink. As she continued to sing the bridge worse than even we did, we looked at each other, shrugged, and started singing again.

We heard Keesha's feet hit the ground just before she dramatically bust out the stall, her head flung back, her eyes closed as she sang into her fist. She had Mary's movements down pat.

A senior cheerleader walked into the bathroom, gave us an odd look, and turned and walked back out.

We all stopped singing, looked at each other, and burst out laughing.

The three us have been inseparable ever since.

"Why don't we go to the shore," I suggested, changing the direction of my thoughts to the beaches of South Jersey.

Dom immediately rolled her slanted mocha eyes heavenward as she reached in her Dolce & Gabbana bag for her always on-hand soft pack of Newport cigarettes. She lit one quickly, her peach-tinted lip gloss staining the butt. "This is my first weekend off in a month, and for one, I ain't even trying to be around kids screaming and playing in that dirty-ass ocean all day. Secondly, if I'm gone to give up chillin' with my man for y'all, it gots to be for more than South Jersey, ya heard me?"

A long and narrow tunnel of exhaled smoke followed her declaration.

I was used to Dom's supposed tough-girl exterior, so I ignored her. "Moët, we already know you cannot go. So, Alizé, what do you think?"

"Let's go to Myrtle Beach for Biker's Week," came a soft reply.

All our eyes darted to Moët in surprise.

"Big Mo," Alizé teased, raising her hands to the roof with two quick pumps.

Dom watched Moët through eyes that she squinted against the silver sliver of smoke. "What the hell you gonna tell Reverend Ike and Sister Shirley Caesar?" she asked, her raspy voice condescending.

"Dom, I told you not to call my parents that," Moët snapped, her round pretty face twisted with irritation.

Dom just shrugged a slender ebony shoulder, running her two-inch acrylic nails through her short-cropped hair before she exhaled more smoke from her nostrils.

I was wondering how long it would take for me to Febreze all the cigarette odors from my apartment. I glanced pointedly at the cigarette, and Dom pointedly ignored me. I rose, walked over to the large bay windows, and flung them open wide.

"An-y-way," Moët said. "Y'all down or what?"

"Ain't nothing but a thing. Let's ride," Alizé said, fingering her necklace. "Rah gave me some money to go shopping today. I only spent a hundred of it, so I still got plenty left."

I studied the chain Rah gave Alizé just two weeks ago. Even though it was probably from one of those Chinese-owned jewelry stores downtown, it still was a nice piece. I preferred Cartier, Cassis, Tiffany & Co., or the custom pieces of that brother Chris Aire. I could not afford it, but I definitely preferred it.

"That man spends that money, huh?" I asked, tucking my bare feet under me on the couch.

Alizé gave me a look like "Say what!" "Shit, getting money out of him is easier than rain in April," she bragged, with a little feeling good shimmy of her shoulders.

"That's all well and good, but I still could not deal with thugs," I told her as I reached for Dom's steadily disappearing pack of cigarettes and put them on the end table by me.

"Rah's out the game, Cristal."

I looked at her and raised a perfectly arched brow. "Yes, but in or out of the game he still has the clothes, the mean face, and the attitude of a thug. But do you."

"Oh, and you know this," she answered, knocking her leg against my knee.

"Yeah, but is he still whack in the bedroom?" Dom asked, a sly smile on her lips.

Alizé laughed. "Girl, *please.* His thing looks like a damn gherkin."

We all joined her in laughter.

I could not help but picture Rah standing with his hands on his hips, with all his business—what little there was—hanging out.

"*Shit,*" she said, drawing out the vowel. "I pray every time we do the do that his ass don't give me a damn D & C."

"I can't stand an itty-bitty short-dick man for no amount of money," Moët added.

"Are you getting *any* kind of dick, Mo?" Dom asked as she tapped her cigarette ashes into her hands.

I did not have ashtrays. Dom refused to get the hint.

"I got a man, thank you."

"I'm just saying, you never talk about him."

"Don't worry. He got twelve inches and plenty of money, Dom," Moët snapped, her eyes flashing.

"How about Atlanta?" I suggested, trying to change the subject before an argument ensued. Plus, I wanted to steer my girls to the high road, away from the upcoming freak central in Myrtle Beach. I mean *please.*

Biker's Week, the largest rally for African-American motorcycle riders, was held at Atlantic Beach in Myrtle Beach, SC. It was more for a man's enjoyment than a woman's. Lots of bikes, loud music, wall-to-wall bodies—most half-naked females. Since I did not care for motorcycles, nor did I plan on shaking my derriere in front of *anyone's* video camera, there really was no need for me to go there. Okay? All right.

"Ain't Ludacris and Usher from ATL?" Dom asked with a wicked lick of her lips.

"I'll take that as a yes for Atlanta from Dom," I said, turning to Alizé. "Cool?"

"Cool," she answered.

"Moët, you sure your ass can go?" Dom asked.

Good point. I looked at Moët, and I could see her embarrassment. Her parents were sickening.

"I'll think of something," was her reply.

Enough said.

"Ladies, now that we have chosen our destination, I have to get my hands on some money," I admitted. Being in between "friends" had put a definite strain on my resources.

"Call Ezekial—" Alizé began, reaching in her purse and pulling out her compact and tube of IMAN lip gloss.

"Everett," I corrected her on the name of my last companion.

"Yeah, whatever. Call him. He's a big-time corporate lawyer," she stated as she applied the gloss to her lips.

"But don't tell him what you really want it for," Moët added, her voice soft—almost fairylike. "Tell him you got a bill due or something."

It was funny that little Moët was trying to school *me* on men. Inside I was asking the same question as Dom: just who *was* Moët's mystery man? I asked once and I did not get an answer. I was not going to ask her again. I guessed she would tell us in her own time.

"Cristal, you gonna call him?" Alizé asked.

"I do not deal with him anymore." I unfolded my slim frame to walk over to my desk, reaching for my black crocodile address book.

Dom used slender fingers to hold her cigarette. "You need to leave them damn corporate suits alone."

I glanced over at her, pausing in my perusal. "What should I do, get a thug in my life?"

"Damn right," Alizé and Dom said in unison, finishing that off with a round of pounds and high fives.

"Alizé, is this the same corporate world you are salivating to get into? I can sure see a man like Rah attending all those corporate functions with you." Yes, I meant to sound sarcastic.

Alizé flipped me the bird. Humph, truth hurts.

"Look here, bougie," Dom said, leaning forward on her slender knees to look at me with a devilish hint of a smile in her slanted ebony eyes.

"Put her d', Dom," Alizé added.

I started to tell Dom that someone should put her down, and that she needed to move her child out of the projects, but I refrained. Instead I closed my address book, using my finger to mark the page, and leaned my hip against the desk as I faced my more than outspoken friends.

"A brotha that works on a job every damn day ain't feelin' givin' up that money like a thug. And you know why?"

"Do tell," I said sarcastically.

"Because a thug don't give a shit about that easy money. You know what I'm sayin'?"

Dom looked to Alizé and Moët for backup.

Moët reluctantly nodded in agreement.

"She's right, Cristal," Alizé chimed in like a sidekick, pulling a grape Blow-Pop from her purse to smack loudly upon.

"To Rah, or my baby Lex, it's like a part of their street cred to lace they women with nice shit. They *wanna* give up that loot. But a brotha gettin' up out of his bed every day, bustin' his ass doing forty or sixty hours a week for a check, ain't feelin' it."

Dom had a habit of hitting one slender fist into her open palm as she spoke, like she was trying to hit her point home. And although I understood fully what she was saying, I was not getting involved with a grown man whose main ambition in life was to develop his street credibility.

I wanted a man who was husband material and not jail material. I wanted someone who could offer what I lacked the first eighteen years of my life: stability. A man who played outside the law was not any more stable than someone walking a tight rope in the middle of a hurricane. I wanted more than a friend who would spend his money on me. I wanted a wealthy husband. Period. I was talking permanency and security, because *if* my future husband left me, there was always alimony. Okay? All right.

The girls kept on lauding their street warriors, and I politely tuned them out, turning my attention back to my address book with a "whatever" look on my face. Using a clear-painted nail, I traced down my list of names.

Each and every man I ever dated or slept with was listed with a brief bio, and a photo if I had one. I used dollar signs to rate how free giving they were with their money, and stars to rate how good they were in bed. Five dollar signs was a true spender, and five stars was a too-good-to-be-true lover. A combination of both and he was *almost* a true keeper. I had only one or two of those.

The man I chose to call had absolutely nothing to do with making me climax until I fainted. This call to Townsend Lakes was all about the Benjamins, baby.

I met the defensive tackle for the New York Giants about a year ago at one of the label's release parties. I was not able to get any passes for the girls, and I definitely did not want to carry sand to the beach, so I went alone.

Looking ever so fine in a red silk Diane von Furstenberg strapless dress that originally retailed for $1,250.00 (I caught it on clearance for a mere $300.00), I stood out in the crowd of half-dressed groupies and overdressed industry elite. That dress drew Townsend straight to me.

Better known as The Enforcer, he rated two stars

and five dollar signs. He was a wall of muscles except where it counted. Unfortunately for him, a four-star, five-dollar-sign man had beat him out; thus ending our five-month relationship.

It was only Tuesday. I had until Friday morning to get him eating out of the palm of my hand . . . again.

"Cristal, we'll save money if you just drive your whip," Dom offered.

I shook my head. "No, thank you. I am not putting all of those miles on my ride. Why not yours?"

"It's a coupe."

True, but I still was not driving, and my face showed that. Not even bothering to address the issue further, I turned my back on them and picked up my cordless phone.

I had not spoken to Townsend in a few months, but I knew he would remember me well. I made sure of that . . . if you know what I mean.

"Whaddup."

"You as always, Huggie Bear," I purred into the phone, quickly referring to my black book for the nickname I gave him.

He paused for only a brief second. "Long time no hear from, Cristal," he said, pleasure obvious in his deep, Barry White like tone.

"I was so hurt when I heard you were getting married. I decided to help you be faithful to your future wife," I lied, twirling a lock of my bone-straight auburn hair around my finger.

"Married?" Townsend balked. "Who told you that lie? Marriage ain't nowhere in my vocab."

Ahem, yet another reason why I dropped him. Even though he loved to spend the money, three hundred pounds with a short penis *and* no sight of legal commitment did not make me a happy woman.

"Just a little rumor I caught in the wind," I told him, turning to wave my hand at the girls as one of them muttered something about me being a good liar. "As soon as I found out it was a lie, I knew I had to call you," I said softly.

"You shouldn't have ever stopped calling me."

Okay, my big fish took the bait.

"I regret listening to that rumor now."

"I regret it, too, baby."

He was nice and hooked. Now it was time to reel him in. "I guess we have a lot of lost time to make up for."

"You damn right."

I gave my girls a thumbs-up.

7

Moët

No one could deny that The Greater Temple of Jesus Christ is one of the most grand and beautiful churches in Newark. Massive stained glass walls depict religious scenes straight from the Bible. The pews and woodwork are a gleaming mahogany. Brass adorns every possible accent piece.

The grandest of it all was the pulpit. It took up the majority of the front of the church and had a feel that was more royal than religious.

Every Sunday our charismatic leader, Reverend DeMark, held two services to accommodate his ever-growing congregation. Leave it up to my parents to attend both, as well as devotional services and Sunday school. Of course, that meant I was supposed to go to it all as well.

On the inside, I smirked as he preached on being a good Christian soldier. Mind you, he'd already given me our special signal from the pulpit for me to meet him in his office between services.

My mother was ushering today, and my father was on the front pew with the other deacons, so their hawklike eyes weren't on me. I eased off the pew and slipped out of the back door five minutes before his first sermon began to wind to an end. The sound of the organist backing up his ever-increasing words followed me down into the basement level apartment that served as both his office space and parsonage.

Using the spare key he gave me, I shivered in anticipation as I entered his domain. The door opened directly into the converted living room that served as an office for both him and the part-time secretary. A locked door—for which I had no key—led to the rooms farther into the apartment that were for his private use.

I moved freely about the spacious and elaborately decorated room as the shouts, stomps, and organ music filtered down through the floor. Everything in his place spoke of wealth—a testament to the money he made from shitting innocent people.

His wealth. *His* people. *His* flock.

They paid for it all. The sprawling house in Maplewood. The Lexus. The tailored suits. The jewelry. The trips to the Caribbean. The cash he so generously gave me. All of it.

Not that the Rev's money was all that drew me. At first there was a lure associated with his position that I couldn't resist. I enjoyed his heated hands *and* cold hard cash.

I walked over to the mahogany Italian leather sectional in the corner. I remembered the day I lost my virginity and my faith on this couch.

When Reverend DeMark mentioned to my parents that

he wanted to hire some additional help to clean his offices, my parents readily volunteered my services; another testament to their devotion to God, their church, and their minister.

They made the task seem like such an honor that I was actually nervous about doing it. I wanted his praise. I considered it the start of my paying tithes to my church. It wasn't money, but it was my time, and at seventeen time was all I had to give.

That first afternoon, I used the key my mother had proudly pressed into my palm and unlocked the heavy door leading into the office. I was shocked and surprised to find the Reverend sitting at his desk, his reading glasses in place on his long aquiline nose as he read from the leather-bound Bible open before him.

"I'm sorry, Reverend DeMark. I didn't know . . . I mean your car wasn't out—" I stammered, edgy in his presence because I thought I made a mistake.

"No, no, Latoya. Come in, come in," he said, removing his glasses with a serene look on his face. "My car's at the detail shop. It'll be delivered when they're done. I hope I didn't scare you?"

"I can come back another time—"

"No, Latoya. You're okay. Did you walk over from school?" he asked, leaning back in his chair slowly as he tented his fingers beneath his chin.

"Yes, my daddy's going to pick me up on his way home from work."

"Good, good," he said, resting those deep eyes on me as I nervously stood there. "I was waiting on you."

"Yes, Reverend?" I asked, shy and nervous, my heart pounding wildly in my chest.

He had a way of looking at me that made me feel that way . . . shy and nervous.

"God is good, isn't he, Latoya?"

I nodded, still standing in the doorway with one hand holding the knob and the other tightly grasping my book bag.

"Come in," he demanded, beckoning me with a bend of his fingers.

Still clutching my book bag, I closed the door, my black pumps clicking against the ceramic tile as I walked over and stood before his desk.

"Are you a good Christian, Latoya?"

I nodded, my eyes locked with his, and said, "Yes, sir."

"Pure?"

Flushing with embarrassment, I answered quickly. "Yes, Reverend DeMark."

He turned in his maroon leather swivel chair and stood suddenly, coming around his desk to stand beside me. He was so close that I could see the tiny flat mole near his mouth and feel his cool breath against my forehead.

Anxious, I took an automatic step back and looked up at him.

"Are you afraid of me, Latoya?"

"No, sir," I stammered, hypnotized by his eyes.

Slowly he raised his hands and grasped my face. "You've grown to be a very beautiful young lady. Very innocent and . . . tempting."

I was a virgin, only pretending to be as cool and hip as my friends so that I would fit in. I didn't know much about men, or even boys for that matter. Yet, I knew at that moment, as the Reverend continued to stroke me with his eyes, that he wanted to kiss me.

I gasped slightly as my nipples hardened at the very thought of his lips on mine. Remorse and shame quickly filled me.

"Do you believe that He is a forgiving God?" he asked,

his voice strained as one hand moved down to my buttocks to press the lower half of my body close to his.

I nodded, completely under his spell.

As his head lowered and his warm lips met mine, he guided my shaking hand to his erection; I could only pray that He was indeed forgiving.

The sound of the doorknob rattling brought me from the past with a jolt. I knew Reverend DeMark had a key, so either it wasn't him or he wasn't alone. With a quick look over my shoulder, I dashed into an oversized armoire.

"Reverend DeMark, your words were truly inspirational."

My eyes widened into mini saucers at the breathy sound of Sister Rebbie Labelle's voice. Curious, I eased open the door of the armoire just a crack and watched as the voluptuous woman, clad in a lilac suit with matching fur stole, sashayed past the Rev into the office.

"I'm glad that you enjoyed the sermon," he said, still standing with the door ajar.

Her wide-brimmed hat was tilted to the side and covering part of her face, but nothing could hide the slick smile that spread across her face like butter. "This sure is a nice conversion of the basement into an apartment, *but* it needs . . . a woman's touch."

I saw his eyes darting around the office, probably wondering where I hid. "I'm quite comfortable the way that it is actually. Uhm, I want to look over my notes before the next sermon, Sister Labelle. Is there anything else?" he asked politely, while pulling the door open wider.

Sister Labelle pouted as she pranced back over to him, lightly swinging the gloves she carried. "If there's anything I can help you with—and I do mean *anything*—just call on me, Luke."

I tensed at her use of his first name.

With one last stroke of her hand against his cheek and a long, meaningful stare into his eyes, Sister Labelle finally took her leave.

I waited until he closed the door and locked it before I left my hiding place. "It's good to see you have so many willing servants."

He turned. Slowly he nodded as he removed his elaborate gold-trimmed robe.

"Sister Labelle seemed quite eager to please," I pressed, unsuccessfully hiding my jealousy.

Preacher or not, Reverend DeMark put it down *so* good that I just didn't want to share, okay?

He took the seat behind his desk, steepling his fingers and then resting his chin on the tips. "Don't make assumptions, Latoya," he ordered in a steely tone. "Jealousy doesn't become you. The Song of Solomon states: 'For love is as strong as death, jealousy as cruel as the grave; its flames are flames of fire. A most vehement flame.'"

I felt properly chastised.

"Come," he beckoned, his elbows now resting on the open pages of the Bible on his desk.

Eager, but not wanting to show it, I walked slowly to him. His eyes pierced me. I felt he could see through my bones and flesh to my very soul.

"Undress," was his next command.

I was already hot with want and anticipation as I removed my pristine black dress and cotton undergarments. A draft from some unseen crevice breezed across my nude body, tightening my nipples into chocolate buds.

"Come and kneel at your altar," he demanded, turning in his chair to expose his erection to me as he kicked his pants away with his feet.

I shivered as I obeyed him, my knees pressing into the plush carpeting as he pulled my head toward him. I knew his wants without him speaking and eagerly took his shaft into my mouth.

He taught me so well.

I enjoyed the hard feel of him against my tongue as he chanted prayers of forgiveness for our sins and weaknesses. "To the Lord our God belong mercy and forgiveness, though we have rebelled against Him."

When he ordered me to take my position so that he could fill me with his heat, I didn't have thoughts of how wrong it was to let him fuck me. I climbed my ass right up on his desk, exposing my throbbing core to him.

I gasped as if drawing my last breath as he slid his dark inches into me with one deep thrust.

His fingers tightly gripped the cheeks of my ass as he stroked inside me deep and fast. I bit my bottom lip to keep from crying out in sweet pleasure.

"Therefore let it be known to you, brethren, that through this Man is preached to you the forgiveness of sins," he whispered harshly, his sweat dripping down onto my quivering buttocks.

He clasped one hand over my mouth as he paused midstroke. His tip throbbed like a pumping heart against my walls. "Don't move. I don't want to come," he gasped.

My heart beat a furious rhythm in my chest. The bud between my legs throbbed with a life of its own. My head dropped to the desk. "God, it's good," I whispered, struggling for air.

"What did you say?" he asked, his voice hoarse as he panted, his sweat like a slow drizzle down the back of my thighs.

"God, it's good," I repeated, reaching out to grasp the edge of the desk as his stroking continued at a furious and almost punishing pace.

He laughed low and deep in his throat. "Oh, no, sweet angel. God *ain't* doing this," he said.

I gasped as he pushed so deeply into me that the soft hairs around his dick tickled my buttocks.

"*Who's* doing it?" he demanded, delivering another deep and powerful thrust.

"You," I answered, biting my bottom lip.

"Oh, no, you know the drill. Now who?"

"Reverend DeMark."

Another hard thrust. "Who?"

"Reverend DeMark!"

We both hollered out roughly as we came together.

"In Him we have redemption through His blood, the forgiveness of sins, according to the riches of His grace," he chanted softly.

Tears flew down my face as I closed my eyes and whispered, "Amen."

8

Dom

"Wake up, Mommy. Mommy, wake up."

Now, I love my daughter to death, but if she don't stop bouncin' her ass up and down on my bed, I'm gone whup her. Okay, no I won't, but that ain't the point.

I opened my eyes and peered into a face that looked just like mine. My own Mini-Me.

"Mornin', girl, with your bad self," I told her, my mornin' voice soundin' way too mannish.

"Diane said to get up, Mommy."

Yes, Kimani called my mother by her first name just like I did. So?

"Go tell her I'm up."

I sat up in bed and looked around me as she went running out of the room at full speed. Clothes were everywhere: on the floor, at the bottom of my small-ass closet, atop my damn dresser, and across the foot of the bed. The only thing hangin' up in my closet was this red fake fur that I don't even wear no more.

To hell with it.

Alizé was always gettin' up in my business about *my* shit. She ain't got to live here, and she can't fit my clothes, so why the hell she care? Humph, she'll be the hell okay and so will my clothes . . . right where they at.

All four of us all weekend in one suite? Oh, I know I was calling dibs on roomin' with Mo—if she really was going. With Rev Ike who knew?

Damn, it was fucked up the way her parents treated her. Didn't they know how hard life would be on Moët if she really did walk around all day every day lookin' like a f'ing Quaker?

Matter of fact, that same dumb shit was the reason we all pulled Mo right into our clique.

"Look at her. Can you believe the clothes she wearing?"

"Girl, I ain't seen somebody rockin' opaque stockings and Mary Janes since I was six."

Monica, Danielle, and I were sitting at the lunch table behind these two upperclassmen, listening to they dumb ass as they ragged on Latoya James. She was sitting at a table alone, her head damn buried in her tray, looking so lonely she was 'bout to cry.

As loud as them upperclassmen were talkin', she probably overheard them.

"I heard she supposed to be saved," one of 'em said.

"Somebody need to save her dumb ass from them clothes," the other replied.

Monica, Danielle, and I all looked at each other and then glanced over at Latoya. That girl didn't bother nobody, and the only time she talked was to answer questions in class. And sure her clothes *was* jacked the fuck up, but who the hell told them somebody gave a flyin' fuck what they thought.

I was already in a f'ed-up mood 'cause I wanted a blunt, so I wadn't hardly in the mood for pickin', even if them tricks wasn't talkin' to my ass.

I jumped to my feet. Before Monica and Danielle could blink, I walked over to Latoya's table and sat down. "Whaddup, Latoya."

She jumped like I scared her, and I had to stop myself from rollin' my eyes. "Hi," she said back with a soft smile.

"Why you eatin' by yourself?"

She just shrugged.

"Well, we want you to come sit wit us, a'ight?" I stood up and grabbed her tray.

She looked over at Monica and Danielle. They waved and she waved back. She looked back up at me. "Really?"

Okay, I couldn't stop myself from rollin' my eyes that damn time. "Girl, come on."

She looked relieved not to be alone and scrambled off the bench, nearly trippin' over herself.

I heard snickers, and my head whipped around to find the upperclassmen laughing. I shot dey ass a nasty look, and trust me the snickering stopped like that. Trust me, these Hillside, Vaux Hall, Union, and Elizabeth living bitches knew I wasn't shit to fuck wit. Freshman or no freshman I handled mine.

Latoya followed me back to our table.

"Hi, Latoya," Danielle said, sliding over to make room for her.

"What's the deal," Monica greeted her.

She smiled. "Hi."

I slid on my seat on the bench. "Now let me see if somebody think it's comedy hour up in dis bitch," I said with a nasty attitude loud enough for the upperclassmen to hear me.

Monica, Danielle, and even Latoya all giggled.

The three of us been watching out for Mo ever since.

I lit up a blunt I didn't finish last night. I inhaled, letting the weed fill my lungs. Besides good clothes and great sex, ain't nothin' better than gettin' high.

My bedroom door swung open and in walked my mother.

Diane's a forty-five-year-old woman goin' on twenty-five—in her damn mind anyway. I gotta give her her due 'cause she look good for her age. She dressed young, acted young, wore her hair young, liked hangin' around young people, and slept with young men. Everythin' about her ass was young *except* for her real damn age.

She's more like one of my friends than a mother, and the girls always been jealous 'cause Diane just don't give a damn. She's always down for whatever.

Her eyes zoomed in on my blunt like a fly to shit. Damn! I ain't in the mood for her BS this mornin'.

Diane closed the door and strutted her wide-hip

self over to my bed like she some runway model. I sucked my teeth and rolled my eyes as she stuck out a hand with a "don't even play with me" look.

"Puff puff give," she said, imitating Smokey from the movie *Friday.* "Don't fuck up the rotation, bitch."

Takin' one last hit, I used my long acrylic fingertips to pass it to her with another eye roll.

"Holdin' out on me?" She laughed, before she took a deep pull.

Oh, yeah, Diane smoked weed. Shee-it. She got f'ed up on the regular. As long as I could remember, Diane got high. First it was rolling with E-Z Wide papers and then Philly Blunts. Hell, I even saw her and her friends smoke it out a bong. A spliff and Smirnoff Ice and she was straight as hell for the day. Mess around and she ain't got either and she moody as hell. For real.

I'm the same way. I don't find a damn thing funny when I ain't high. I guess the limb don't fall too far from the tree.

I started stealin' her roaches—that's the butt of the joint or blunt from the ashtray at eleven. My grown ass was curious as hell about the little cigarettes Diane always smokin'. My first hit and I was hooked. I got f'ed up before school, during school, and after school. Gettin' high was my homework, and I got straight A's. When I went to high school, I started buyin' my own stash, and I introduced my friends to the wonderful world of weed.

I was seventeen the first time Diane caught me smokin'. She told me I was almost grown and pass the blunt. I swear.

Diane started coughin', and I cut my eyes over

to her as I climbed out of bed in nothin' but a thong. "You know your ass can't hang. I don't why you try."

With her eyes all red and watery, Diane passed me the blunt. Wasn't shit left but the end. What the hell she think I want with it? I know some older cats who eat the ends, but it ain't even that serious. Y'all feelin' me?

I just dropped it in the ashtray on the floor by my bed. It was already full up with dull ashes, cigarette butts, hardened wads of gum, and an ass of blunt ends.

"Give me a hundred dollars," Diane demanded, finally gettin' her shit under control as she stretched her hand out like I'm a ATM.

"For what?" I bent over to dig in a big black garbage bag of dirty clothes.

"The rent is due, that's what," Diane snapped, pickin' up a black Via Nicci sheer camisole that still had the tag on it. "This will look good with my new low-rider jeans."

She was always wearin' my stuff. We the same size on top, even though her hips and butt was way bigger than mine.

Reaching over, I snatched it away from her. "Oh, no. I don't think so. And the rent's only fifty."

"Well, it's two months behind."

Did I mention that Diane ain't had a job since I was 'bout two?

When I turned eighteen, the government stopped payin' her bills. She turned to her men, and me, to pick up the slack.

Now see, I knew she had money, but she didn't wanna spend her own cash. Diane kept money 'cause she kept a man who kept money. Point blank.

She was singing "No Romance Without Finance" long before the song ever hit the airwaves.

And she taught me well. Ever since I was old enough to remember, she been schoolin' me on men, money, men *and* their money, and why the two should always go hand in hand.

Yeah, Cristal's uppity butt always talkin' smack 'cause we live in the projects.

It's by choice.

Why pay eight hundred dollars or more a month for a one-bedroom apartment when we livin' just fine in our two-bedroom for fifty dollars a month. Oh, section eight is a son of a bitch. A *damn* good son of a bitch.

Our apartment was decked out. The whole livin' room was black and silver with one of those nice-ass leather sectionals, a sixty-inch big screen TV, and a glass entertainment center with a matchin' dining room set. Mirrored walls. Black carpet you could lose your toes in. Even a mini chandelier Diane got from Sears.

Hell, I even got a forty-inch TV and a two-thousand-dollar bedroom set in my room.

Yeah, we liked nice things and we got nice things. If it meant me shakin' a little T & A to keep my Lexus, my clothes, and a new hairdo every week, then I'm a shake dat ass. Ya heard me?

I picked up the jeans I wore last night and reached in the back pocket. I turned my back to her as I counted the money. Three hundred and eighty dollars. I peeled a fifty, a twenty, and three tens from my roll.

"Huh," I said, reaching back behind me to push at her.

Rememberin' I needed her to watch Kimani while I went to ATL, I peeled off three more twenties. "Huh."

Diane smiled like a cat. "That's my baby," she sang, before steppin' over the piles of clothes on the floor to leave my room. "And you need to get some of this shit up off *my* damn floor."

I just looked at her 'til the door closed behind her. Straight crazy.

I started throwin' clothes I wanted to take with me in two piles. One to pack and the other to wash. I gotta lot to do today. Wash clothes, go get a half ounce from Mookie, and drop by Antoinette's to see what she boosted from the mall last night, 'cause that girl can cop clothes like nobody else.

Ah, what the hell we got here?

I closed my fist around my find as I pulled my hand from the pocket of them vintage Versace jeans I wore to the club last week. I'd bought a bag of weed from this kid standin' outside the club. How could I forget?

Smilin', I opened the tiny Ziploc-like pouch, steppin' over the mounds of clothes to grab my Gucci purse from the foot of the bed. I kept my purse and my glove compartment full up with cigars 'cause you never knew when you gone be in the mood to smoke. Nothin' worse than rollin' up to the corner store and findin' out that Papi's all out of cigars.

Sittin' cross-legged on my bed, I used my car key to bust the cigar down the middle. Seconds later I had that mother rolled, licked, and lit.

I held the blunt like a cigarette as I threw some clean things in this Gucci duffel bag I bought from Antoinette for a bill.

I damn near packed my bag and smoked half the blunt before I started to feel it.

Damn.

Either I'm smokin' too much or that kid's weed ain't no damn good.

Nah, must be a bad batch, 'cause you can never have too much weed!

Girl Talk

"What star would you freak for one night?" Alizé asked, stirring her apple martini as the ladies lounged at their VIP table in the Orange Room of the upscale and trendy Vision Nightclub in Atlanta.

"Denzel," Moët answered without hesitation, blushing before she sipped her Amaretta and orange juice on ice.

Three sets of eyes turned on her.

"I think older men are sexy. Don't sleep," Moët warned playfully.

"Needless to say I would be more than pleased to give Sahad Linx a taste," Cristal added, crossing her legs on the suede banquette.

"We know about him. Who else?" Dom asked, lighting a Newport.

"Okay, okay. Sean Combs," Cristal admitted with a smile.

"Oh, so if they don't own a record company, you ain't feelin' 'em?" Dom asked.

"Do not hate because I'm ambitious," Cristal told her with a raised brow. "What about you, Alizé?"

"I want me some of Nelly so bad that it don't even make sense," Alizé sighed, fanning her face and then between her legs jokingly.

"Okay, Miss Dom Perignon, what 'bout you?" Cristal asked as she reached in her purse for her wallet.

Dom blew smoke through her nostrils, already moving her upper body to the music thumping loudly against the walls. "Question is who *wouldn't* I do."

"Dom!" Moët exclaimed.

"Let me run into Ludacris or Usher in this joint and y'all have the answer to your question. Hey!" She rose and did her signature "Juicy" ass shake. "They can't stand it! They can't stand it!"

"Dom, your ass is so crazy," Cristal told her, before they all broke out with laughter.

9

Cristal

One Month Later

"**P**latinum Records."

"What you doing?"

"I'm working, Alizé. What are *you* doing?" I said into the phone.

"Girl, I ran up on a good piece last night!"

"A good piece of what?"

"It damn sure wasn't cake."

"So Rah's ah . . . skills are improving?"

"What my man got to do with it?"

"You broke up with Rah?"

"Hell no."

I did not say another word. I was not a prude, but sleeping with two men will wear your walls out. Okay? All right.

"Listen, Cristal, Rah's cool. The money is lovely. But if he want fidelity, he got to step up his game in the bed."

Deciding not to school my friend on letting her hot spot out rule a cool head, I moved on. "Where are you?"

"I'm on campus. Why? What's up?"

"Where is Mo?"

"At work at the Student Center. I think she got a class at twelve."

"I just spoke to Dom a little while ago."

"Dom was up before noon? *Do,* Dom!"

I laughed, looking around the lobby to ensure I was alone. "I woke her up to see if I could take Kimani to an indoor block party the label is having this Saturday. Since Mr. Right is nowhere in my future for me to have my own husband and child, I have to latch on to our godchild when I feel motherly."

"What happened with Townsend?"

"We still go out, but it is not anything serious. Besides, I told you he is not a husband candidate," I told her as I flipped through my new *Essence* magazine.

"Stop hunting for a husband to make you a BAP and you'll be all right."

There was nothing wrong with being a Black American Princess to me.

If I yearned to marry a wealthy man—preferably African-American—and live the life of Riley, what was so wrong with that? Take Patricia Lawrence, now Patricia Smith, current wife of professional football star Emmitt Smith, and ex-wife of multimillionaire actor and comedian Martin Lawrence. Not only did the woman marry well, but she married well *twice.*

"What did Dom say?"

I did an uncharacteristic eye roll. "You know Dom is forever searching for a babysitter."

Alizé laughed. "Dom's so crazy. I still can't believe she got us thrown out of Vision's last month."

I frowned at the memory. "What possessed her to get up on the bar and start stripping?"

"I don't know. She must've thought she was in *Coyote Ugly*."

We both laughed.

The intercom buzzed from Alyssa DeSanto's office. Alyssa was Sahad's executive assistant—his right-hand woman. Humph, I would love to be his right hand so that I could wrap it around that ebony penis!

"Alizé, I have to go. I will call you later."

"Make sure you call so I can tell you all about that big mule—"

I hung up the phone on her with a laugh, pushing the button on the intercom. "Yes, Alyssa?"

"Mr. Linx is expecting a delivery from Tiffany's in about forty-five minutes. Just buzz me when it arrives and I'll walk out to get it."

"Not a problem."

Sahad was currently dating Tyrea, an up-and-coming singer whose first release, *Tease Me, Taste Me*, was #1 on the Billboard R & B chart. I saw a picture of them in the *New York Post*'s Page Six section. Tyrea *was* attractive in that "if you like that look" kind of way.

What if it was an engagement ring?

Oh, no-no.

* * *

That night I was at home alone, sipping on a glass of Chardonnay and looking out my bay window at the still night below. Everything was quiet. So peaceful. So unlike the rowdy streets where I grew up.

And I was glad for that.

I was mugged twice at gunpoint when I was sixteen and living on Sixteenth Avenue by Westside Park. Hell, I am lucky to be alive.

Do not get me wrong, I was not as ashamed of growing up in Newark as everyone thought. I just decided to move on from the liquor stores on every corner and the thugs hanging out in front of the bodegas. The noise. The littered streets. The unemployed wanderers. The dealers. The addicts. The criminals. The projects.

Unfortunately, I seemed to shift from one foster home to the next in nothing but those bad areas. I always felt like I did not belong. The gritty urban environment did not suit me. I never liked playing in illegally opened fire hydrants on hot summer days, or sitting on the stoop, or playing kickball in the street.

When I was a little girl, I used to dream that my parents were rich and living large somewhere grand like Beverly Hills or the Hamptons. I swore that I had been stolen from them and that they were looking for me so that I could return to the wonderfully rich life I deserved.

I got older and the dream faded with age.

Suddenly the phone interrupted my thoughts, and I was glad for the diversion. No need dwelling on a past I could not change. The future? Well, the future was all in *my* hands.

I picked up my cordless phone. "Hello?"

"Cristal?"

"Dom?" I set my precious Waterford crystal goblet on the windowsill.

"Yeah, this me. You got a dude there?"

"No. It is just me, myself, and I. Why?" I asked, straining to hear her clearly on her cell phone.

"Me, Alizé, and Moët are on our way up there."

I loved my girls, but the only thing on my schedule for the night was maxing and relaxing. I wanted to focus on my strategy for sexy Sahad since I "accidentally" opened the package from Tiffany's and discovered it was just one of those trendy I.D. bracelets for Tyrea.

Not a ring.

"Something wrong?" I asked.

"You not gone believe this bullshit."

"What?" Goose bumps raced across my body in a rush.

"Guess who's knocked up."

I could tell that Dom had a cigarette in her mouth, but I could also hear her anger. "Who?"

"Be there in five."

The line disconnected, and she left me in suspense.

Pregnant? Who? Alizé? Moët? Oh, God, not Dom?

Grabbing my goblet, I walked over to the bar and poured myself another full glass of wine. I finished it in one gulp.

Three minutes seemed like an eternity when you were staring at a Fact Plus pregnancy test stick. All four of us were in my bathroom . . . watching and waiting. Would the pink line appear in the result window?

"Ain't this 'bout a bitch," Dom said for the tenth time from her spot on the edge of the tub.

Me? Well, I was busy praying, "Please, Lord, do not let it show," and cursing, "Do not show, you son of a bitch," and warning, "You better not show."

All to myself, of course.

The timer I used for my facials went "ding."

All my praying, cursing, and warning did not work. There was that damn pink line coming in big, bold, and bad as hell.

10

Moët

One Month Later

The day I killed my unborn child, a huge part of me died. I regretted my decision even as I lay on that table. For days afterward nightmares filled with graphic images of what I had done chased me from my sleep.

Thirty days later and it still hurt like a sharp blade through my heart to even *think* about it.

What's thirty days anyway?

I knew I should pray for forgiveness, but I had no faith. My ties to the church and God were as visible as a strand of hair. Living under my parents' roof, I pretended to listen, pretended to care, but I felt too numb inside.

I knew all the commandments. I studied the Bible and sang the hymns, but I didn't *believe* anymore. Somewhere along the line I learned to lie and deceive about my faith and blind trust in the Word, the church, and its ministers.

Religion was such a huge part of my life. What choice did I have? None at all. Maybe that was the whole point: I never had a choice.

I *had* to go to church.

I *had* to be Pentecostal.

I *had* to be on the usher board.

I *had* to go to every church event in a twenty-mile radius.

I *had* to smother my own creativity and wear "appropriate clothes."

I knew my resentment was bred from my lack of freedom. A religion that centered around the lies and manipulations of a no-good, scheming scoundrel like Reverend Luke DeMark.

How could I believe in the Word when my spiritual and moral leader obviously didn't believe or follow the verses that *he* spoke?

He preached from his mighty thronelike pulpit about premarital sex being a punishable sin, yet *he fucked me* and we sure wasn't married.

He shouted to the rafters about abortion being murder in God's eyes, yet he convinced me to kill our unborn child.

I didn't have pain anymore when I thought of his cold indifference when I told him of our "blessing." That night, his words cut me like a knife. . . .

"I'm pregnant," I blurted out in a soft and hesitant voice as I lay in his bed still naked and sweaty from his sex.

He said nothing, but his body went as stiff as a board beside me. Seconds later my eyes widened as he jumped from the bed and jerked on his discarded slacks. "You're . . . you're what?" he asked, his tone sharp as he looked down at me with angry eyes.

I clutched the damp sheet to my naked body as I sat up in bed. "I'm pregnant," I repeated, even as my heart nearly raced out of my chest in slow-rising panic.

"Aren't you on the pill?"

My lips shaped the word "no," but I didn't have a chance to let it free from my mouth.

"If this is some kind of trick to get me to marry you, you can forget about it," he said in a nasty tone as he paced back and forth before the bed.

I said nothing more. I couldn't have even if I wanted to. Being told by the man you loved that you were good enough to fuck in secrecy but not good enough to marry—or to be happy that you were pregnant with his child—had a way of making a person shut the fuck up.

I rose from the bed to search out my clothes, hating the tears that burned first the back of my throat and then my eyes.

"Where are you going?" he asked sharply, reaching out to tightly grasp my upper arm like a vise grip.

To be honest, as I looked up into his eyes, I saw anger and fear. I became afraid. I didn't know what he would do to keep his secrets from being told.

I nervously licked my lips. "I'm going home," I said in a voice I hoped was calm.

He must have seen the fear of him in my eyes because he suddenly released me and backed away, wiping the fine sheen of sweat from his upper lip. He was a coward. To hell with him.

I knew then I was in it alone, and alone was not a good place to be.

Quickly I got dressed.

"What are you going to do?" he asked, now sitting on the edge of his bed looking older than his mid-thirties.

I was at the bedroom door and turned to look at him. "I'm getting rid of it—and you."

Still, I hoped he would stop me and tell me we would get through this together.

He didn't. "That's the best thing," he said, not meeting my eyes.

I walked out of the house and haven't been back to it or him since.

To dare accuse me of trying to trap him into a marriage by "getting myself in trouble."

Is he crazy?

I'm a senior in college with a part-time work study job paying just $5.65 per hour. I live with my religious parents who will disown me if they ever discover this secret. I long since sinned against God. My lover rejected me.

I lay down with a dog and came up with fleas.

I was so glad to have my friendships with Alizé, Cristal, and Dom. How would I have gotten through *it* without them? They all went with me to the clinic, held my hand, and told me everything would be okay. Never once did they ask who the father was or why he didn't help me pay for . . . for . . . *it*.

I felt weak.

Even with my girls' support, I felt so alone.

11

Dom

Shit with our little crew was gettin' mad hectic.
Moët's straight trippin' 'bout the abortion. Hell,
I had two and I ain't never felt as bad as she does.
And she still ain't tell us her who her baby daddy
is . . . was . . . whatever. Cristal thought it was an
undercover freak nasty professor. Alizé said she
can't even guess who it could be since Moët never
talked about a man. I said whoever the m'fer was,
he's a broke-ass joke since *we* had to pay for the
abortion.

Now on to Alizé. Just found out she's steady givin'
up the rhythm to some cat on the low behind Rah's
back. Riskin' all that good money Rah be givin'
her for some dick. Stupid.

And Cris. I thought I saw her ass grinnin' and
chinnin' with some white dude last night. I ain't
had time to ask her, but I know she ain't lookin'
for no cream to go up in her coffee.

But I ain't even got time to worry 'bout nobody

else's shit right now. I got mad problems of my own. Peep 'dis. Lex bust out last night—*after* I done sexed the hell out of him—and told me to stop dancin'.

Say what? Say who?

Seems some of his boys saw one of my shows and was braggin' 'bout all my skills up on the Ave. Now he's straight lost his mind talkin' 'bout it's him or strippin'.

When we met six months ago I was dancin', so why all the drama now?

Some people are doctors, nurses, teachers, or preachers. Me? I'm a stripper.

I've been dancin' ever since Dawn, my crazy-ass cousin from Florida, put me d' to the mad loot she make dancin' down in Tampa. So I took a G-string, a smile, and a copy of my birth certificate to Club XXXcite—the hottest strip club in the Tri-state area. I auditioned, makin' sure I shook the hell out of what Diane gave me. I got the job on the spot. That was two years ago.

Shee-it, I still remember my first night onstage in nothing but that same G-string and a smile. Dem fellas foot-stompin', hollerin', and applause vibrated against my body. I got loose and made that money. Five minutes later I strutted my ass offstage with four hundred dollars in tips and a bunch of knuckle-heads trying to holla at me after the show. The owner had been on me like I was his next big money-maker. All of the glory went to my damn head, and I been shakin' it like a saltshaker ever since.

I waited about two months before I clued Diane and the girls in on my new career. Cristal stopped speakin' to me for about two weeks—like I really gave a fuck. Alizé told me as long as I didn't shake my business all up in one of her boyfriends' faces, then she was straight with it. Moët, who I thought was an undercover freak, was just actin' nosy askin' me a bunch of questions. And Diane, well she had a fit 'til I dropped two bills in her lap.

I never sold my ass.

I never gave blowjobs in one of the private rooms.

I never put on a lick fest with another bitch.

I never even gave hand jobs.

I NEVER CHEATED ON THAT M'FER.

Why he trippin'?

Needin' to talk to some damn body, I rolled out of bed and walked barefoot into the living room. Diane and Kimani were watching *Hustle & Flow*.

"My Mama's 'wake," my child yelled out, runnin' over to me at full speed.

I caught her and swung her up on my hip. "Lex wants me to stop dancin'," I told Diane, ploppin' down onto the couch next to her.

"And who the hell died and made him your daddy?" Diane reached for the remote to put the TV on mute.

My daddy was another damn story. Sometimes I thought about his cracked-out ass . . . most times I didn't.

"I thought I schooled your ass, but you up in here tellin' me 'bout what some *man* want you to do?"

"Oooo, Mommy, Diane mad," Kimani sang, her hands playing in my jet-black, shoulder-length weave.

"Damn right, I'm mad," Diane yelled. "You got a child to take care of and bills to pay. To hell with what Lex want. If his behind can't get with the program, then drop his ass. What you call yourself, in love or sum'n'?"

I ain't even get a chance to answer.

"See what love got you the last time," she told me, lookin' over at Kimani.

The doorbell rang and I was glad that somethin' shut her the hell up. Why I opened my big mouth thinkin' I could talk to her?

I got up off the couch with Kimani's heavy self still wrapped on my hip.

"Who?" I asked, looking into the peephole.

"Lex."

"Don't be a dumb ass your whole life," Diane mumbled from behind me.

I ignored her and opened the door. Lex was standin' there lookin' too fine with his high yella self smelling good as hell and dressed to kill as always in vintage jeans and a striped button-up with a baseball cap and black leather coat. My pussy lips went to smackin'. I just loved me a red man. "Hey, baby. Whaddup?"

"Nothin'." He walked in and took Kimani from me to put on his own hip.

"Whaddup, Lex? What you got for your mother-in-law, son?" Diane asked with a big Kool–Aid grin.

Damn, she phony as hell.

Lex stopped ticklin' Kimani to reach into the pocket of his RocaWear jeans. He pulled out a wad 'bout big as a fist. "You know I can't front on you, Ms. D." He took off the rubber band and peeled off five fifty-dollar bills.

My mother stood up to come take Kimani and

the money from Lex, givin' me a hard stare behind his back.

"Gimme some," I told him, holdin' out my hand.

Lex put the money away and left me hangin' as
he sat on the sofa. "You made your mind up or
what?"

Damn, he gettin' straight to the point.

I think of the pimped-out silver Escalade I knew
was parked downstairs, the trips we took to places
my ass ain't even had the sense to dream of, the
shopping sprees, the way he took care of Kimani
like she was his seed, the goodness of his sex, and
the *fab-u-lous* way he ate me out.

But . . .

What if he left me?

What if he get locked up for pushin' major
weight?

Where would that leave me?

For sho not up in Mickey D's.

Knowin' Diane's nosy behind was listenin', I
stood. "Let's go downstairs."

We left the apartment, and the heavy metal door
closed behind us. Somewhere on the floor somebody's bad-ass kids was runnin' up and down the
hall. We stepped on the elevator, and I covered my
nose with my hand. The smell of piss was strong
enough to make your damn eyes water. Ain't no
way I was openin' my mouth 'til we got the hell off
this oversized toilet, and Lex knew that.

"So what's the deal, Dom?" he asked as soon as
we stepped into the lobby.

"Why you trippin'?" I asked, stalling.

He looked at me like I was crazy. "I don't want

my girl to be the talk of the damn block," he shouted, pushing his hands into the pockets of his jeans.

"I was dancin' when you met me."

"You know what, Dom? I ain't even feelin' all that noise you talkin'. Choose."

We stared each other down, and I didn't say a word.

Silence ain't never been so loud.

"You know what? Fuck it. Shit. Do you, a'ight?" Lex waved his hand and turned to walk away from me. Or was it *us*?

"So what you sayin'?" I asked with attitude, fakin' like I'm tough. On the inside I'm cryin'.

Lex turned at my question.

People were starting to come inside the lobby and watch us argue.

"You wanna be some nasty ass—"

Oh, no . . . the hell . . . he didn't. "Nasty?" I snapped, anger fillin' me in waves.

"Keep strippin' and I'm through wid your ass, Dom," he said, givin' me one last long look before he walked out the building.

Even though I'm pissed 'cause he put our business all on front street before these nosy-ass people, it hurt me like hell to see him walk away. "What the hell y'all lookin' at?" I yelled at the top of my lungs at the onlookers.

Somebody from the back of the crowd yelled back: "You."

I stormed out the door behind Lex into the bitter winter air, but he was already gone. The only thing I heard was the squeal of his tires as he sped away.

Damn.

12

Alizé

In two weeks Moët and me would graduate from Seton Hall. I had my gigs for the upcoming months all lined up. Summer internship. Grad school in the fall. Everything was on track when it came to getting my professional thing together. It was my personal life that was jacked up.

Rah and me were still together, but this new cat in my life, Lionel, was sexing me strong. Thing was, Lionel was starting to catch feelings and wanted more of my time. I could tell he was on the verge of saying those three words I damn sure didn't want to hear.

And they said women can't separate love and sex?

I met Lionel in my dance class. He had just moved to N.Y. from D.C. to grab his moment on the Great White Way. He started class on a Tuesday, and after the next class on Thursday, I was in his bed giving him the best that *I* got.

He was fine as Morris Chestnut *and* Boris Kodjoe rolled together—pretty-boy fine. That brotha could throw down like nobody's business. He had this trick he did with a string tied tight around the base of his dick, and he would count down from ten, and just as he reached one, he would come. Have mercy! As a dancer he was flexible, and he could twist and turn his body while he twisted and turned me out.

Yeah, I'm sprung on his sex—I'll admit that—but there was no way I was letting a good piece come between my good provider and me.

Lionel was broke as a joke but ain't a damn thing funny. He worked as a waiter at a small, nondescript restaurant that Cristal wouldn't even spit at. He lived in a studio apartment in Brooklyn that was furnished with a second-hand sofa bed and a tiny dinette set. He ate bologna sandwiches and Oodles of Noodles to save money. And if he wore those Adidas sweatpants to class one more time, I was going to fucking scream.

Last week I started to buy him a new outfit, but that was a no-no. I wasn't spending my money on a grown-ass man who can't even afford to take me out to a hot dog dinner.

Now I just had to decide how to split my time: more great sex or even greater money.

I was so busy juggling finals and my three lovers—Rah, Lionel, and dancing—that I hadn't seen the crew in a minute. I worried about Moët mostly because she wasn't the same since the abortion. The innocence we all loved about her was gone. She was cold, indifferent, and distant. It was like she didn't care about anything. At least she did stop hanging around Cristal's apartment during the day, skipping classes and took her ass to school.

Avant sounded from my Longchamp canvas bag. I looked over at Lionel to make sure he was sleeping before I climbed out of the lumpy sofa bed. Naked, I reached in and grabbed my cell phone, checking the caller ID. I smiled.

"Hey, Daddy."

"What's the deal, Ladybug?"

I loved that my father—my daddy—still called me by the nickname he gave me as a child. "Nothing much. What's up with you, old man?" I teased, lowering my voice as Lionel turned over in his sleep.

"Dinner. You and me."

I smiled. My daddy left the house and the marriage, but he never left me, thank God. When I was younger, I spent the weekends with him at his small apartment, and he never missed a holiday where he came by to either take me out or bring me presents. Anytime I needed him, he was there. He called me all the time, and he never stopped letting me know that he loved me. But love for your daughter and love for your woman were two different things.

I graduated from high school, and my parents graduated from marriage to divorce. I wasn't surprised when it all went down. I had nearly fifteen years of seeing them fade into indifference. Arguments behind closed bedroom doors became total silence.

"How 'bout Friday?" I asked.

"Uh, no-no. I got a date."

My mother's not going to like that. Even though

she claimed not to care, I knew she *still* loved Daddy. See, that lingering "love" had her life on lock while Daddy was living it up "La Vida Loca."

I'm not blaming my father for trying to meet someone special. Even though they've been divorced for four years, he just starting dating again. He didn't leave my mama to rip the streets and run through women. He left her so they both could be happy in their lives.

"Okay, Thursday after my dance class, Casanova," I teased him with a soft smile.

"Why you whispering, Ladybug?"

"I'm in the library on campus," I lied, crossing my fingers.

"Oh, okay. Thursday's good. I'll cook a lasagna. And don't bring Rah; he makes my ass itch," he said with deadpan seriousness.

I just laughed. My father ain't buying the "Rah was a businessman" deal. Although I denied it, he swore Rah was nothing but a lowlife. "Just me, Daddy. I'll see you Thursday. Love you."

"Love you more."

I flipped the phone closed, and Avant sounded off again almost instantly. It was Rah. I flipped it back open. "Hey, you."

"Where you at?"

"Just about to walk into dance class. Why?"

"Catch a cab over to the new store after your class."

Rah and one his "struggling to get out the game" friends were opening a new clothing store on Lennox Avenue here in New York.

"Why?" I asked, thinking that my plans for some more sexual healing from Lionel were 'bout to get jacked.

"Just do it, Ze."

I frowned at the phone as irritation caused my eye to jump.

Rah was getting bossier lately. Do this. Do that. Come here. Go there. Hell, last week he made me change outfits before we went to a concert at the PAC because he thought it was cut too low in the front. It was my favorite silk camisole, but instead of arguing I just changed.

"Okay, I should be there before nine."

"A'ight."

I flipped the phone closed.

"Who was that?"

I turned to find Lionel standing behind me. His nude body was like a sculpture, and his strong penis hung like a true third leg.

"That was my daddy," I lied, hitting the power button to turn the phone off before I dropped it back into my purse.

Lionel looked suspicious. "Why'd you have to lie to your father?"

I walked back to the bed and climbed onto it. "And what should I say? I'm lying naked in bed with a man?"

He climbed on next to me, and I curled my body close to his, leaning forward to suck his bottom lip.

The thin sheet tented as he got hard, and I knew I had to have just one more taste of him before we left for class. He wanted me to spend the night, but that was a no-no.

Lionel moved to lie on his stomach between my legs, and I had no shame as I spread them wide. With a delicious sigh, I pressed his cool, wet mouth closer to my core and shivered at the first feel of his tongue against my clit.

As he brought me to one and then another achingly slow climax, I knew that at least for now, this one was a keeper.

Girl Talk

"What's more important, love or good sex?" Moët asked as the four friends all lounged at Dom's after an afternoon of getting their 'dos done at Compliments Hair Studio on North Maple Avenue in Irvington. The name of the salon was on point because every time they stepped out of the joint, they got nothing but compliments.

"Definitely good sex, 'cause love is a nasty little four-letter word just like shit and fuck," Alizé immediately chimed in, rising to walk into the kitchen.

"Don't listen to her, Moët," Cristal told her, staring her naive friend in the eye. "If you find the right man, you can have both, and you won't have to choose."

"Bullshit."

Cristal and Mo looked to Dom.

Alizé sat back down on the sofa with a soda in hand. "Preach, Dom," she boosted her friend.

"Uh-uh. Don't group me with your man-hating

ass, Alizé. No harm, no *fuck-ing* harm, but I love men."

"So what's your point, Dom?" Cristal urged.

"If I do recall, Miss Find a Right Man, didn't you love Erick?" Dom asked boldly.

Alizé took a sip from her soda. "Oooh, that's a name I haven't heard in a while."

Cristal looked uneasy. "I loved him . . . so?"

Dom lit a cigarette, her eyes squinted against the smoke. "And didn't you say he was good in bed?"

Cristal fidgeted. "Yeah, and?" she snapped.

"Guess love and good sex with Mr. Right went out the damn window when you kicked his broke ass to the curb, huh?"

Cristal raised a finely shaped brow. "Neither love nor good sex pay the bills, baby."

13

Cristal

"Do these shoes match, Cris?"
I turned my head and looked at the Stuart Weitzman stacked sandals Moët held in her hand. I moved over toward her, lifting the edge of the Macy's embossed plastic garment bag to reveal the hem of the FDJ denim trench coat I had purchased.

They matched perfectly and I told her so.

"Excuse me. Can I have these in a nine and a half?" I asked the slender salesman standing nearby.

It was not until he disappeared into the storage area that I peeked at the sales price on the sole of the shoe. They were marked down to one hundred and five dollars and with the twenty-five-percent-off sale, the shoes would be about eighty dollars. That was not bad at all, and I figured I had that much left on my Macy's credit card.

We were at The Mall at Short Hills, taking full advantage of Macy's one-day sale—which really was a two-day sale since the sales price always went in effect the day before—just a little hint from the shopping diva.

"You did not see anything else, Moët?" I asked, moving to take a seat beside her.

"Those Via Spiga boots killed my little one hundred dollars," she joked, raking her fingers through her jet-black, chin-length bob.

I noticed that ever since the abortion she did not have spending money like she used to. I assumed that whoever the faceless and heartless baby daddy was had also ended the relationship. She did not seem to be in any rush to replace him either. In fact, she was not in a rush to do much of anything.

"You're graduating soon and will be making all that big money," I told her as the salesman handed me the box of shoes.

Moët just shrugged. "I'm so tired of pretending to be something I'm not. Hell, I'm tired of not really knowing who I am."

"I know that is right," I chimed in, moving toward the register with my charge card already in hand.

"Will this be all for you, Ms. Johnson?"

"Yes, thank you."

I watched as he rang up my purchase and swiped my card, bagging my shoe box as he waited for authorization. I was busy picturing myself in that coat at work. Professional but feminine.

"I'm sorry, Ms. Johnson, but your card was denied."

Oh, hell no.

"Excuse me?"

He handed over my useless card. "The purchase

was denied. Would you like to use another charge card? Check? Cash?"

I felt like the women in line behind me were staring.

"There must be a mistake on your company's behalf. I need to speak to someone—"

"You'll have to step out of line and use one of our customer service phones."

Gone was his polite and pleasant disposition to be quickly replaced with cool indifference once he realized his chance at a commission was fading fast.

"I'll just pay cash," I asserted, opening my Coach wallet to remove five crisp one-hundred-dollar bills.

It was my car payment money that I had no real intention of dipping into, but he had no way of knowing that.

"Very good, Ms. Johnson. I'm sure you'll look just lovely in them," he fawned, his kiss-ass attitude back in full effect once he saw the cash.

I just smiled coldly as he rang the purchase again.

Spitefully, I waited until he had bagged the shoes once again to push the money back into my wallet. "You know what? I changed my mind, but you have a blessed day."

I walked away, head held high, to retrieve my packages from Moët.

"Where's the shoes?"

"I decided not to get them," I lied. "Let's go find Dom and Alizé."

Dating a white man was not as perplexing as I thought it would be. Winthrop and I were just two adults enjoying each other's company. Just two friends. Uh, friends *without* benefits.

I enjoyed our dinner dates, going to the theater, and sightseeing like a tourist around New York, but I just could not bring myself to be intimate with him. And so far, he had not pressured me for more than what I was willing to allow.

Winthrop Blanchard IV was a prominent divorce attorney practicing in Livingston. He graduated from Harvard Law at the top of his class. Single at thirty-three, he leased an apartment in my building, wanting to be close enough to visit his parents in his hometown of Maplewood but far enough for his privacy.

I would see him in passing while entering or exiting the building or underground parking garage, but it was not until a tenant meeting on the newly enforced security measures that we had our first real conversation. I found him to be charming, handsome, and funny, so when he offered to take me sailing, I easily said yes, surprising myself.

In our short time together I had had more culture-filled dates than I had had in my entire life. Museums, art galleries, historical tours. It was all new to me, and I actually enjoyed myself because this was how I envisioned wealthy couples.

Of course, I wished it was Sahad and me enjoying each other. He still starred in my sexual fantasies, and the more I saw him saunter around the offices, the more I wanted him. Unfortunately, he was still deep in his relationship with Tyrea. Winthrop was just a diversion.

Tonight he was fixing me dinner in his apartment, and I was trying to decide what to wear. I finally opted for casual elegance: an ivory silk blend, off-the-shoulder sweater and matching slacks, both by Ellen Tracy.

I was twisting my shoulder-length hair up into a loose chignon when my telephone rang. I recognized Townsend's cell phone number on the caller ID, so I let the answering machine pick it up. I had moved on from him once again.

I decided to cut him loose for good when I saw him and a light-skinned beauty on the red carpet of a televised awards show. I did not play second fiddle to another woman. So I cut him and his money loose, thus my return to bad creditville.

Slipping my feet into a pair of Unutzer flats, I snatched up my keys from the marble table by the door and left my apartment. I tapped the button for the elevator. Seconds later it slowed to a stop at my floor.

"How you doin', Ms. Danielle?"

Startled, I looked up from the piece of lint I was removing from my clothes. It was Mohammed Ahmed. "Hello," I greeted him shortly, stepping onto the elevator beside him. I pushed the button for the fourteenth floor.

I did not miss the curious look he gave me at my selection, but I ignored him anyway.

Mohammed was the handyman for the building. He was a nice enough guy and even attractive with his over-six-foot muscular physique, but the Jamaican flirt was not my style, no matter how much he wanted to be.

He didn't make over thirty thousand a year. (Huh?) He owned a home, but it was on Stuyvesant Avenue in Newark. (Big deal.) He had a head full of shoulder-length dreads. (Haircut anyone?) He drove a dilapidated 1994 Chevy Blazer. (Hello, it's 2007.)

The elevator slid to a smooth stop. "Have a good evening," I told him politely, not bothering to look back as I glided off the elevator toward Winthrop's door.

"Only if I can follow you," floated through the steadily closing doors.

"Negro, please," I mumbled, pushing Winthrop's doorbell.

"Winthrop, I really love your apartment."

"Thank you. I take that as quite a compliment from such a stylish woman."

I smiled at his compliment as I carried my wine goblet from his rugged dining room table to the wraparound leather sectional of his living room. "The neutral tones are fabulous."

"I hired an interior decorator," he said, coming to sit on the sofa beside me. "All I had to bring were my clothes and a toothbrush."

"Here's to hiring good help," I told him, raising my goblet in a toast.

A comfortable silence fell between us as we sipped on his vintage wine. I could not remember the name of it, and to tell the truth, I didn't know the difference between it and Mad Dog 20/20, but I did not tell him that.

"How about a movie?" he offered, setting his glass down to move over to the large mahogany armoire in the corner. He opened the doors, and there had to be hundreds of DVDs on the bottom shelf. "So what's your pleasure?"

Knowing full well that he did not have any of my all-time favorites in his collection—like *Imitation of Life*—I left the selection up to him. I silently prayed to be able to grin and bear it. "Whatever you choose is fine with me."

I watched him over the rim of my goblet.

Winthrop was handsome with deep olive skin and jet-black wavy hair. His blue eyes seemed illuminated in his face. His features were model worthy.

I didn't want to be attracted to him.

So what in the world was I doing here?

14

Moët

"Your grades have slipped considerably, Miss James," Dr. Frost said. "Is there anything I can do to help you?"

I looked at my psychology advisor where he sat behind his desk in his cramped, book-filled office. Then I looked down at the red letter D on the final exam I took last week.

Since my days at University High School, I had been a straight-A student. This was my lowest grade ever.

And I didn't give a damn.

I shrugged my shoulders, the look on my face blank and nonchalant.

Dr. Frost studied me with his dull brown eyes before shaking his head sadly.

Standing, I slipped the paper into my Coach satchel before leaving the office.

I left the building and debated whether to go to work at the Student Center or not. To hell with it.

I had already missed every day this week so far. I just didn't want to go. I didn't give a damn.

I passed the chapel on my way to the front of the campus. Two robed seminary students walked ahead of me.

The same God that allowed a devil like Reverend DeMark to walk the earth and use his position to seduce young, impressionable women. Seduce. Impregnate. Desert.

I hated that sacrilegious son of a bitch.

Just the thought of him made my feelings plummet. That was how much of a rollercoaster ride my life was these days. Depression. Furious anger. And back again.

I kept walking until I left the front gates of the campus on South Orange Avenue and crossed the street to the bus stop. I didn't have to wait long before a #31 bus headed in the direction of Livingston Mall pulled to a stop in front of me.

I sat in the front near the bus driver. A group of teenagers got on about three blocks up from the campus. As they flashed their bus passes and moved to the back, one of them stepped on my favorite Christian Louboutin boots.

"Excuse me. I'm sorry."

Instead of getting angry, I just shrugged and thought, *Shouldn't be wearing four-hundred-dollar boots and riding the bus any damn way.*

As soon as I got to Cristal's apartment, I changed into my ankle-length skirt and blouse, slipping into Latoya the Christian. I lay down on the couch, feeling sleepy as always.

I put on a front for my girls, but most of the time I just wanted to be left alone. I didn't deserve fun. I didn't deserve an education. I didn't deserve friends.

I didn't even deserve to live.

Hours later, after I finally found the strength to get off Cristal's couch, I went home.

"Look who's here for dinner, Latoya."

Closing the front door to my parents' house behind me, I headed straight for the stairs. "I'm not hungry," I called out, just wanting to go to my bed and sleep some more.

"Latoya!"

My father's stern voice echoed around me on the stairs. I paused before I turned to face him where he stood at the foot. The anger on his face was evident.

It's always amazing to me that I can feel the same pains of "daddy hunger" as a child raised without a father's presence in her life. I used to feel starved for his affection, craving the hugs and kisses most little girls got from their daddies. He never came to any of my school functions, or read me any bedtime stories, never taught me to swim or ride a bike.

Nothing.

His devotion to the church far outweighed his devotion to his children in my eyes. My father just didn't have time to be a daddy. And there was a difference.

With dull eyes I gazed down into a face that I'd inherited, knowing my hunger would never be fed.

"Yes, sir?" I finally answered.

"Come into the dining room," was all that he said before turning to do just as he instructed me.

I wanted nothing more than to go to my room, but I knew they would nag me and interrupt my rest, so I made my way to the dining room.

"This sure is a mighty fine meal, Sister James."

What . . . the . . . hell?

I froze in my tracks at the sound of *his* voice. The Good and Honorable Reverend Luke DeMark. That conniving snake in the grass had the fucking *audacity* to show his face in this house I was forced to call home?

After the pregnancy, he stopped his weekly dinners here. No more signals from the pulpit for our freak sessions. I only suffered through his presence in church, being sure to avoid his no-good ass.

"Sister Latoya. It's good to see you."

My eyes locked with his, and I didn't back down. In fact, he looked away first. And you know what, I kinda felt a little surge of power. Maybe I'd make this demon squirm.

I smiled softly at my two younger sisters, Latasha and Latrece, before taking my seat next to Satan. The scent of his Gucci cologne blended with the aroma from the steaming bowls of collard greens, white rice, macaroni and cheese, and fried pork chops. I had long ago lost my appetite, but I fixed myself a plate to keep away a hundred questions.

"Bless your food, Latoya."

The fork paused midway to my mouth at my mother's words. Closing my eyes, I pretended to say grace.

"Reverend DeMark, our Latoya is graduating from college this next week. God is truly good," my mother gushed, closing her eyes and thanking God right then.

"In this age of promiscuity, teenage pregnancy, and an escalating high school drop-out rate, that is truly a blessing."

I froze, about to force another bite of food down my throat. In the words of Dom: "Ain't that 'bout a bitch?"

"I'm proud of her. I'm proud of all my girls," my mother continued.

I looked down the table at my father, who was busy shoveling food into his mouth. *What about you, Daddy? Are you proud of me?*

"Now that she has her education out of the way, she can find a nice young man, get married, and start a fami—"

"Ma! Uh, could you pass me the rolls . . . please," I shouted out, cutting her off before she could finish.

She looked at me oddly. "There's no need to yell, Latoya," she said, passing the napkin-covered basket.

"I'm sure Sister Latoya will make someone a beautiful wife and an excellent mother," the devil piped in.

Unable to hold my tongue, I turned my head to look at his handsome, lying face. "Do you really think I'll make a good mother, Reverend?"

It pleased me to no end to see him flush with color.

"Latoya, first you have to become a wife," my mother added somewhere in the distance.

"Oh, yes, Ma. I'm a good Christian. I would never sin and have a baby out of wedlock. Right, Reverend DeMark?"

He cleared his throat. "Yes, right . . . right," he stuttered.

Tears threatened to fall, but I blinked them back as I focused my attention back to the food on my plate.

"Are you all right, Latoya?" my sister Latasha asked.

I looked up at her and smiled, giving her a wink at the look of concern on her face.

"Reverend DeMark, how are the preparations for the annual convention coming along?" my father asked.

Leave it up to Daddy the Deacon to be concerned only with church business.

My sisters began to fill me in on their school day, and I forced myself to look amused when all I really wanted to do was be alone. I was taking a sip of my lemonade when I felt a familiar hand warmly grasp my thigh beneath the table. Without blinking an eye I pretended to accidentally drop my fork on the floor just as he slid those probing fingers beneath the band of my underwear. I bent to pick up the fork and held it like a weapon as I sharply dug it into the fleshy meat of his calf.

"Ow!" he yelled out in pain.

I calmly cleaned my fork with a napkin and continued forcing myself to eat. My parents questioned the devil with concern, and he made up a quick excuse of a muscle cramp as his hand slid away from my body.

That'll teach the son of a bitch!

For the first time in a long time, I felt a little peace.

15

Dom

Club XXXcite was packed as always. The bass of the music echoed downstairs into the dressing room as I smoothed some sweet-ass raspberry glitter lotion all over my body. Just gettin' ready to give them hardheads what they want. I'd have dem tongues waggin' for a taste of Juicy.

"Dom, you're up next," Dogg, the new muscle-bound bouncer, yelled down from the top of the stairs.

"A'ight," I yelled back, taking one last swig of my Dom P. champagne straight from the bottle.

I double-checked my reflection in the small mirror hanging on the open door of my locker. My short, spiky do was tight, fresh from a trim and curl at Compliments. My makeup perfectly in place. My smooth chocolate complexion gleaming from a fresh rub of cocoa butter. Gold jewelry gleaming from my ears and neck.

Shit, I looked f'ing good.

"I don't know why your black ass always in the mirror like you cute."

The words from my past caused my eyes to dull, and the image in the mirror changed. It was me at eight years old. Hair wasn't as long as a finger snap. Face ashy. Eyes filled with fuckin' pain that I still feel today.

Tears filled my eyes, and I blinked to keep 'em from fallin'.

Growin' up black, bald-headed, and poor wasn't easy for me.

I took another sip of the champagne, and when I looked in the mirror again, Li'l Dom was gone. *Damn.*

"Dom!" Dogg called down to me again.

I ain't have time to let my f'ed-up past keep me from makin' dis money. Since I didn't trust any of these scandalous bitches as far as I could throw they trickin' asses, I put my padlock on my locker. I'll be damned if they up in my champagne, smokin' my weed, or "borrowin'" any of my damn clothes while I'm upstairs shakin' dat ass.

I climbed the stairs slow as hell so that I wouldn't fall in my new five-inch glass stilettos. "Whaddup, Dogg." I ignored the once-over he gave me.

"You working that thong with your sexy black self."

It pissed me the hell off when somebody called me black. Not Black like my race but black like I'm dark-skinned. The shit always sounded like an insult, especially when some idiot would say, "She's pretty . . . for a black girl."

Dumb, right?

Ignoring his ignorant ass, I stepped through the

break in the curtain onto the dark stage. It was time to make dat money.

"Yo, Dom!" Dogg hollered at me as I strutted by him in the dimly lit club.

He leaned down, the flashing neon lights reflecting off his bald head. "You got a request in the Balloon Room."

Looking up at him, I rubbed my index and middle finger against my thumb, giving him the sign for money.

"He gave me a hundred just to tell you. Go 'head and make that money, gal," he yelled into my ear before slapping my ass.

I gave him the middle finger before I turned and made my way straight to the back of the club. There were three private rooms, each decorated with its own theme and shit. The Fur Room was decked out with nothing but white fake furs, even down to the walls and floor. The Champagne Room had a big-ass champagne glass in the middle of it filled with bubble bath. And the Balloon Room was filled with nothing but a bunch of balloons floating to the ceiling and all on the floor.

I pulled my thong from so deep up in my ass and walked into the room from the dancers' entrance, stepping right up on the mini stage. I took my spot with my back to my private freakazoid as "Juicy Fruit" by Mtume—my signature song— came on. I knew how to work my hips and ass as I gave it to him full force, undoing my bra and letting it slip to the floor.

"This what the fuck you won't give up for me?"

I was just easing my thong down over my hips when my ass froze. Turning, I covered my titties with my hands and looked dead into one pissed-off face. "Lex!"

"I just wanted to see for my damn self what your ass love so damn much 'bout dis bullshit!" he shouted, his face twisted in anger.

"How long you been in here, Lex?" I asked, 'cause I didn't know what else to say.

"Long enough to see your nasty ass squat on a Heineken bottle."

"Why you actin' like this? I ain't fucking none of these niggas," I shouted back, picking up my bra from the stage.

"I can't tell. You was about to get naked just now."

Suddenly the door opened, and there stood Dogg with his big cock diesel ass. There were video cameras in each private room so that the bouncers could make sure none of these hardheads got out of line with tryin' to rape or attack somebody or some shit.

"Everything a'ight, Juicy?"

Lex stared at me for a long-ass time. "Who he? Your f'ing pimp?"

I stepped down off the stage and reached out to slap the hell out of his ass. It echoed like a firecracker in the room. Even Dogg made an ugly face.

Lex reached into the pocket of his jeans and searched until he found three one-dollar bills in his roll. Ballin' it into his fist, he threw it in my face. "Make sure he get his cut," he said in a nasty voice, before pushing past Dogg to leave the room.

"You a'ight, Dom?"

I just shook my head as I pushed past him to run behind Lex. My tits were swinging free as I dropped my bra in the fucking commotion. By the time I reached the door, his SUV sped off down the street.

I still can't believe this shit.

"Are you okay, ma'am?"

I looked up at the police officer as I sat on the curb. I saw him but I didn't see him, you understand? I didn't know if I would ever be okay, but I nodded at him anyway.

After Lex left the club, I kicked off my heels, raced downstairs, and changed clothes. Five minutes later I was in my car and headed toward the direction he drove off. I had barely gone a mile before the sound of sirens was all that I heard. The closer I got to the scene, the more I slowed my car.

I damn near wrecked my own shit when I saw the SUV twisted around the light pole. I slammed on my brakes and ran into the middle of traffic to get closer. As soon as I saw the license plate, I nearly passed the hell out.

It was Lex's truck.

I tried to get past the cops to get to him and make sure he was a'ight.

But it was too late.

Lex was dead, and it was all my fault.

Girl Talk

The four friends stood together in front of the open casket. The room in the funeral parlor was filled to capacity, and all eyes were on Dom as she looked down into Lex's face. Mo, Alizé, and Cris surrounded her, offering silent support.

"What the fuck I'm gone do without him, y'all?" Dom asked, her raspy voice breaking up.

Cris and Mo exchanged a look behind her. It was a difficult question to answer.

Alizé took the lead, taking Dom's slender hand into her own. "You keep living and loving him, Dom."

Moët placed her arm around Dom's thin shoulders, pulling her closer to her side. "You stop blaming yourself, because it was an accident."

"You rely on us because we will always have your back," Cristal offered. "Always."

PART TWO

"What About Your Friends?"
—TLC

16

Alizé

"Welcome to Braun, Weber, Monica."

I rose from my seat and firmly grasped the hand of the vice president of Mergers and Acquisitions, Cameron Steele. "Thank you, Mr. Steele. I certainly look forward to this invaluable experience of working with you and your team this summer."

I sounded like Cristal, right? Well, I was smart enough to know that in the workplace all of my *ain'ts* don't belong, and cursing wasn't appropriate. I could flip the script with the best of them.

Cameron Steele was not at all what I was expecting. Young, virile, handsome, and beautifully B-L-A-C-K. He moved with confidence and strength. He spoke with intelligence. His smile was nice and charming. He definitely was the Head Negro in Charge and wasn't a damn thing wrong with that.

Everything about him spoke of a Black man headed up the corporate ladder. The sharp navy Brooks Brother pinstripe suit, with a crisp tailored white shirt and rust-print tie. Diamond cufflinks in place. Handmade shoes which I knew were Gucci.

But as handsome as he was with his six-foot-four athletic frame and rugged good looks, he was definitely not my style. Any concern I might've had for falling for my boss vanished instantly.

Thug appeal still had me hooked.

"Delaney, will you come in here for a moment," he spoke into his intercom.

Seconds later his administrative assistant appeared, opening the office door. "Mr. Steele?"

"Please escort Monica to her office and help get her situated."

"My own office?" I asked, clutching my new Longchamp briefcase in my hands in front of me as I followed the short, plump woman out of the office.

"Don't get too excited. It's more like a walk-in closet with a desk," she told me with a conspiratorial wink of her green eyes.

And that was exactly what it was.

After she left me alone with some office supplies, I removed the navy tailored jacket of my Marithé François Girbaud pantsuit and rolled up the sleeves of my white shirt. The outfit was nothing at all like the hood rich gear I preferred, but hey, when in Rome. . . .

I took a spin around my office, taking everything in all at once, which wasn't hard. The entire space could fit in the corner of Mr. Steele's stylish workspace. I guess I should feel lucky I even got an office and not just a cubicle. A few pictures and I would get my spot straight.

Taking a seat behind the desk, I wondered what

I should be doing. I picked up the phone and dialed Cristal's work number.

"Platinum Records."

"Hey, girl. Guess who?"

"Not Ms. Madison Avenue."

"The one and only. I'm calling you from my office."

"Oooh. I'm scared of you."

"Don't be. It's 'bout as big as a matchbox."

"You got to creep before you crawl, Alizé."

"Yeah, I know, I know. Girl, guess what?"

"What?"

"My supervisor, the VP of Mergers and Acquisitions, is a brother."

"Get out."

"Uh-huh. He cute, too, in that chocolate-dipped
white man sorta way. Definitely more your type than
mine."

"Single or married? Straight, gay, or bi? Rich or
surviving?"

"Girl, I don't know. I just met the man today," I
told her, opening a drawer to find it empty. "We
should meet for lunch one day. Just two sistahs working hard for the money in the Big NYC."

"That is fine with me. Just not today, I am meeting Winthrop at Le Bernadine."

"Ooh, Le Bernadine. I'm scared of you." I teased
her about the very popular four-star restaurant.
"So white boy still hangin' in there, huh?"

"We are just friends, Alizé."

"Whatever."

"It is true."

"Denial damn sure ain't just a river in Egypt.

When you want to do lunch?" I asked her, reaching into my briefcase for the matching agenda and my favorite Movado pen, all graduation gifts from Rah.

"How about tomorrow at one o'clock?"

I jotted the info onto my calendar. "Cool."

"Maybe we should invite Mo and Dom. It's been a while since the four of us got together."

"Yeah, not since your graduation. I'm worried about both of them. Wait . . . hold on a sec."

Delaney knocked again before she stepped into the office. "Grab a pen and a pad. Meeting in five minutes."

"Cristal, I have to go. Got my first corporate meeting. Girl, I'm so excited."

"Hey, Ze."

"Yeah?"

"I'm proud of you, girl."

I was touched. "Thanks, Cris. Thanks a lot."

My thoughts were on Dom when I pulled Rah's Benz into the driveway where I lived with my mother. I was worried about her. Lex's death had crushed through that hard shell she kept around herself. Seeing her weak and defeated at his funeral had pained us all.

That was a month ago, and although she puts on a brave front, I still don't think she's recovered. If anything, she seems even more distant and hostile, even at times lashing out at the three of us.

In fact, it had been about two weeks since I'd even seen Dom. We spoke on the phone, but no shopping excursions or going out to eat. We were all so busy, there never seemed to be time.

Still, friendship was about making time.

Not even bothering to get out, I put the Benz in reverse and backed out into the street.

I was just turning onto Springfield Avenue when my cell phone rang. Seeing Lionel's name and number displayed on the caller ID, I switched the call to voice mail. I'd decided a couple of weeks ago to cool things down. My little undercover lover wanted too much, too soon, with too little money.

He even asked me to move in with him!

That little one-room studio wasn't hardly big enough for him, far less me, him, *and* my wardrobe.

Besides, Rah was picking up his game lately, and he was just too good to me. I got free clothes from his stores, he got my hair done once a week at Compliments, I drove his car like it was mine, and he bought me nice things all the time. In the end I had to decide what was more important: a man who could financially provide or a wet ass?

So goodbye to Lionel and those ten inches.

"Hey, Diane, how you doing?"

"Well, damn, Alizé, it's been a minute since I last saw your ass. Still jiggy as hell, I see. That's a bad-ass suit you sportin'."

We gave each other a hug as I walked into an apartment that looked like it belonged on the Upper East Side of New York and not the projects.

"Thank ya. Thank ya. I wore this for my internship. Is Dom here?"

"Yeah, she up in that room as always," Diane threw over her shoulder as she headed to the kitchen.

Following behind her, I glanced at Dom's closed bedroom door. "How she doing?"

Diane just shrugged and waved her hand as if to say, "Who cares."

Growing up we always thought Dom had the coolest mom. She dressed like we did, knew all the latest songs and dances like we did, partied at the hottest clubs like we did, smoked weed with us, and talked about sex and men with us. She was more like one of the girls. More like Dom's sister than her mother. No curfews. No questions. No rules.

We all had wanted Diane to be our mother.

But when I heard her mumble under her breath, "That bitch needs to get up and get over it," I questioned the wisdom of my youth.

I walked out of the kitchen and over to Dom's door. I didn't even bother to knock as I opened it and walked in. I started coughing from the massive weed smoke trapped inside them four walls. The stench of alcohol was so strong that I felt I could swallow the air and get a damn buzz. As always clothes were everywhere until you couldn't even see the floor. "Dom?"

She was sitting in the windowsill wearing nothing but a thong, a blunt in her mouth and a bottle of half-empty Hennessey at her feet. "Hey, Alizé. What's up, girl?"

I could tell she was high as hell. I mean, why else would she be sitting damn near naked in front of an open window. True, their apartment was on the twelfth floor, but still. I wanted to check her on it, but I held my tongue.

"I just came by to check on you. Where's our godchild?"

"Moët took her to some festival or some shit at their church."

"You gotta work?" I asked, stepping right atop her clothes to sit on the foot of her bed.

"Not at the club. Me and this other chick doin' a private set downtown."

I reached down and picked up an empty Apropo leather fringe purse. "I thought you didn't do those private shows? Dom, you have got to be careful."

"Don't tell me what the fuck to do, a'ight?"

I did a double take at her tone. I got mad and flung the purse back on the floor along with the rest of her shit.

"Bitch, don't throw my shit on the floor."

Standing, I grabbed my car keys. "You the bitch. You done lost your mind. Call me when you find it."

She said nothing, and I left the room.

"What that bitch doin' up in there? She better be getting ready to carry her ass to work. Life ain't forever, but bills is."

I kept on walking to the door. "I'll see you later, Diane."

I closed the door behind myself as my anger toward Dom disappeared. She was still my friend, and although she just pissed me off, I knew I would never give up on my friendship. We been through too much for that shit.

I drove straight home, not even bothering to turn on the music. I walked into the house and straight into the kitchen where I knew I would find my own mother. "I love you, Ma," I whispered in her ear, hugging her little body close from behind as I placed my face on her back.

I felt her tears shaking her shoulders before I

heard her sniffles. "Ma, what's wrong?" I asked, turning her to face me.

"Janice saw your father and some high yella woman all hugged up at Mahogany's last night."

Damn. My heart ached at the redness and puffiness of her eyes. I hugged her close and said nothing. What could I say? I didn't want to take sides. I didn't want to admit that I knew about my father's girlfriend. I didn't have the heart to tell her to get over my father because he wasn't coming back.

Love ain't nothing but a no-good son of a bitch.

17

Cristal

Well, well. What a sudden and totally unexpected turn of events. I arrived for work at my usual 8:45 A.M. which gave me time to flip through the *New York Post*'s Page Six gossip section and sip on my cafe latte from Starbucks before the phone lines started ringing at exactly nine. I was already feeling good and looking good in this Moschino linen fit-and-flare dress I wore with a cardigan. The platinum bangle bracelet Winthrop gave me last night was the perfect accessory, and my infusion weave was tight.

So when Alyssa called me into her office around 9:30 A.M. and informed me that she and her boyfriend of five years were going to Jamaica for a wedding/honeymoon trip and that I would be her replacement during the week she was off, I nearly fainted.

"Mr. Linx is out of town vacationing in the Hamptons, but he'll return tomorrow evening for Bones's new video shoot."

I nodded, my face neutral and not showing my excitement. "I will not let you down, and congratulations, girl."

As she began to go over my duties, I was busy thinking of the five fabulous outfits I would buy to wear next week . . . after I returned Winthrop's bangle for cold, hard cash today.

"Dinner was delicious, Dani." Winthrop moved from the kitchen to take a seat on my sofa after our dinner of pheasant stuffed with wild rice.

"Thanks."

"Where's your new bracelet?"

I looked over into his blue eyes. "You know I keep all my valuables in my security box downstairs," I lied, moving across the room to the bar to refill my wineglass.

He placed his hand inside the pocket of his chinos, nodding with understanding. "That's a good idea because I don't trust that maintenance man. What's his name?"

"Who? Mohammed?"

"Yeah, him."

I moved to take my seat next to him on the sofa. "Why?" I asked, looking at him over the rim as I sipped my wine.

"Why what?" he asked, distracted as he set his briefcase on the coffee table and opened it.

"Why don't you trust Mohammed?" I persisted. I didn't even like the man, but I certainly didn't think he was a thief.

Winthrop looked confused. "Where is this coming from? I didn't mean anything by it."

"I would think as an attorney you would know better than to prejudge someone, that's all, Winthrop."

"You're right and I'm sorry."

Why was he apologizing to me?

He sat back and pulled my feet up onto his lap. "You look fabulous in that dress," he said as he removed my shoes and began to massage my bare feet.

"Thank you." He gave the best massages. I set my glass on the table and let my eyes close as I lay back on the sofa.

"You're a very beautiful woman, Dani."

I knew what was coming next.

"I'll be glad for the day we can take our relationship to the next level."

Nothing but sex was on *that* next level.

"But I respect your wishes."

No, he had not gotten into my precious silk panties yet. I was running that prim-and-proper role on him. Men like Winthrop loved good girls.

Not that I was not physically attracted to him. He was a fine white boy, and my awareness of his tall, dark good looks had first drawn my eye and led me to accept that first date.

We had fun together. We had chemistry between us. He was sweet and romantic. He showed me things I had only dreamed about or seen on television. Still, I could not have sex with him. As much as I told myself that I did not care that Winthrop was white, I knew that was not true. Why else did I have my goodies on lock?

I did know that eventually he would insist on that next level.

"I want to make love to you, Dani," he said softly, shifting his position on the couch. His hands worked up my legs underneath my dress to slide my panties down over my hips and down my legs. He spread my legs. "For now this will have to suffice."

The first feel of his lips on my pussy was cool, but as he sought out the bud with his eager tongue, I felt myself respond to his licks. I even clutched his silky hair as I arched my hips for more. He used his finger to open my lips and expose my clit. I began to break out in a sweat, my moans echoing his own as he sucked me so deeply that his cheeks caved in.

"Your pussy is so hot and sweet, Dani."

I could have done without his words because they reminded me that it was him and not Sahad licking away like a cat to milk. My body convulsed with the first wave of a climax, and I lay back as my come filled his mouth, enjoying each delicious moment of it.

"Aah," I sighed as heat shot through my pussy just as he stiffened his tongue to fuck me with it.

If nothing else this white boy knew he could eat the hell out of pussy.

"Touch my cock, Dani," he urged afterward, shifting again to rise from the couch.

I heard his zipper and then the rustle of his pants falling to the floor. I dared to look and came eye to . . . ahem eye with his long, red, and angry-looking penis as he knelt by the couch.

"Suck it," he ordered thickly, stroking it.

"What?" I shrieked as he touched the tip to my cheek.

"We don't have to fuck. Just suck my cock good for me."

I scrambled off the couch completely, pulling my skirt back down over my hips. "I know damn well you did not just tell me to suck your . . . your . . . ? Are you crazy?"

Winthrop's erection shriveled as he stood and jerked up his pants in frustration and anger. He picked up his goblet and downed his drink in one gulp. "Oh, but it's just dandy for me to lick your clit whenever you snap your goddamn fingers, right?"

"I ain't never asked your white ass to do a mother-fuckin' thing." I was more angry than ever as I slipped and sounded more like Dom than myself.

He raked his hand through his hair and then pointed his finger at me accusingly. "This whole virgin bit is getting a little old, don't you think, Dani? Hell, you act like you've never done it before. I'm sure one of the brothers—"

I slapped him, leaving an angry red handprint on his cheek. "Get the hell out," I shouted, storming to the door to open it wide. "I do not appreciate you calling me a whore on the sly just because I will not put your skinny dick in my mouth."

He flushed with embarrassment. "Sorry, I don't have a huge gorilla cock."

"What?" I shrieked, seeing red—all variations and different hues of reds.

"Is there a problem, Ms. Danielle?"

I whirled around, and there stood Mohammed, very calm and cool in his blue uniform.

Winthrop walked over to the door to stand beside me. "This doesn't concern you."

Worried that Mohammed would do something to lose his job or get arrested, I placed a restraining hand on his chest. "Mr. Blanchard was just leaving."

Never once breaking his stare with Winthrop, Mohammed stepped aside.

Winthrop glanced at me angrily before turning to grab his briefcase and leave in a huff.

Soon the elevator dinged with its arrival, and I knew he was gone.

"Choose your friends more carefully, Ms. Danielle," Mohammed warned with his lilting Jamaican accent before walking away.

I closed my door, securely locking it behind me. I was a bundle of nervous anxiety. I wanted to call my girls. Picking up the phone, I dialed Alizé. Her mom said she was at Rah's. She was with her man so I let her be.

Dom had already left for work, and besides Ze told me how Dom tripped on her, so I had already decided to give her some space.

Moët was barely allowed phone calls, and her cell phone was off.

Resolved to saving the juice until tomorrow, I ran a bubble bath and slipped beneath the depths with a sigh. I was adjusting my eye mask when I realized that I had not even told Mohammed thank you.

18

Dom

I'm f'ed up. Big-time.

The junior suite at the Hilton downtown was packed up with about thirty fellas. I was damn near blinded by all the diamond jewelry them cats was sportin'. Nothin' but ballers. It was a bachelor party for one of these fools who called himself gettin' married in the morning.

Matter of fact, it was the same little thick brother over there eatin' Cherry out on the floor in front of the lit fireplace. A bunch of his boys surrounded them cheerin' his ass on. The way she was hollerin', she either was a damn good actress or that little m'fer was hittin' the right spot, ya know?

I was high as hell, laughing to myself when I thought of his future wifey kissin' his nasty-ass mouth in the mornin'. The bitch ain't know it, but she'll be tastin' Cherry's twat.

Now I was busy givin' some cat a hellified lap dance in the corner, wearing nothing but thigh-high boots, a thong, and pasties on my breasts. I was twistin' my body, damn near doin' a head stand so that I popped that coochie all up in his face. And he was steady puttin' them bills down inside my boots.

When he stopped givin' up the money, I politely got my ass out of his face. No money, no honey, ya heard? I stood up, and the next fool sat down in the chair behind my back. I started backin' that ass up until I sat down on his lap. His hands touched my hips as I bent over to touch my toes and bounce on him like a low rider.

The crowd around us went wild, shoutin', "Damn!" in unison as I worked hard for the money in a way Donna Summer didn't know shit about. Some of the knuckleheads yelled out some rude shit, but I ignored them. I was too high to care. Too numb inside to give a fuck. Anyway, the m'fers with big mouths either had a small wallet or an even smaller dick. I ain't had time for either.

Without standing, I twisted around on his lap and then set my legs on his shoulders. I looked into his face and froze. "What the hell you doin' here?" I asked. My eyes were half closed from the liquor and shit.

He kissed both of my thighs and held my legs with his hands so I couldn't move. "I won't tell if you won't."

Lex's death really fucked with me. Deep down I knew it was all my fault that he got into the accident, because he was mad with me and lost control of the SUV. All mine.

The first few days were hell for me. My ass realized too little and too late that I really loved that nigga. I LOVED him. I missed him. And sometimes I felt like I wanted to be with him in death.

It got to be that I could go to sleep only if I was drunk or high. Seein' him in that casket had really shook me up.

My bedroom door cracked open, and I could slap myself for not locking it when I got home this morning.

"Mama?"

I held my blunt down on the side of my bed. "Get out of here, Kiki," I yelled, my patience shot to hell.

She peeked her little head in any damn way. "Ma?"

"Do what the fuck I said, Kimani!"

The door shut, and I stuck my blunt in my mouth as I wiped my eyes with my hands. Guilt filled me.

Guilt over Lex's death.

Guilt over the way I treated my child.

Guilt over what I did last night.

I still can't believe I fucked that dude.

My door swung open. "Look here, bitch. I don't give a damn what you do, but you ain't gone have my grandbaby cryin'."

I turned my head to look at Diane, but I ain't say nothin'.

She pointed her finger in my face. "That's your child. No man, dead or alive, is worth you ignoring her. You understand?"

I turned my head to look out the window and still ain't said shit. I was too busy lookin' at the sunrise. Too busy feelin' like shit.

"You better get your act together. I heard 'bout

how wild you been actin' down at the club. Every time I see your ass, you drinkin' or smokin'—"

"And you don't?" I asked in a dull voice, turning to look at her.

Diane's body got stiff like "Oh, no you didn't."

I knew it was coming, and I looked back out the window.

"Look here, bitch. I'm in control of my shit. Don't throw what I do in my face. See, you can pack all your shit off the floor and get the hell out if you don't like the way I run this f'ing show. This is my shit, and I do what the hell I want to . . . in . . . *my* . . . shit."

I kept looking at the peach, blue, and lavender surrounding that red-ass sky and said absolutely nothing.

19.

Moët

I absolutely loved the summer. The heat pressed against my body like a passionate lover, roasting my warm banana complexion to a bronzed pecan tan that I welcomed. I would sneak out into the backyard when my parents were gone, rub my body with suntan lotion, and baste like a bird on a rotisserie.

Summertime in Newark was a joy to me. The city was different, and you could tell when the summer fun was nearing without looking at a calendar. There was a different feel in the days. Freedom from long school hours had children laughing. Music being pumped from car radios thump-thumped as people drove down your block. And there always seemed to be more vehicles on the road when the heat reigned.

And the people. You never knew just how many people lived in your neighborhood until it got hot. The beautiful mosaic of people on the streets, stoops, and porches seeking relief from the heat of an apartment or house. All welcoming the death of winter and the vibrant life of the summer season with a smile.

The block parties. The ice cream peddlers driving around the neighborhood. The open fire hydrants children played in to escape the heat. The rugged b-boys playing ball on the blacktop courts.

I loved it all.

I sat cross-legged on my bed and gazed out at the boys playing football in the street down below. A car slowed to a stop, momentarily ending their game as they all scattered to either side of the street to let it pass. On the sidewalk four little girls were doing steps, chanting, "The devil did it to me," as they clapped their hands and stomped their feet.

"Yeah, me, too," I muttered to myself, hating that I even thought of the Good and Honorable Reverend Luke DeMark.

My cell phone vibrated from near my pillow. I rolled off my bed and wedged a book under the closed door. There were no locks on any of the Jones's doors. No, that book wouldn't keep them out, but it would give me time to hide my phone.

There were no TVs, radios, or telephones in our bedroom for me to use to drown out my voice in case my wardens happened by my room. Twenty-one and still sneaking. Ridiculous.

I reached for it and flipped it open, glad that Cris let me borrow the money to pay the bill and turn it back on. "Hello," I answered, lifting the screen on my window to stick my head outside.

"Good morning, Mo."

"Hey, Cristal. Why didn't you call on the house

phone?" I asked, waving at the kids who caught sight of me and yelled my name.

"I did. Your mama said you were sleeping and then asked me why I don't go to church."

Rolling my eyes, I swallowed back my irritation. "What's up, girl?"

"Remember the day you came by here last week?"

"Yeah."

"And remember the guy you rode up in the elevator with?"

"That rapper Bones?"

"Yes."

Oh, I remembered. He had been too fine with his sexy black self.

"He asked me for your phone number, but you know I had to check with you first," Cristal said. "Then he gave me his number to give to you."

"He did?" I asked, surprised. "What should I do, Cris?"

She was quiet for a minute. "I know you took what happened a few months ago really hard. I would have, too, but it is time to go on with your life the best that you can. Just be more careful this time."

I looked at the kids in the street and realized that eight years from now that would've been my son playing ball or my daughter being grown and doing steps with her friends. My eyes and my heart got sad.

"He is just a phone call away, Mo," she said softly. "He just went into a meeting with Mr. Linx—"

"Mr. Linx?" I asked at her formality.

"I am at work," she reminded me. "Anyway, what do you want to do?"

"Okay, but give him my number."

* * *

Twenty minutes later my cell phone vibrated. I carried it with me into the bathroom while I got ready for an afternoon summer class. I didn't get out of my funk soon enough to pass one lousy class. So I won't officially graduate until the end of first summer session. Thank God I was still allowed to march with the rest of my class.

Another secret I kept from my parents.

Flipping the phone, I turned on the shower and sat down on the toilet. "Hello," I answered in my most feminine voice.

"Moët?"

"Yes."

"Hey. This is Bones."

I shivered. He had a voice like Jah Rule, a body like Ginuwine, and the looks of Tupac. A triple threat.

20

Cristal

Professional but sexy. Respectful but attractive. Noticeable without appearing to want to be noticed. A perfect selection.

I knew from the once-over Mr. Sahad Linx gave me when I walked into his office that morning that the smoky lavender Lafayette 148 wrap dress was an excellent choice. The V-neck top and just-below-the knee skirt perfectly accentuated all of my attributes.

My infusion weave looking glossy and perfectly coiffed in a straight style that was sleek and well suited to my round face, I was looking good, feeling good, and ready to finally catch that man.

"Good morning, Mr. Linx." My heart pounded just from being in his presence.

He cleared his throat. "Morning, Danielle."

"Your car will be downstairs in twenty minutes to take you over to the video shoot at Madison Square Garden," I told him, looking down at his schedule for the day as I closed the agenda Alyssa left for me to stay abreast of his swamped schedule.

He was busy scribbling something into his own agenda, so I took the time to look around his sprawling office. I liked the masculine black, gray, and maroon tones with chrome furnishings. The framed platinum- and gold-selling albums on the walls were testaments to his success and power in the music industry.

Everything spoke of all the trappings of wealth.

"Will there be anything else, Mr. Linx?" I asked, wanting his attention on me.

Sahad looked up in surprise like he forgot I was standing there at all.

I wanted to shoot him my "I want you" look, but I kept my face composed and cool. I was not a groupie.

"I'll need you to go with me to the shoot."

I nodded, even though my stomach did a flip-flop. Alyssa had explained that she did accompany him to a lot of his appointments. Assuming that was all, and not wanting to seem eager to be in his overwhelming presence, I turned to leave.

Snagging a man like Sahad was about playing it cool.

Call it ego—call it whatever you like—but I had the feeling that his eyes were definitely on me as I left. Back in Alyssa's office, I double-checked my makeup in the portable mirror she kept in her desk. Needing only another light coat of my Chanel Glossimer lip gloss, I put the mirror away. I lightly sprayed my wrist and cleavage with my favorite perfume, Glamour by Ralph Lauren, hoping to finally have the glamour and the man I craved.

Of course, if he did make a sexual advance, I would politely resist with just enough interest to let him know I was attracted to him . . . but not easy. You must remember that every man kept one notion in his head when it came to women: you can not make a whore a housewife. Ahem, Rule #1.

And that was my goal: marriage. Period.

"All set?"

I looked up, and there he stood looking quite handsome in a very casual plaid shirt and khaki shorts. I liked the ensemble. Casual but not thuggish. It was something a successful Black businessman could easily wear to the Hamptons or Harlem.

I grabbed my Ria handbag and my Fendi rimless shades. "Ready."

Sahad, his publicist Savionne, and I rode his private elevator down to the underground parking lot. We exchanged no words because he was busy on his steadily ringing Blackberry. In the back of the limousine the calls continued, but I did not mind. Just being in his presence as the limo sped through the congested New York streets was enough.

"No one was able to reach Dom?" I asked.

"Not me," Alizé yelled from my bathroom.

"I tried to call, but all I got was her voice mail, and Diane said she hadn't seen her. I left a message."

That was Mo, looking quite stylish in a peach drape-front tank and stretch sequin jeans of the same hue. The color looked fabulous against her tanned skin and minimal makeup.

My first two days working as Sahad's assistant went so well that he rewarded me with four VIP passes to one of the artists' release parties. Of course, I was taking my girls. I just wished that Dom could have made it as well. Her raw energy would have made it even more fun.

"Tah-dah."

Alizé walked out looking like the true hip-hop diva she was dying to be in Gucci logo hot pants and high-heeled sandals. She did have the legs.

"Wonder what your Madison Avenue bosses would say if they saw you in that outfit?" I teased, because it was so different from the professional image she presented at her internship.

"I'm like a chameleon. I adapt to my environment, thankyouverymuch," she informed me with a ballerinalike spin and a kick of her leg.

"You ever thought about auditioning to dance in a video?"

Alizé pushed her shoulder-length hair behind her ears, showcasing her retro door-knocker earrings. "You see all that rump shaking those girls do? And the clothes? Have you seen the clothes they wear?"

I looked pointedly at her shorts which were a designer logo away from being stank. "Yes, we have seen the clothes they wear. They look like what you are wearing."

Mo laughed. "Yeah, don't bend over, Ze, or we'll see all of your business."

Alizé flipped us both the bird. "My dance instructor said I was good enough to audition for the Dance Theatre of Harlem, so picture me having my ass up in a video, leaning wit it and rockin' wit it."

First off, I was shocked for more than the obvious reason. Who knew Alizé was that good? She never invited us to any of her sacred dance classes. She hardly even talked about dancing. It was one thing about herself that she kept to herself. I had always respected her privacy.

"Come on. Let's roll. I want to see your Mr. Linx and your Bones face-to-face."

Mo and I exchanged a look at the way Ze changed the subject, but neither of us said a word.

"A'ight, bitches. Let's do this shit," Moët said suddenly as she stood up, sounding like our crazy-ass Dom.

We all walked out of the door laughing.

Music was thumping against the walls of Jay-Z's 40/40 Club, and a mass of bodies was gyrating on the dance floor. With our glossy VIP passes in hand, we headed straight through the crowd swarming around the burly bouncer at the foot of the staircase behind the velvet rope.

Just as we all walked up, a scantily clad woman boldly pulled her shirt up and shook her breasts at the bouncer. Nothing but a groupie willing to do anything, or rather, everything, to get past that rope. These women made it the main priority to chase celebrities, be it athletes or musicians. They were as much a part of the music and sports industries as flashy cars, clothes, and homes. They journeyed to nightclubs, parties, hotels, parking lots, and any other event sure to pull the well-known in the hopes of meeting the celebrity of their choice. Each groupie's goal could be different, some just to be able to brag to their friends that they slept with a famous rapper, others were looking to snag a celebrity as a husband, and some still yet saw it as their own claim to fame and celebrity.

Oh, we celebrity watched with the best of them, but we were not groupies. Yes, I desired to marry well, but I was not going to sleep with the security personnel of a famous person just for him to allow me a chance to then sleep with the actual celebrity. I had standards.

Reaching around the shirtless wonder, I flashed my laminated VIP card, and the velvet rope was immediately removed. "Right this way."

Smiling sweetly at him under the colorful flashing strobe lights, I pulled first Alizé and then Moët forward to head up the stairs. "Thank you," I mouthed to him, following behind my girls as the people at the bottom of the steps clamored to squeeze past him.

The bouncer held them off, and the rope was replaced.

We all held our heads high, knowing that all those left behind were jealous of our immediate entry. And we did not have to show a breast or promise some man sex. Like I said, we were not groupies.

I looked around at some of hip-hop's Black elite, and I was not ashamed to admit that I was impressed. Russell Simmons, Damon Dash and his crew, P. Diddy, and Andre Harrell, just to name drop a few. And there was Sahad, looking sexy as hell, even though he had Tyrea draped around his arm like a bad accessory.

He looked in our direction and did a double take. I had a feeling he was about to invite us to his already crowded table. I waved and quickly turned my back. The last thing I wanted to do was spend time in Tyrea's company. One hit record and the woman thought she was Aretha the way she strutted into the office. She was a diva before her time.

Moët wanted to find Bones, and Alizé left to find a quiet spot to call Rah. That left me standing alone.

"I'm paying you too much, Ms. Johnson."

My nipples hardened in a heated rush at the very sound of his voice, and I took a calming breath before turning to face him. "Why do you say that, chief?" I asked, looking up at him with a soft smile.

"You dress better than the wives of some of the record execs."

I was pleased by his compliment. Pawning another of Winthrop's platinum trinkets had made it possible for me to wear the melon, white, and gold stretch halter top with a plunging neckline and print stretch pants, all by Roberto Cavalli.

Now, a wealthy man who was possible husband material would feel somewhat less on guard if you appeared confident, attractive, and already well off and put together before you met him. Ahem, Rule #2.

"Just a little something I threw together."

"Well, you look beautiful." His eyes traveled up and down my body, and I felt this energy pulse between us. There was no denying his interest.

"Thanks, chief," I responded, keeping it light.

"Enjoying yourself? Need something to drink?" he asked, his eyes intense.

"I was going to call it an early night. I'm not really a club girl. I just wanted to show my support for the label."

"I'll have a bottle of champagne sent over for you and your friends," he told me, reaching for the cell phone on his hip.

I laughed.

"What's so funny?" he asked, now smiling as he held the vibrating cell phone in his hand.

"Nothing. My friends and I all have the names of champagnes as nicknames. Mine is Cristal. It is ghetto, I know—"

He laughed as well, and his eyes crinkled at the corners in the most delicious way. "No, no. It's cute," he said. "Hold on one sec."

Sahad turned away a bit as he placed the phone to one ear and his finger to the other.

"What's cute?"

I turned as Tyrea walked up and draped herself around his bent arm.

I did not even bother to answer her. "Excuse me," I said, walking away.

I was not in the mood for a cat fight, verbal or physical.

Besides, Tyrea was insignificant because Sahad's ebony eyes stayed on me all night.

Girl Talk

Postponed until further notice.

21

Alizé

"What the hell?" I snapped as I jiggled my key in the lock again.

Nothing.

My key to Rah's apartment didn't work.

I carelessly dropped my Louis Vuitton duffel onto the floor and dug into my purse with both hands for my cell phone. My heart was racing as I dialed.

"Whaddup?"

"Rah? Where you at?"

"In New York at the store. Why? Where are you?"

"At your apartment . . . locked the hell out," I screamed, kicking the door in frustration with my sneakered foot. "Why my key don't work?"

The door across the hall opened a crack, and I turned my back on Rah's nosy neighbor.

"Oh, I had the locks changed 'cause I lost my keys."

I rolled my eyes heavenward. "When?"

"Huh?"

My attitude shot up a notch. "When?"

"The super changed it for me this afternoon."

"You couldn't call and tell me that?" I snapped, glaring over my shoulder as the nosy neighbor opened their door a little wider.

"I know, baby, but I didn't know you was going to the apartment tonight. You got my car, right?"

I was pissed off. "Yes, *and*?"

"Go on home and I'll call you when I get there. Cool?"

"Whatever, Rah," I mumbled and then hung up the phone straight in his damn face.

I reached down and pulled my duffel over my shoulder, gave the nosy neighbor a glare, and stormed to the elevator. Something smelt fishy, and it damn sure wasn't me.

I didn't love Rah. I don't even think Rah really loved me. But we said the words. Went through the motions. I was not about to be played by some thug whose shoe size was higher than his level of education. Aw no, hell no. This sistah definitely was not having it.

On the ride down in the elevator, I was busy thinking like Angela Lansbury on *Murder She Wrote.* I tapped my foot and watched the lit numbers decrease.

Oh, I was getting in that apartment. Tonight!

Think, Alizé. Think, girl.

The elevator reached the ground level. I smiled as the doors opened and my gaze fell on the security booth near the front entrance of the building.

If Rah had been in New York all day getting ready for their grand opening, he was not here when the lock got changed. His copy might be waiting at the security desk for him.

A brotha was sitting inside the glass office in his generic rent-a-cop uniform. The same brotha who had tried to tell me how fine my behind was looking in my pale pink JLo velour shorts when I first walked in the building. Too bad I gave his butt a nasty-ass eye roll like I was Miss America. That's cool, just a little extra work to do.

Smoothing back my already slick edges with my palms, I dropped my bags outside the elevator and made my way over to him with a big Kool-Aid grin. "Hey, Brian," I said, after quickly checking out his name tag.

He looked up at me in surprise and then pleasure.

Got him.

He wasn't a bad-looking guy. He kinda resembled an even lighter skinned Ludacris. But I just knew that with his little job he wasn't pulling but eight, maybe nine dollars an hour tops. Chile, please.

I wasn't up in his face to make a love connection. All I wanted was that fucking key.

"Brian, I need a little favor."

This time when I stood before Rah's locked door the new key was glistening like gold in my fingers.

I unlocked the door, turned on the lights, and strolled in like I owned the joint. I didn't know what I expected to see or find out, but a sistah had her eyes on everything like an eagle even before I shut the door behind me.

Rah was hiding something. I was sure of it, and I was going Inspector Gadget to find out what. I headed straight for the bedroom and hit the lights once I walked through the door. Four large steps had me standing by the bed, and just that quick his ass was busted.

For one, whoever made the bed did a shitty job at it. Even Rah was anal enough that he made his bed every morning.

Two, my picture that usually sat on his bedside table wasn't there.

Three. Some perfume that wasn't mine clung to the covers. I couldn't quite name the scent, but I knew it wasn't mine because I only wore Happy by Clinique.

I snatched back the covers, flinging them to the floor in one swoop. Okay, there wasn't none of the telltale crusty spots on the sheets from love juices, but that didn't mean shit to me. I fixed the covers back, checked out the bathroom, and then left the room to snoop through the rest of the apartment.

No extra dishes in the sink. No female hairs in the bathroom. No odd phone numbers or messages on the answering machine. So what? I had seen enough to be suspicious but hadn't found anything to say I put my hands on him.

I turned out all the lights in the apartment and locked the door behind me. On the elevator ride down I was busy trying to picture who the little heifer could be. Everybody knew Rah was my man;

thus, whoever she was knew she was stepping on my toes and f'ing with my money.

I was gonna drain his ass before I kicked his ass to the curb. Oh, he was going to learn a lesson for trying to play me. Disrespect *me?*

I did my dirt, but I gave him his respect. I would never have another man in the bed we shared.

This was about my respect and money, not love.

But still it hurt.

I thought my juicy had his ass crazy. I never thought he would cheat on me. I honestly didn't believe any woman could outdo me.

Just imagine if I *had* let myself fall in love.

See the main reason why I don't mess around with loving no man? I learned a long time ago that love don't love nobody.

I put the disc inside the CD player in the corner and then strode over to take my position in the middle of the floor in front of the mirrored wall. And those mirrors might as well have evaporated, because as soon as the first sweet refrain of Stevie Wonder's "Ribbon in the Sky" floated into the air, my eyes drifted closed. In my mind I entered my own little paradise.

Nothing mattered in here. Nothing but the music and me. Not Rah's funky attitude lately. Not even my worrying about Dom. Nothing.

This was my therapy, my remedy, my one love.

Each turn, every twist, was like a drug to me as I tried so hard to recreate the steps I choreographed in my dreams. I hadn't come up with the ending yet, but every minute up to that point was absolutely divine.

During the hour I rehearsed my dream dance, or just practiced my reggae grinding in the mirror, it was all about enjoying myself. Just me and the music.

22

Cristal

"**D**amn it! Damn it! Damn it!"

Frustrated, I hit the steering wheel with my fist. Taking a deep breath, I made myself calm down and tried to crank my car again.

Nothing.

Now definitely was not the time for this. I was going to be late getting to work at this rate, and that was a no-no. I pulled the lever to open the hood and climbed out of the car. I had no idea what to look for or how to fix it even if I did.

"Mornin', Ms. Danielle. Can I be of service?"

I stiffened where I stood. When I turned my head to the right, I looked right up at Mohammed. "Good morning," I said, forcing a smile. "My car will not start."

"Lookin' sexy fine as always," he said, giving me a once-over that made me feel naked.

"What does that have to do with my car, Mohammed?"

He laughed, low and husky, a broad smile on his face. "What seems to be the trouble?"

I wanted to say, "If I knew that, why would I need you."

Mohammed moved to stand beside me, and I smelled his fresh soapy scent. As he leaned down to fiddle with something, I noticed that those dreads that I thought were funky were not so funky after all. Instead they smelled faintly of cocoa butter.

He moved suddenly and walked around the car to slide into my driver's seat. He just as suddenly jumped out. "You just need a jump, pretty lady. You left your lights on."

I winced in embarrassment.

"Be right back," he said before striding away in the garage.

Glancing at my watch, I reached into the car for my cell phone. I dialed the private line to Sahad's office, leaving a voice mail to let him know I was running late.

"Long time no see, Dani."

Turning, I did not bother to force a smile to my lips. "Hello, Winthrop," I said, my tone evident of my continued annoyance with him.

He was on an all-out campaign to get back in my good graces. Phone calls, uninvited stops by my apartment with gifts and flowers, notes pushed under my door. Now here he was blocking my car in with his Range Rover in our deserted underground parking garage. He was really plucking my last good nerve.

"Car trouble?" he asked, stepping out of his SUV to walk over to me in golf attire.

I gave him a nasty look that he chose to ignore. "I have someone assisting me, but thank you."

"Funny, I don't see anyone," he joked, pretending to look around. "Let me call my mechanic for you."

I heard Mohammed's old clunker roaring toward us. "Here is my help now," I said with relief, stepping past Winthrop as Mohammed parked his jeep in the space next to mine.

"Him?" he spat, obviously perturbed by the other man's presence. "Does he ever go home?"

"Hey, baby." I fawned over Mohammed as he walked to the front of my car with cables in hand.

He looked at me oddly.

"I missed you just that quick." I sighed, wrapping my arms around his neck.

Before he could protest in that lilting accent of his, I pressed my lips to his. My eyes warning him to play along. I just hoped he would not get any oil on my silk Liz Claiborne sundress.

"You asked for this, little Danielle," Mohammed whispered against my lips, unceremoniously dropping the cables to grasp my hips with his hands as he deepened the kiss.

He took advantage of my plight as his tongue caressed my lips softly before circling my own in a wicked fashion. He pressed my lower body closer to his, and I felt his dick growing as it pressed into my stomach with way too much thickness and length.

Soon Winthrop stomped to his SUV and pulled away with a squeal of his tires.

I yanked my head back and broke the kiss. "You can let me go now," I ordered him, prepared to knee him in the groin if I had to.

"See what you do to me, sexy lady?" he asked thickly.

"One—" I began.

He just smiled. "Now, come on, Danielle. You know you liked it—"

"Two—"

"I heard you moan, Ms. Danielle—"

"Three!"

"Okay, okay."

And he released me.

He smacked his lips. "So you had coffee for breakfast?"

"Just give me a jump," I snapped and immediately winced at how that sounded.

"Gladly, sexy lady—"

"Mohammed."

He laughed good-naturedly as he worked on connecting the cables to my car battery.

I wrapped my arms over my breasts. No need for him to see that my nipples were hard as acorns.

"You have a daughter, right?"

I looked up at Sahad at his question. I shook my head. "No, I do not have any children."

He leaned back in his office chair and looked across the desk at me as he rubbed his chin. "Oh, I thought I saw you with a little girl at the Family Day event."

I smiled. "That was Kimani, my goddaughter."

"Oh, okay . . . okay."

"You're putting the carriage before the horse, Mr. Linx—"

"I told you to call me Sahad, Danielle," he said with a smile.

"Okay, Sahad. I am not married, so children are not in the picture. I am not into the baby father drama."

"I hear that."

"You do not have any kids, either, right?" I asked as I looked back down at his schedule for the day.

"I guess we have something in common, because I am not feeling baby mama drama, either."

We fell silent after that. I wanted to strip down to my lacy French thong and climb right onto his lap. That would be fine if I was just looking for a one-night stand to brag about to my friends. I remained cool, calm, and confident at all times. I did not fawn over him and play into his ego. My thinking was that it would be as much a pleasure for him to date me as it would be for me to date him. Never let a wealthy man think he was doing you a favor. Ahem, Rule #3.

"Uh, Danielle . . . I mean Cristal. Do you have plans for lunch?"

My heart double skipped, but I just looked up at him with the most innocent face. "No. Why?"

He dropped the pen he was using to sign payroll checks and looked over at me. "I thought we could grab a bite together."

"Okay, just tell me where. I will call and make a reservation. How many?"

"Just two."

Our eyes locked.

"Just you and me?" I asked softly.

Sahad nodded with clear intent in his sable eyes. "If that's okay with you?"

"What about Tyrea?" I asked boldly, laying it on the line.

"It's over."

I wanted all or nothing. "How do I know that for sure?" I asked, tilting my head to the side to meet his heated stare.

Sahad leaned forward in his chair to put his phone on speaker and dialed a number quickly.

Three rings.

"I thought you said it was over, so what the fuck you calling me for, Sahad?"

My brows raised at the angry voice of Tyrea.

Seconds later the line disconnected, and the dial tone echoed in the quiet of the office until Sahad ended it.

My pussy throbbed as he rose to come around and lean against the desk. My eyes traveled from the enticing sight of his dick outlined by the linen shorts he wore to his handsome face. I was turned the fuck on by his power, his wealth, and his pure sex appeal.

Still . . . I had to play this right if I was going to play it for keeps.

"You're so damn beautiful," he said, picking up my hand to pull me to my feet.

"I don't want to be played," I told him softly in the heat between us as he urged my body close to his and lowered the mouth I had dreamed of to mine.

"Neither do I."

I quivered as his strong arms wrapped around me and he pressed his soft lips to mine. My hands rose to lightly grasp his lapels as he suckled my

tongue like he was thirsty. My heart pounded li[
wild drum, and my nipples ached as my breasts w
crushed against his solid chest. My clit tingled a
gave him just as much passion as he gave me.

Victory never tasted so sweet.

23

Alizé

"If there's nothing else, I say we call it a night."
I felt mentally drained, and I didn't want to show it, but I was happy as all get-out at Cameron's statement.

He looked around the cherry boardroom table at his mergers and acquisitions team. "Good night, everyone."

I chanced a look down at my Movada watch. It was going on 9:00 P.M. I had been up since 6:00 A.M. and had hoped to get my behind in bed early tonight. An impromptu meeting to prep Cameron for a trip to Chicago in the morning had put a stop to that with a quickness. Even though I was just an intern, Cameron had encouraged me over the last month to see everything and miss nothing as a part of my learning process.

All of the girls were busy with their own lives, and being at Rah's beck and call was no longer of interest to me, so I enjoyed the invaluable experience that I knew would benefit me in the end.

"Plan on spending the night?"

I looked up to find Cameron standing above me. Everyone had left, and the meeting room was now empty except for him and me. Lost in my thoughts, I didn't even notice everyone take their leave. I gathered my things and smiled as I rose. "Definitely not," I answered.

"How's everything going so far?" he asked as we walked together.

"Great. I think this internship will help me so much when I start graduate school," I told him as we neared his office, surprised by the scent of his cologne lightly tingling my senses.

"I hope you decide to apply here when you graduate."

We stopped at his closed carved mahogany door.

"Thanks, I'll take that as a definite compliment from *the* Cameron Steele," I teased, looking up at him with a smile.

"You do that."

We fell silent.

"I better head on home. Good luck with everything tomorrow."

"Thanks."

I walked away, heading to my own office for my briefcase and purse. I instinctively felt Cameron's eyes on me.

"Monica."

Uh-huh, I thought so. Turning, I looked at him with a questioning gaze.

He looked like he wanted to say something, but then he shook his head. "Nothing. Never mind."

"See you in a few days, then."

"Bye, Monica."

I turned back and continued on to my office. When I glanced back over my shoulder this time, he was gone. I couldn't help but wonder what he had started to say.

Cameron reminded me of a few of the guys I went to high school with. The kind that went to college and pledged white fraternities, dated white women, and listened to Michael Bolton, Barry Manilow, or Kenny G. I wouldn't be surprised to see him dressed like Carlton from *Fresh Prince of Bel Air* in chinos and deck shoes. He was definitely a nerd. A gorgeous one, but a nerd nonetheless.

I wanted nothing more than to go home and take a hot shower and crawl into my own bed, but I had promised Rah I would spend the night at his apartment. Since I was steady trying to work his ass for my own car in my own damn name, I steered his Benz toward his apartment. Once I had it, I was gonna ride away from his ass.

I was so glad that Brian the rent-a-cop was not at the security desk when I signed in. The last thing I was in the mood for was his weak-ass plays for my affection. I rode up in the elevator and used the key Rah *finally* gave me to unlock the door. "Rah, I'm here," I called out, setting my Coach briefcase and purse atop the leather bar.

"I'm in the bedroom," he called back.

Who gives a shit? I thought as I strolled in there. He was sprawled out on the bed, watching the flat screen television and smoking a blunt. Not wanting the scent in my work clothes, I removed my

Donna Karan suit and blouse at the door before hanging it up in the closet.

He smiled up at me like he was pleased as punch to see me, patting the spot on the bed next to him. "Come here, baby," Rah urged.

As I crawled on the bed and lay beside him, I was wondering if some stank hussy had laid up in the very same bed screwing my sorry-ass man while I was working. He didn't have to worry about getting up in my stuff raw dog anymore. There was too much shit out there to catch from a cheating dog. I lied and told him that I couldn't take my pills and we had to use condoms until I got on different birth control. The lie worked like a charm.

When he left the bed to go and fix himself a sandwich, I picked up his cordless phone and scrolled through the numbers in his caller ID. "Why didn't you tell me that Dom called for me?" I yelled when I spotted her cell phone number.

Rah walked back in carrying a black plate with two sandwiches on it. "Oh, I forgot. I'm sorry," he said, quickly eyeing the phone in my hand as he offered me one of the sandwiches.

I shook my head at his offer and dialed Dom's cell. It rang several times before automatically switching to voice mail. "Damn, Dom, you finally know how to call somebody, huh? I hope you feeling better. Call me when you get this. Oh, this Alizé if you don't recognize my voice. Call me, heifer."

I hadn't spoken to Dom in at least two weeks—maybe more—and even then I had to always call her. Maybe this weekend I'd round up Cris and Mo and we'd bum rush her. It was definitely time to see what was up with Dom and Kimani.

"I'm going to shower," I told him as I rose with effort from the water bed.

"Let me finish eating this sandwich and then I'll eat you."

I just smiled at him before walking into the bathroom. Once the door closed behind me, I rolled my eyes. I wanted to confront him, question his behind, and corner him, but I had no real proof. I had to put my hands on him so that he couldn't pull a Shaggy and say it wasn't him.

I've done my dirt on him, true. Knowledge of his shadiness had me call Lionel, and we had one helluva lunch date yesterday. If Rah wasn't bright enough to catch on to my game, then that was his damn problem. Right?

I stripped off my underclothes and stepped under the pulsating hot spray of the shower. I heard the bathroom door open and froze with my soapy loofah paused over my outstretched arm. My eyes widened as first one hairy masculine leg peeked through the curtain and Rah climbed into the shower with me. He was naked and already hard, his dick looking more like a condom-covered gherkin pickle than a cucumber like Lionel's.

"Come give me some sugar, baby," he moaned, pulling my wet body against his own.

"Rah, you gone mess up my hairdo," I screeched as water hit my hair.

"Just go to the shop and get it fixed."

I jerked out of his grasp and slipped past him to stand at the back of the tub. "I just went yesterday," I told him, holding out a hand to his chest.

Rah smiled as he jerked my body to his and then stepped back under the spray. "You are so sexy,

Ze," he whispered as he rubbed his hands over my body.

The suds and the heat actually intensified the feel of our bodies together as he sucked on my neck and squeezed my buttocks. I surprised myself when I moaned in pleasure. His thing was whack, but Rah did know how to use that tongue of his.

As he moved down to suck wildly at my nipples and the water beat down upon us, I actually didn't care that my perfectly coiffed hair became plastered to my head, neck, and shoulders with wetness.

All too quickly he moved back up to my neck, which was his usual speedy style. He pressed his erection into my stomach. "You want this bad, don't you?"

I bit my bottom lip to keep from telling his ass the truth as the warm fuzziness he started cooled with a quickness. "Yes, daddy," I moaned, lying big-time as his finger played in my sudsy pussy.

"Say please," he ordered, taking my hand to circle around his gherkin.

"Please, poppy," I said with a bad Hispanic accent.

As he lifted my leg and pushed the gherkin up inside of me, I went along with the motions and even faked a nut or two. The only thing on my mind as he grunted and tried his best to please me was the perfectly good Doobie I wasted for yet another sorry lay. Then I thought of the cherry red Chrysler Sebring convertible I wanted and faked another one. "You the best, Rah," I lied, clutching his neck.

24

Moët

"Say cheese!"

Bones, Sahad, Cristal, and I all smiled for the paparazzi, wanting to look our best for whichever entertainment magazine would publish the photos. And to think my parents thought I was away for a weekend orientation for graduate school. I had to come up with some lie so that I could spend some serious time with Bones, including attending the Los Angeles premiere of a hot new movie starring a lot of hip-hop entertainers.

It was so funny because Cris and I were trying hard not to act like we were star struck, but we would pinch or nudge each other when we spotted some of the biggest faces in the entertainment industry from Jay-Z and Beyonce, Trina, Mary J. and her husband Kendu, Will and Jada, and anyone else you could think of. It was the Who's Who of Black Entertainers. We were *loving* it, especially when we were introduced to the many celebs who chatted with Sahad and Bones as we all made our way down the red carpet.

And we looked great. Cristal wore a short Roberto Cavalli spaghetti-strap print dress, and I wore the strapless satin Bella top and vintage jeans.

"Girl, look over there. It's Usher," I whispered to Cristal as Sahad, Bones, and the entourage spoke to a correspondent from E! Television.

Cristal coolly looked over in that direction and nodded like she belonged in the presence of the rich and super famous celebrities. "Don't look now but Sahad's ex, Tyrea, is over there."

The guys moved on from Patrick and came back toward us, so I didn't get a chance to look anyway. I smiled up at Bones, who was looking too fine in casual Sean John wear. He worked the red carpet, waving and smiling at the screaming fans and posing for pictures like the star he was meant to be.

"Having fun, shorty?" he whispered into my ear as we posed for yet another picture.

"I sure am. Are you?"

"Just part of the job, ya heard."

As we moved forward, I heard a reporter ask the label's publicist who I was. My stomach felt warm when I heard her say, "That's Bones's girlfriend, Latoya James."

That was news to me but good news at least.

I hadn't even given him any yet, but that would all change this weekend. In fact, it would be the first time I did the do since . . . since the Rev. But I refused to think of him and all of the bad memories that went with him.

As I felt Bones's warm hand on my bare lower

back urging me forward with him into the spot-light, I felt like a much younger version of Stella, 'cause I was ready to get my groove back.

"Yes, I said my prayers, Ma."

"Thank the heavens for that. Are you sure there isn't a phone there where I can call you?"

I rolled my eyes heavenward. My mother acted like I was twelve instead of twenty-one. That was so aggravating. "No, Ma, I'm calling you from a pay phone."

"Reverend DeMark says—"

I faked a yawn, cutting her off. "I'm so tired, and I have to get up early. I'm going to bed."

"Your father and I worry about you, Latoya. You're so different lately."

"Like he cares," I muttered, instantly regretting speaking my thoughts aloud.

"Latoya!" she exclaimed. "What a hateful thing to say. Of course your father cares what happens to you."

"I know, Ma."

"Honor thy mother and thy father, Latoya."

I knew she'd get a scripture in there somewhere. "Ma, I have to go. I'll call you in the morning. Tell my little sisters I said good night. Okay. Bye-bye."

And I hung up the pay phone in the lobby of the hotel in my mother's face. A fact I would deny tomorrow.

Hours later Bones curled his naked and muscu-lar body close against mine in the middle of the messy bed. The moon was our only source of illumination. The heat of our sex still clung to the air.

"You sleep?" he asked as he lightly kissed my shoulder with those delicious lips.

I shook my head and then remembered he couldn't see me in the ebony darkness. "No, I'm not sleep."

"I'm glad Cris hooked us up, baby girl," Bones said, his words caressing the back of my neck as his hands found a comfortable spot on my hip.

"Me, too," I whispered with a smile. I was enjoying every moment.

Bones had made love to me. That kind of slow, sensual, emotion-filled lovemaking that could really get inside a woman's head. It wasn't sex at all. It was nothing like the nasty moments the Rev and I shared on his desk. This was a man putting his mind and his body into making sure that I was pleased.

Every kiss on my lips and face. Each stroke inside of me. Every suckle of my breasts. The soft touch of his hands on my thighs, my butt, my clit. Sweet Jesus!

He had made the most sweet and gentle love to me like he had forever.

I knew I was in love.

25

Dom

"*Damn, Dom, you finally know how to call somebody, huh? I hope you feeling better. Call me when you get this. Oh, this Alizé if you don't recognize my voice. Call me, heifer.*"

BEEP.

"*Bitch! If you don't get your ass here and get this girl, I'm gonna call D.Y.F.S. on your ass. What kind of mother are you when you ain't seen your child in two days? I done told you before that you made her and you gone raise her. What the hell—*"

BEEP.

"*Uh-huh. You thought I was through, but I ain't. I don't know what the hell you trippin' off of, but you better get your ass here ASAP. I got D.Y.F.S. on speed dial!*"

BEEP.

"Dom, this is Mo. I was just calling to check on you. Did I do something to make you mad? Call me."

BEEP.

"Whassup, chocolate. I'll be in the room in 'bout an hour. Go 'head and get that thing ready for me. I feel like eatin' 'bout a pound of it."

BEEP.

"Pick up this phone, Dom. Your daughter wants to talk to her sorry-ass mama." Pause. *"I never knew I would have such a slack-ass child."*

BEEP.

"Juicy? This Dogg. The boss wanna know when you coming back to work. Call a nigga."

BEEP.

"Dom, this Alizé again. Cris, Mo, and I just left your house. Your mom is trippin' so we're takin' Kiki to Chuck E. Cheese. Here Ki." Pause. *"Hi, Mama. You miss me? I miss you. Diane said you on a trip. When you coming home, Mama? I wuv you."*

Beep.

"This Ze again. The phone cut off. Dom call one of us. I can't really talk now with Ki here, but what's up with you? Bye."

I dropped the cell phone back in my purse, ignoring all the nagging-ass voice mails as my new man walked up behind me. He put his hands all over my body as we fell back on the bed together. He moved to bury his head between my open legs, his tongue Frenchin' my clit like it was goin' outta style. The way he was a groanin' and moanin', I knew Juicy had him good and fucked up.

This nigga knew he could eat that thang just right!

Sweat dripped from my body as I moved my hips up against his mouth. "Ooh, I'm comin', baby," I shouted as my pussy walls vibrated and I filled his mouth with my nut.

He sucked harder at my clit, and I hit a high note like an opera singer.

He rolled onto his back, and I moved to straddle his hips, slipping his dick inside me. He grabbed my titties as I rose dat ass like a pro. I looked down into his face all twisted from the feel of me.

"Who the best?" I asked him, reaching behind me to massage his balls.

"You!" he shouted.

"Better than her."

"Hell, yeah."

I laughed, even though my ass knew wasn't a damn thing funny.

26

Alizé

Rah was getting on my nerves.
It was our anniversary. One year since we hooked up and he insisted we celebrate by having dinner at one of my favorite soul food restaurants, Neicy's in South Orange. Just too bad the company was not as great as the surroundings.

I looked across the table at him and wished I had stayed my black ass home. To think I skipped dance class for this. His attitude had stunk since he picked me up, and things had just gotten worse as the night progressed.

The waitress brought out steaming plates of food, setting them down in front of us with a friendly smile. "Enjoy."

My smothered pork shops, macaroni and cheese, collards, and corn bread looked and smelled good. I usually watched what I ate to keep the figure slim, but I was going to splurge with the calories because I was determined to enjoy *something* about the night.

"This shit ain't even done!"

I looked up in surprise and a bit of shame at Rah's loud complaint just as he roughly pushed the plate away.

Looking around I saw that every eye was on us. "Rah, just ask the waitress to take it back," I said, leaning forward to talk in low tones to him.

"Hell with it. Let's go somewhere else," he said, his eyes angry and sullen—and glassy as hell—as they rested on me.

He was high. What else was new?

"Monica?"

At the exact moment that I heard that cultured and educated voice say my name, I wanted to shrink to the size of a tennis ball and roll my ass out of there. Forcing a smile and saying a quick prayer that Rah wouldn't act any more ghetto than he already had, I turned my head and looked up at Cameron and his date standing by our table. "Hi, boss, enjoying a night out?"

"Yes, we were just about to sit. Uh, this is Serena Lemons. Serena, this is Monica Winters, a new intern at the firm."

I held out my hand to the woman, who looked liked an ebony Barbie doll. "Nice to meet you. This is Raheem—"

"Rah," he interrupted rudely, glaring up at Cameron like he was a pile of shit on his new butter Timbs.

Serena looked a bit uneasy before she, too, forced a Kool–Aid grin. "Nice to meet you both," she said, her voice refined.

She crossed the *t*'s and dotted the *i*'s in her diction.

Cameron cleared his throat, placing his hand at the small of his date's back. "We'll leave you to your dinner. Monica, I'll see you in the morning. Rah, nice to meet you, man."

"Yeah, whatever," Rah mumbled, reaching for his glass of fruit punch.

They walked over to their table, and I counted to ten.

"Why were you rude to my boss?" I hissed, losing my appetite for the chops.

Rah turned and glanced at Cameron just two tables away. He turned back to me and then had the audacity to shrug.

All I could do was stare at that bastard like he was a creature from another planet.

"No . . . he . . . didn't."

"Yes, he most certainly did."

Cris and I exchanged a troubled look over our table at Justin's the next day for lunch. "I told you about those thugs, even one who has supposedly gone legit. He still lives and acts like a roughneck. I'm sure even MC Lyte has matured beyond the craze."

"Say what you want, Cris, but there's an aura around a thug—"

"That aura is the ghetto."

I signaled for the waiter. "I damn sure don't see myself with a man like Cameron."

"Why not?" she asked, taking a sip of her lemonade.

"One word: boring." The waiter came to a halt at my elbow. "Can we have the check please?"

Cristal reached inside her wallet, but I waved my hand. "My treat. I snuck a grand from Rah's stash. A gift to myself."

She shook her head at me as she slipped one of her beloved credit cards back into her wallet. "What's wrong with an educated man, especially since you're an educated woman?" Cris asked, looking over at me with confusion in her eyes.

"Girl, I just love me a thug."

Cristal almost looked like she felt sorry for me.

When Cameron invited me to a business dinner he was hosting, I was very reluctant to go, but he had taken on the role of my mentor which was an important tie I didn't want to sever, so I decided to attend. In business it was just as important who you knew as what you knew. I was going solo. Cris and Mo were both busy with their men, and there wasn't a snowball's chance in hell that I would take Rah. So it was just me, myself, and I.

All I could envision was stilted and boring conversation, elevator music, weird appetizers, and a room full of bougie people who would look down their noses at someone from the Bricks like me.

When I walked up the stairs of Cameron's three-story brick town house in South Orange, I was surprised to find that it was in a predominantly Black neighborhood. Inside, I was immediately impressed by the warm, masculine décor and the vast amounts of African artifacts and art adorning the walls.

I particularly admired a colorful abstract in the foyer.

"Are you a fan of Romare Bearden?"

I looked over my shoulder to see Cameron leaning in the doorway of the living room with a snifter of brandy in his hand. "Whom?"

"Romare Bearden. He was a preeminent African-American artist. In fact, all of my art is by various artists of color."

Okay, I must admit that impressed me.

He gave me a brief history of each author and painting as we strolled along the corridor and into his library. Surprisingly, I wasn't bored by his presence. In fact, I was intrigued by the passion in his voice as he gave me an impromptu art history lesson.

I learned about more than just art, though. A lot of things about Cameron surprised me that night. Who knew that Mr. Sell-Out would live in a predominantly Black neighborhood, collect African American artwork, and socialize with other people of all economic makeup? Hell, there was a brother there who worked for UPS!

"You look surprised, Monica?"

I took a sip of my white wine, resting the crystal goblet in the palm of my hand. "I do?"

He watched me over the rim of his snifter as he swallowed his own liquor.

"I guess I never thought of you being into Black art," I admitted as I looked around at the artwork adorning every available space on the walls.

"Why's that, Monica?"

I shifted my eyes from his and shrugged. "No reason."

Cameron shook his head regretfully. "Why's that, Monica? You think I'm an Uncle Tom, a sell-out, an Oreo?"

He must have seen something in my face, or maybe he was overly defensive, but I was shocked by the restrained anger I heard in his voice. I turned my head to look up into his face. "Cameron, I—"

A muscle in his cheek tightened as he clenched his teeth. "I guess I don't act Black enough for you, Monica. Maybe I should give back my Harvard education and settle for a GED."

I hadn't meant to piss him off. "No, Cameron—"

"Would I be more Black if I wore Timbs all the time, acted ghetto in a restaurant, smoked a blunt, and called you a bitch."

"All right, Cameron, I apologize, so don't go there."

"Sorry I'm not serving forties and playing music that degrades women, but try to enjoy yourself anyway," he threw over his shoulder as he turned and strode out of the room.

"Cameron—"

He paused in the door frame, turning to look at me with eyes that were filled with pity for me. "You know what, Monica? For an educated woman you have a lot to learn," he said, before leaving the room.

Now, what the hell was that supposed to mean?

27

Cristal

"**H**appy birthday, baby."

I looked up in surprise at the gift Sahad was holding in his hand.

"Sahad, my birthday's not for another few days," I protested lightly.

"Take it, baby," he urged, moving with ease to sit at my feet on the sofa.

And I did take it, letting the book I was reading rest open against my chest as I did. He smiled at me, looking so handsome with his head newly shaven and wearing the Calvin Klein gray silk sweater and slacks I bought him. You got to give a little to get a lot, okay. Ahem, Rule #4.

"Open it," he instructed me.

Carefully, I removed the silver wrapping paper from the long slender box. His eyes moved from my face to the box and back up to my face again. I opened the black leather box, and my eyes widened into circles. "Sahad," I said softly with surprise and pleasure.

The diamond bracelet was exquisite. Quickly I eyed it at a total weight of three carats.

With a soft smile, I leaned forward and kissed him deeply. "Thank you, baby," I whispered against those divine lips.

He took the box from my hands, removed the bracelet, and snapped it around my wrist.

My body tingled where his fingers lightly skimmed across my skin, and my heart raced at the sight of the diamonds glistening brilliantly in my eyes. "My birthday is not until Monday. Why are you giving this to me now?"

Sahad scooted down on the sofa and pulled me easily onto his lap. "I have to go out of town to-morrow, so I'll miss your birthday," he said regret-fully, his hand massaging my inner thigh.

Disappointment and hurt clutched at my heart. All my visions of enjoying a romantic dinner on my birthday vanished. "Business again?" I asked lightly, trying hard to hide my disappointment.

"Yeah, I freed up some time to be in the video for my newest group. The shoot's in L.A. and it's gonna take a few days," he told me, nuzzling his mouth against my neck. "You understand, don't you?"

Not wanting to rock the boat just yet, especially with that bracelet glistening on my wrist, I just nodded and turned into his strong embrace.

His lips sought mine, and I purred like a kitten as his tongue danced around mine. My hurt feel-ings dissipated in the heat we created as my fingers tugged at the edges of his sweater to pull it over his head.

His hands rose to pull the clasp from my hair, and it fell around my shoulders in soft auburn waves. "Sexy ass," he told me thickly.

I felt his dick press up against my core, and I ground my hips against it with a wicked smile. "Your sexy ass," I countered as I lightly raked my fingers through the soft hairs of his muscled chest.

He pulled the edges of my stretch T-shirt from my jeans and lifted it above my breasts. "Why your nipples so hard?" he asked as his fingers lightly tweaked them.

I grunted softly in pleasure. "Why your dick so hard?"

He laughed. "Shit, what you think?"

I laughed with him, lowering my head to taste his lips again. "You are so hard to resist, Sahad Linx."

He began to massage my breasts and tease my nipples like he had been doing it for years. "Why resist me?" he asked, pulling me down to suck wildly at my nipples through the lavender lace of my LaPerla brassiere.

"Shit," I swore as heat rose from my pussy up to warm my neck like a schoolgirl blush.

I reached between us to unzip his pants and free his dick.

He hissed at the feel of my hands as I massaged the stiff length of it in a slow and steady rhythm that made his tip drip. "Damn, Cris, I want to get so deep inside you," he groaned against my cleavage as he worked his hips against my hand.

Yes, I wanted to strip naked and set my pussy on his face.

Yes, I wanted to feel every inch of his dick against my tongue.

And God knew I wanted to slide down on that dick and ride it until it was white from our come.

But I was trying to play my cards to win.

"I just want to make sure what we have is going to last before I give it up. I do not believe in casual sex, Sahad."

He looked frustrated. "Damn, baby, make this motherfucker come then. Shit."

I pulled my breasts free from the cups of the bra and guided one to his hot open mouth, and I kept gripping and stroking his dick. He suckled my whole breast into his mouth, and his tongue had the quickness of a snake's as he tasted my nipples like they were the sweetest candy.

Sweat coated my body, and I felt like I could come from him just sucking my nipples. "Suck 'em," I groaned, drawing in air as I closed my eyes and rested my head against his.

"Come on, baby. Damn," he moaned against my flesh before taking my other throbbing and aching nipple into his mouth.

A jolt of pure electricity shot through my body, and I whimpered as my clit swelled and my pussy dampened the seat of my panties.

The phone rang suddenly.

I was glad I remembered to turn down the volume on my answering machine. Last thing I needed was for him to overhear one of those sickening creditors leaving one of those nasty "you better pay me my money" messages. There was no way I was letting him know that my financial situation was not together.

The ringing ceased.

"This bitch gone come."

I used some of his juices to wet my hand, making the up-and-down motion of my tight grip slick and hot as I picked up the pace.

My heartbeat raced. My nipples tingled like they were rubbed with ice. My pussy was so wet that my lips smacked against each other, and my clit was so thick that nothing but the slightest motion would make me come until I cried.

Wanting release, I bit my bottom lip and shifted on his lap until my pussy pressed against the side of his firm thigh. As I stroked him like a fiend I began to rock my hips back and forward on his leg, causing the hard seat of my jeans to rub my clit.

A little of that freak I was hiding from him came out as I cried out roughly when I felt my come squirt from my pussy like bullets fired from a gun. I rode his leg harder. "Suck my titties. Suck 'em now, motherfucker," I cried out as I flung my head back.

"Aaah," he cried out as his hips jerked up off the couch and his seed shot up like a geyser and coated my shirt, my chin, and his rigid stomach.

Even as my own nut subsided, I shivered as I worked his dick muscle until it was drained and lifeless in my moist and sticky hands.

Sahad's face was damp with sweat as he cocked one eye open to look at me and shake his head like "Wow."

Ding-dong.

My eyes popped open, caught a little off guard by the doorbell. But then I relaxed. No one would have been allowed upstairs without my permission, so it was probably a neighbor. At least I knew it wasn't Winthrop. The little impromptu scene with Mohammed that day in the parking garage had ceased all his efforts to reconcile.

Ding-dong.

"I'll get rid of whoever it is," I promised, my throat dry and sore from breathing raggedly. My legs were still quivering as I rose, and I had to pause and give it a count of five with my eyes closed because I was dizzy. I pulled my bra up over my breasts and my shirt down over my chest.

Sahad flung his drained dick back inside his boxers and zipped his pants.

I did not miss the quick look he gave his diamond-encrusted watch as I made my way to the door. Platinum Records' offices were closed in observance of Independence Day, but a man like Sahad never took a day off. I was still surprised that we had enjoyed the morning together without any interruptions.

Up on my toes, I looked out the peephole and saw him. My heart double pumped twice, and I hated that the kiss we shared had left such a impression on me. There was no way I would ever get involved with a man like Mohammed. No way in hell.

I took a deep breath before I opened the door. "Yes," I said, meaning to be distant as Sahad looked on from the couch.

Mohammed, catching sight of the other man, checked his usual flirtatious manner. At least I assumed that was why he did it. I even assumed he would get excited at the sight of the rich and famous celebrity, but he did not.

"Whassup, man," was all that he said with a nod of his head before turning his attention back to me. "I'm here to fix your kitchen sink."

He did not even call me Miss Danielle like he usually did.

"Actually, could you come back? I'm busy—"

Mohammed handed me the clipboard. "No problem. Sign in the pink area."

Even though the man of my dreams was waiting for me, I was put off by Mohammed's cool demeanor. "Sign for what?"

"It says that you refused to allow me entrance to make the repair," he said in that lilting Caribbean accent, looking down at me with eyes that were blank.

"I am not refusing to allow you entrance—"

Mohammed took a step forward, and the scent of cocoa butter surrounded me.

I placed a restraining hand on his chest. "But I have company."

"This is the day you requested because you knew you had the day off," he told me, handing me that clipboard again. "Sign."

Sahad appeared behind me suddenly. "It's okay, baby. Let him in."

"Fine," I acquiesced, stepping back.

"Sahad," he stated, offering the other man his hand.

Mohammed took it with a wide smile. "Mohammed. It's nice to meet you, man."

With that he walked into my kitchen, his dreadlocks swinging down his back as he did. Soon the sound of his work echoed into the living room.

"I am so sorry about this," I told Sahad, reaching my arms around his waist as he shut the front door.

"I'm sorry I'll miss your birthday this Monday,

but business is business, baby," he told me, giving me a hug back that I knew was a farewell. "Listen, I have to run. There's a lot of shit I have to tie up before I leave in the morning."

Again I felt disappointed. "How about I fix dinner for us tonight?" I asked, hating the pleading tone in my voice.

"I'm sorry, baby. I have a dinner meeting with my lawyers."

Again that pang of regret. "Good thing I trust you, Sahad."

"Baby, the only thing on my mind besides you is making money and keeping my eyes on my money," he teased, lifting my chin with his hand. "How about a trip when I get back?"

Now that piqued my interest. "Just you and me?"

"Just us, baby. Anywhere you want to go," Sahad promised, kissing my forehead. "And I have another surprise for you."

I looked down as he reached into his pants pocket and pulled out a Gucci logo key ring. My face became confused. "It's the key to my penthouse."

Gotcha!

Having that cold key pressed into my warm grasp lifted my spirits considerably.

28

Moët

Life was good for me.
I got an A for the class I took during June, so I was officially a college graduate.

I was studying hard for my New Jersey teaching certification, but in the meanwhile I had an interview for a long-term substitute position with the Essex County school board.

I would work and save money to get my own place. Soon I would have the one thing I wanted the most. Freedom.

I was in love with a man who lavished me with gifts and affection like I deserved.

I didn't think anything could bust my bubble.

Anything except going through my daily planner and noticing that I didn't have my cycle last month. My period was as regular as clockwork. Hell, you could set time to it. For the past nine years of my life there was only one other time that it didn't appear as scheduled. I didn't even want to think of that time.

Maybe it was just stress.

Then again maybe it wasn't.

I felt weakened by the possibility of being pregnant . . . again. I couldn't help but think of the child—my child—that I murdered. There was no way I was going through that again. No way in hell.

Grabbing my purse, I pushed the buzzer on the bus for the next stop before working my way through the standing crowd to the front of the bus just as it pulled to the curb. Four blocks from my house I walked into a small corner pharmacy and purchased my second home pregnancy test in my life.

As I started home, my purchase safely hidden in my book bag, my mind was focused on my dilemma. I moved like a robot. I waved to passers-by who spoke to me. I stopped at the corners until the street light switched to WALK. I did it all without really knowing that I was doing it.

"I might be pregnant," I said to myself as I climbed the brick stairs of the house/jail I'd lived in for every year of my life.

Pausing at the front door, my hand slid to my book bag for my cell phone. Thinking twice, I let it drop back into my bag with my book and the pregnancy test. I'd started to call for Cristal or Alizé to come and get me, but instead I just went inside.

What was I going to say? "Hey, girls, guess what? Remember that abortion I had, the one y'all paid for, well, I might be pregnant again."

And what about Bones?

And what about me? A piece of me wanted to replace the baby that I killed, and the other part of me was afraid like nothing else.

"Something wrong, Toya?"

My youngest sister, Latrece, was coming down the stairs just as I entered the foyer. Seeing the concern on her face, I wiped away my worried expression and threw her a big smile. "No, nothing wrong. Where's Mama?"

"At the church," Latrece told me over her shoulder as she walked into the kitchen.

My father was at work, and my mother was putting in her hours for the Lord. Good. Perfect time to do the test without my wardens busting in on me. I headed straight for the bathroom at the top of the stairs.

I breezed through the steps to do the test this time, eventually placing the cap on the stick before I quickly carried it and the empty box into my room. My heart was beating like a drum as I jammed an old shoe under my door.

I placed the stick flat on the bottom of my dresser drawer. I felt nauseous as the control window turned pink. In three minutes I would know for sure whether my ass had wrote a check I couldn't cash.

My hand moved to my flat stomach. "Another baby," I whispered aloud.

It had been just three weeks since that first night we spent in Los Angeles. Was it possible? Wasn't it too soon?

If I had another chance to be a mother, I would not throw it away. This time would be different because Bones and I were in love. Didn't he say he felt lucky to have met me that day at Platinum?

Didn't he make love to me like no other woman could satisfy him?

I smiled as I got caught up in my visions of his reaction to the news. He would kiss me and shout for joy. He would be too busy touring to go to every doctor's appointment with me, but that was fine as long as he was happy. I could see him buying little designer clothes for the baby and taking publicity photos to be released to the press.

Maybe he would even propose!

Then I could really get the hell out of this prison and run my own house, raise my child my own way, take care of my family.

Yeah, this time would be different.

If I was pregnant.

I moved from where I had been looking out my bedroom window. Wiping my sweaty palms on my knee-length navy skirt, I moved toward my fate. I reached in the drawer and picked it up, holding the test stick in my hand. "Well, that's that."

29

Dom

I drove my car up the Ave., my eyes looking left and right for Antoine's ugly ass. I couldn't find Jarvus, my regular supplier, so now I had Antoine on my mind. I just passed another bodega when I spotted his Magilla Gorilla–looking ass walkin' out the store in my rearview mirror. My palms were sweatin' as I turned the wheel doin' a U-turn in the middle of the street to head back in his direction.

A car behind me blew its horn as I almost hit dey ass, but I ain't care. I *had* to get to Antoine. I felt sick as hell like I could throw up and shit myself all at once.

I lowered the window. "Antoine!" I yelled out to him.

He turned, spotted me, and looked confused before he jogged across the street to me. "Oh, whaddup, Dom?" he asked, his voice gruff and wet sounding like he had spit in his throat. Ugh!

He bent down to lean into the window, and I had

to stop myself from frowning at the smell of old Newport cigarettes, Doritos, and funk on his breath. "Let me get a bag," I told him, holding my breath so I didn't swallow his.

"I don't sell weed, baby girl. Nothin' but the real deal."

"Don't you think I know dat," I snapped, pushing a twenty in his hand.

His face became shocked. "Damn, Dom, I ain't know you got down like that!"

"Fuck the commentary and give me my shit."

He dropped the tiny Ziploc bag of pedope onto my lap. "Do you," he said, unconcerned. To him I was nothing but another customer.

"Yeah, whatever," I said, pulling off as soon as he stepped back from my car.

30

Alizé

"Rah, it's me. I made it to Houston okay. Thought I could talk to you before all of the conference meetings began, uhm . . . I guess you aren't home." I glanced at my newest Gucci watch. "I've been trying to call on your cell since early this morning. I'll just call you back later. Bye."

I released a deep breath as I dropped my silver cell phone into my attaché. I walked around the bedroom of my junior suite at the Hotel Derek near the Galleria Mall. I couldn't help getting pissed as I pondered just what Rah's little slick ass was up to. Did he even stay at his apartment last night or was he just avoiding my calls because he was still upset?

Acting like a straight bitch.

Rah hadn't wanted me to accompany Cameron on the business trip to Houston. This conference was free, the trip was free, and all of it would help my career in the long run. Was I supposed to turn down Cameron's generous offer? Hell no.

Rah was just trippin'. He even accused me of messing around with Cameron, which was the dumbest thing I heard in a long time. Cameron and me? Please.

Rah was just guilty 'bout his own dirt, that was all, and he still had no idea that I was on to his no-good ass. Just like he didn't know about Lionel. What was good for the goose was damn sure good for the gander. Okay?

Bump Rah. If it wasn't for the fact that we actually went car shopping last week, I would've dumped his ass and moved on to bigger and better things.

I was just slipping on the heels to match my pantsuit when there was a knock on the door. Knowing it was Cameron, I grabbed my Gucci purse before leaving the bedroom. "Coming," I called out.

"Hello, Cam—" The rest of the words froze in my throat at the sight of him. *Well, I'll be damned.*

Cameron was dressed casually in a Tommy Hilfiger shirt and jean shorts, both fit loosely around his tall, muscular frame. He even had on a fitted baseball cap and black Jordans. He looked like one of the fellas around the way. Definitely not the tight LeTigre tucked into fitted Lee jeans like I would have expected.

"I feel overdressed," I said, looking down at my silk Norma Kamali suit. I'd assumed he would be similarly dressed in business attire. I grabbed his hand and pulled him inside. "Have a seat while I change."

"Take your time," he told me, moving to pick up the remote and turn the television in the corner to ESPN.

I left him in the living room while I chose a casual outfit. When Cameron had said he was going sightseeing and asked if I wanted to tag along, I agreed. There weren't any meetings until the following morning, and since I wasn't familiar with the city, I didn't want to wander alone.

I hung the outfit back on a padded hanger I brought and pulled on a pair of vintage Versace jeans, beautiful beaded peach tank, and traded my pumps for high-heeled sandals. I swapped all the stuff from my Gucci purse into the tiny beaded clutch matching my sandals. One last check of my hair and I was ready. Not bad for under five minutes.

"All set," I told him as I stepped into the living room.

Cameron rose from the couch, his coal black eyes moving from my head down to my manicured toes. "You look . . . good," he said, abruptly moving to the door to hold it open for me. "You're very stylish. I can't wait to see what you brought to wear to the charity ball tomorrow night."

I froze in the hallway as Cameron closed the door to my suite. "What ball?" I asked, turning to face him.

"Didn't I tell you about it? The company throwing the conference has this big charity ball at the end of the conference every year."

"No, you didn't."

Cameron turned and looked down at me. We were so close that his cologne teased me. I could see that his eyes weren't black but a deep shade of chocolate. "Guess we're going shopping," he said dryly, smiling.

The elevator dinged open. "You, Mr. Steele, are even smarter than I thought," I told him before stepping onto the elevator.

"A ball, huh? Sounds like a date to me?"

I rolled my eyes heavenward at Cristal's words as I finished getting dressed. Cameron was supposed to pick me up in ten minutes. "This is most definitely not a date. It's all business."

"Well, make it risky business," Cristal teased through the phone line. "He is handsome, wealthy, intelligent, and cultured. He is not Rah, and he is not ghetto. Should I continue?"

"He's not my type, Cris."

"Liar, liar pants on fire."

"I don't like him like that," I insisted, realizing that I was trying to convince Cris *and* myself.

Sightseeing yesterday with Cameron had been nice and different. I liked the places we went, the respectful manner in which he treated me, and the conversations we shared.

We started off the day with a breakfast of wings and waffles at the Breakfast Klub—a popular eatery on Travis Street that catered to Houston's local celebrities and politicians. Next we checked out the city's sights. I had a really good time as Cameron filled me in on little historical tidbits as we toured the Buffalo Soldiers National Museum. I had nothing but reverence for the slave documents and replica of a slave ship at the Black Holocaust Museum Exhibit. As we strolled through the Gite Gallery, I admired the fine art and was impressed as Cameron bought several priceless pieces without blinking an eye.

We rounded out the day with an early dinner of Caribbean food at Lagniappe Grill. Who knew you could get shrimp on grits?

All of it had been something I enjoyed and never knew I wanted to explore. It had been a fun day . . . especially shopping for the ball attire. I was quite surprised when he insisted on paying for it. It was his way of apologizing for not informing me of it.

And he went shopping for the dress with me. I modeled them for him, and he became exasperated that I couldn't decide on one. Could I help it that I loved all ten?

My reveries ended when I remembered I was on the phone.

"Cris, I have to go. I'll call you tomorrow when I get back to Newark. Call Mo and try to find Dom and we'll go eat."

"Girl, I can not remember the last time I talked to Dom," Cris said.

"All the more reason for us to find out what's going on with her."

"You are right. See you tomorrow."

"Okay."

"Oh, and Ze? I will take it back to the old school. Cut that zero and get with that hero."

I rolled my eyes heavenward. "Bye, girl."

"Ta-ta."

There was a knock at my door just as I dropped my cell into my new beaded clutch purse. I took one last look at myself in the mirror. The body-skimming strapless gown was a gorgeous and elegant ebony that seemed to make my cinnamon brown skin even more vibrant. A trip to the salon and my hair fell in delicate waves to my shoulders and my makeup was smoky and sexy for an evening look. Stiletto sandals completed my outfit.

Cameron knocked again.

"Coming," I called out, moving toward the door.

I wouldn't admit that I was feeling just a bit nervous about how Cameron would like my appearance. I mean the man did pay for it all—another plus in Cris's book *if* I had told her about it.

"Hey, Cameron," I greeted him.

I looked up at him, and I was at a loss for words. The man looked gorgeous. The tuxedo was so obviously tailored to fit his physique perfectly that there was no way it was a rental. He held a single rose that he offered to me. I accepted it, vaguely wondering if Rah or Lionel even owned or wore a tuxedo. I doubted it.

"You look beautiful, Monica," he said in a deep, husky voice that let me know he totally meant the words.

Did I mention that I suddenly loved the way my real name sounded from his lips?

Uh-oh.

31

Cristal

Some birthday.

Sahad was out of town. Moët was at some church function. Ze was in Houston. Dom was *still* MIA.

A couple of coworkers treated me to lunch. Mostly they wanted to gossip about my relationship with the boss, but at least it was something.

Days like these it really hit home that I had no history, and no family. Thank God for the girls because without them it would truly be just me. A motherless and fatherless child. My parents did not want me, and that was a bitter pill to swallow.

Ever since I was fourteen, I worked for everything I called mine. With the childhood I had endured, I felt I deserved a beautiful apartment, fancy clothes, and a nice car. I was just making up for everything I lacked coming up. A wealthy husband would ensure it all for me with none of my present worries of robbing Peter to pay Paul as I dodged creditors.

What was so wrong with that?

Ding-dong.

I turned from the living room window to look at the front door. Sahad! Quickly I moved toward it, smoothing the silk lounging outfit I wore over my hips. I pulled the door open with a smile. "I knew you wouldn't leave me alone on my—"

My words evaporated into nothing as I looked up into Mohammed's amber eyes. I was absolutely speechless because I had never seen the handyman look quite this way.

"Happy birthday, Ms. Danielle," he told me with a smile.

His dreadlocks were pulled back from his face with a leather strip to flow down his broad back. The linen sports jacket he wore fit his broad shoulders nicely and contrasted well with the crisp white shirt and jeans he wore. The bouquet of lilac roses he held finished the brotha off nicely.

Oh, the little handyman cleaned up nicely.

"Thank you . . . thank you, Mohammed," I said finally, accepting the flowers. "What are you doing here?"

He smiled and looked past me into my apartment. "I hated to think of such a beautiful lady spending her birthday all alone."

"And how did you know it was my birthday?" I asked with a curious expression as I leaned against the door.

"The day I fixed your sink I overheard you and your man talking about it."

"Oh," I said and raised a brow.

He bent down and picked up a plastic bag filled

with take-out containers, a bottle of champagne, and a cake box. "Truce, Danielle?" he asked with a serious tone.

I looked down at the roses and then gazed up at him holding dinner and cake for me. I didn't want to be alone for my birthday. "No strings?" I asked with a warning glare.

"No strings," he agreed, breezing past me into my apartment with confidence and that damn scent of cocoa butter.

"Okay, I'll admit it. The food was good. Too good." I sighed, content and full as we sat at my elegant dining room table.

"I thought you were gonna swallow that bone, you were sucking on it so hard," he teased in that soft Jamaican lilt as he rose from the table with both our plates.

"You do not have to do that," I protested half-heartedly.

"Oh, you really sound like you mean that," he drawled, disappearing into my kitchen.

I could not believe I was spending my birthday with Mohammed, a man who was so different from everything I wanted in a man. I wished Sahad were here, but Mohammed's company had been nice. Real nice. He was funny, good-natured, and a hopeless flirt.

The lights suddenly dimmed, and I was just about to scream for help when Mohammed walked in carrying the cake with lit candles. "Hap-py birthday to you," he sang.

I hid my smile at his off-key rendition. "It's a good thing you're handy, because you have no future as a singer," I teased.

Mohammed laughed softly as he set the cake before me on the glass table. He poured us both a glass of champagne, handing me one. "Here's to many more happy birthdays for one sexy-ass lady."

We touched glasses together as I warmed under his compliment.

"Thank you," I told him softly, taking a deep sip.

"Now make a wish."

I was not an emotional person. The only people I ever deeply cared about were my girls. Still, as I gazed into those tiny embers, the painful truth of my life weighed down on my shoulders, and I felt like crying. "I . . . uhm, never had a birthday cake," I revealed, surprising myself. "Ever since high school my friends and I take each other out to eat or to the club to celebrate birthdays, but I have never blown out candles and made a wish. This is . . . sweeter than you even know, Mohammed."

He reached across the table and covered my hand with his own. "Hey," he said softly, drawing my eyes to his face. "This is your first one, so make your wish extra special."

Smiling away the tears before they could fall, I inhaled deeply and closed my eyes. *I wish that I am this happy on all my birthdays,* I thought to myself, before blowing out every last candle.

"Nothing in this world would have kept me away from you on your birthday," Mohammed told me, his tone as serious as those damn amber eyes staring into mine.

Brrrnnnggg.

We both jumped at the alarming sound of the phone ringing. "I better get it," I told him, moving to the living room.

I picked up the cordless from the base and saw Sahad's cell number displayed on the caller ID. "Hey, baby," I sighed into the phone, glad that he called.

"Hey, how's my birthday girl?"

"Missing you like crazy," I told him, noticing out of the corner of my eye that Mohammed was walking to the front door.

"Wait," I said softly, turning to call out to him.

Mohammed paused in the now open doorway and turned to face me.

"Who there? Who you talking to?"

"Nobody, Sahad. No one's here." My eyes locked with Mohammed's as I lied.

He turned and walked out of the door, closing it quietly behind himself.

32

Moët

"**B**itch, you *must* be crazy!"
My eyes widened as Bones flipped out at the news of my pregnancy. This definitely was not the reaction I dreamt about. As he cussed and fussed about me setting him up to gank him for his loot, it started to feel a lot like Reverend DeMark's reaction.

The same sorry-ass shit.

I felt like crying because it hurt so bad, but I refused to let this ignorant Negro see the pain.

"You ain't gettin' no money, so your ass can forget about it."

"I don't want shit from your sorry ass," I spat, pissed and hurt. I got out of his bed, naked and with a wet ass as I started to pull on my sister Latoya uniform clothes.

My words angered him.

"If *I'm* sorry, why your ass get pregnant," he shouted, getting out of bed to pull on his boxers.

"Fuck you."

"Fuck me?"

Damn, I didn't think I said that aloud. Oh, well. "Yes, fuck you."

I grabbed my purse and stormed out of the bedroom. I felt nauseous, and tension made my shoulders and neck stiff as panic began to set in. I had to get out of his presence before I broke down completely.

He followed behind me. "Who says it's mine? Ho, I don't know who you fuckin'."

"Well, only a jackass would eat a ho's pussy." I kept moving on to the door and didn't break my stride.

"Bitch! Shut the hell up."

I turned and looked at him. I mean, I really looked at this man standing before me. Just ten minutes ago he was diggin' out my pussy and tellin' me how special I was to him. How he couldn't picture life without my smile and my touch.

So I looked at him, and I damn sure didn't like what I saw.

Without saying another word, I turned, leaving his apartment and his life.

It really began to sink home that I was in the same predicament again. Pregnant with a more than reluctant father. What in the hell was I going to do?

All of my bravado and toughness cracked once I was in that elevator. I felt weak with pain and regrets and disappointment and shame. My tears ran like waterfalls, and I stumbled back against the wall, sliding to the floor as my legs gave out beneath me. I felt so engulfed by the pain of his rejection and accusations. I hated myself and I hated him. God, I hated him.

The elevator ground to a halt, but I didn't have the strength or the will to rise.

"What the hell . . . Mo? Mo, is that you?"

I looked up, and there stood Cristal and Sahad. Crying hysterically, I made myself get up and then flung myself into her open and waiting arms. "Help me, Cris. Please, help me," I sobbed, grateful for my friend.

"What happened? Where's Bones?" Sahad asked. "What's going on?"

"What is the matter, Mo, huh? Tell me what happened?" she asked me again as she led me off the elevator.

I cried even harder onto her shoulder at the concern in her voice as she rubbed my back.

"Let's all go upstairs," Sahad suggested, looking around at the curious eyes that were on us in the lobby.

"No!" I yelled, lifting my tear-streaked face to look up at Cristal. "I'm not going back up there. Please, Cris, take me home."

She nodded and looked at Sahad with concern. "I better just take her," she told him softly.

"Take the car," he said, handing her the keys. "I'm going up to see what the hell is going on."

I said nothing as we walked out of the luxury apartment building on the Upper East Side. Not even when we were settled into his Hummer did I speak. It hurt so much to admit to anyone the horrible way Bones had flipped on me. I might as well have been some damn groupie.

"Did you and Bones argue?" Cristal asked again.

"I don't feel like talkin', Cris."

We fell silent after that with Cris handling the powerful and massive vehicle easily through the busy night metropolitan streets. I looked out the darkly tinted windows at the people, the cars, the stores and saw nothing but Bones's angry face and then Reverend DeMark's condemning eyes.

I hated them both with a passion.

"Are you sure you want to go inside? You can stay at my place."

Cris's words jolted me, and it sank through my haze that we were double-parked outside my parents' house.

"I can call Ze, and we can all go to my apartment."

My tears were gone, and nothing but hatred remained. Much as I loved my girls, they would want to talk about what happened, and I was just too ashamed. "I'll be all right. I'll call you tomorrow, a'ight?" I told her with a stiff smile.

I hopped out before she could say anything else. I wasn't going to rely on my girls this time. I had to take care of this for myself. Besides, I was going to make that bastard pay, and they would stop me. I was tired of sorry-ass men who didn't want to take care of their responsibilities. Bones was partly to blame for me now being pregnant, penniless, and hopeless.

I was not having another abortion.

Not this time.

I let my last baby daddy get away with that dumb shit.

Not this time.

I walked into the house and headed straight for the living room. My mother was reading her well-worn Bible, and my father was watching the news on television. The tears that fell from my eyes were real. "Ma . . ."

"Good heavens, Latoya, what's wrong?" she asked as she rose to walk over to me.

I didn't even look at my father because I didn't expect a reaction out of him anyway.

"What's wrong, Latoya?" my mother asked again.

I took a deep breath. "I been raped."

33

Alizé

"Cameron, you wanted to see me?"

"Yes, come on in, Monica."

I closed his office door behind me and moved to take a seat before his desk. "I still cannot believe today is my last day. I'm going to miss everyone."

Cameron signed a few papers with bold slashings and then looked up at me with a smile. "We're going to miss your energy. You really were helpful on a lot of the projects we worked on in the two short months you've been here. Keep working on that degree and soon I'll have to watch my job," he joked good-naturedly.

"Every man for himself and God for us all," I joked in return. I tried to smile but I just couldn't.

"Something wrong?" Cameron asked, his concern obvious.

"Sorry, I just got a lot going on these days."

"Anything you want to talk about?" He rose to come around his desk.

It certainly wouldn't be right to discuss Mo's recent sexual assault or the details of my rocky relationship. "No, I'm okay, but thanks for the offer."

Cameron moved over to the sprawling bay windows of his office. "I remember in Houston you told me how much you loved dancing," he said, looking out at the busy metropolitan streets below.

Yes, I did. As we slow danced under the chandelier of the elaborately decorated ballroom, I had told him about my love, how it flowed in my blood and sustained me.

He turned his head to look over his broad shoulder at me. Our eyes met, and there was a crack in his confident façade as he cleared his throat and retook his seat. "I, uh, have tickets to Dance Theatre of Harlem performances tomorrow night. Would you like to attend with me?"

My face showed my surprise. Cameron was asking me out on a date! He was handsome, intelligent, classy, well dressed, financially stable . . . and not my type. He was better suited for Cristal than me.

I had to admit that we vibed well on the job and when it came to work we had many similarities. We even shared a lot of laughs as we worked. And I felt comfortable around him. More comfortable than I would have thought. But dating Cameron? Or Cameron wanted to date me? I never saw that coming.

For me that "I don't give a fuck" attitude of a thug drew me. Even a thug whom I hadn't spoken to since I returned from Houston last week.

Lionel had filled in the void quite well.

"Cameron, I—"

"Don't think that would be a good idea," he finished, taking the words straight out of my mouth.

"I consider you a friend, that's all," I said, lightly, feeling so put in a damn corner.

Cameron turned down his lips, nodding as if he truly understood.

"I hope this doesn't cause any hard feelings between us."

"I'm not a sexual harasser, Monica," he countered sternly, picking up his pen to return his attention to the files atop his desk.

"No, you are my friend, or at least I thought you were," I told him, actually hating that I may have hurt his feelings. "At least I thought we became friends in Houston."

"Your friend but not your type, right?"

I flinched under his piercing gaze.

"You want to know why I'm so upset right now, Monica?" he asked, tossing his pen onto his desk as he leaned back heavily in his chair.

"I'm gonna go, Cameron," I said softly, turning to leave.

"One day you'll grow up and realize you deserve better," he said.

His words followed me out of his office and remained with me long after my final workday was over.

I turned my mother's car down the street Rah lived on. He was avoiding my calls, and I finally decided to just bum rush his ass at home. If it was over, then I was going to make him be a man and tell me to my face.

The only thing I would miss would be the money and not that sorry-ass itty-bitty gherkin dick, that's for sure.

As soon as I pulled into the gated parking lot, I spotted his car. I felt like throwing my mother's steering wheel Club through his windshield. But I'd seen enough Judge Mathis to know that if Rah sued, I would have to pay to get the m'fer fixed. That's a big nothing.

I parked the car and hopped out, clutching my key. I had a surprise for his sorry ass. I signed in at the security desk and climbed onto the elevator. Soon I was standing at his door, easily unlocking the latch and walking into the apartment.

The scent of weed was strong. As I neared the bedroom, I heard the telltale grunts of two people fucking. I caught his ass! As if he had enough dick to share.

I bust into the bedroom.

"Who's the best?" he asked, sweat dripping down his back to the crack of his butt as he screwed some tramp from behind.

"Sure ain't your sorry ass," I yelled, lifting my foot to kick him straight dead in his ass as hard as I could.

Rah hollered out in pain and surprise as he fell forward onto his mystery woman. He rolled out of her and jumped off the bed to push me roughly out of the bedroom and against the wall hard. "Get the fuck out," he yelled in my face, his hands closing tightly around my neck.

Using the keys in my hand, I attacked his cheek, and he released me. Gasping for air, I slumped down to the ground and then used all the energy I could find to crawl away from him when I saw the crazy and hate-filled look in his eyes. *What the hell is he so mad for?* I thought, feeling the first bit of true fear.

I yelled out as he lunged for me with blood dripping from the deep gouge on his cheek. Futilely I scratched at the cold tile floor as he grabbed my feet and dragged me back toward him. I got one foot free and kicked wildly as I fought like hell to get away. As a kick landed on his arm, he only got angrier. I felt like I was in the middle of a damn nightmare.

"No good trick," he roared, flipping me over onto my back before he knelt and struck me twice in the face with his fist.

I howled out in pain, feeling like a truck ran over my face, as I lifted my hands and arms to block the rest of his blows.

I couldn't believe it. Rah had never hit me. Never.

"Stop, Rah! Stop it. What the fuck you doin'?"

Even through the pain of his blows landing on my body, I knew that voice. I turned my head and looked between my arms at her. "Dom!" I gasped, seeing one of my best friends' naked and sweaty body as she tried hard to pull Rah off of me.

Dom was the bitch fucking Rah.

She yanked him to his feet and stood in front of him. I scrambled onto my own feet, but as I stumbled, I fell back over one of his bar stools. I could taste blood in my mouth, and my body ached like I'd been in a bad car wreck.

Still, Dom's betrayal hurt me worse.

"Fuck that. Fuck that. All the shit I did for that bitch and she gone fuck some nigga on me," he shouted, his face enraged like a charging bull.

Rah pushed Dom out of the way, and her body slammed against the bedroom door. He moved to stand over me. "No-good, bitch," he spat as he raised his leg and stomped down on my left thigh atop the stool.

I heard the bone snap before I screamed out in the worst pain I ever imagined. Pain that caused me to slip right into unconsciousness. I welcomed the black abyss that swallowed me whole because at least I wouldn't feel the pain of a friend's ultimate betrayal.

34

Dom

I wasn't shit. No, no. I was a no-good piece of shit. Tears streamed down my cheeks as I poured more dope on the back of my hand and sniffed up as much of that shit as I could.

It filled my bloodstream and sent me high as a motherfucker.

I didn't want to remember nothin'. Not Lex, not Alizé, not Rah, not even Kimani. Not a damn thing. I wanted to go numb cuz I knew I f'ed up big-time. My man was dead because of me. One of my best friends was in the hospital because I told Rah about Lionel while I fucked him like he wasn't my best friend's man. I wasn't no kind of mother to my fuckin' child. I wasn't shit.

I sniffed more until the second bag I bought was gone, too. I felt like my body was floatin' up to the sky. Smiling, my head nodded forward, and I scratched at my cheek.

"I'm fucked up," I slurred, my lids so heavy that I couldn't open them.

I couldn't even stop my body from falling forward onto the steering wheel, weighin' down on the horn.

I don't remember shit after that.

35

Cristal

My nerves were just about shot as Sahad and I rushed into the emergency room of the University of Medicine and Dentistry of New Jersey on Bergen Street. I was so glad he agreed to drive me because my hands were shaking so bad that I could not even think about handling a vehicle.

"Excuse me, I am looking for my friend," I said to the twenty-something woman behind the admitting desk.

She looked past me to Sahad, and her face suddenly lit up with recognition. "*Daaaamn*, aren't you Sahad Linx?"

I stiffened with anger, and Sahad placed a comforting hand on my lower back. "Excuse me, but we're looking for—"

"My name's Tashi," the woman said excitedly, rising from her seat with pen in hand. "Could you autograph this for me?"

Sahad's two burly bodyguards immediately

stepped forward, forming a wall of pure muscle around us. "No autographs," Hammer ordered roughly.

"Cristal."

I turned and stood on my toes to look over one of the guard's massive shoulders to see Diane. I pushed past them to run to her. We hugged each other tightly. "Where is Dom?"

"They rushed her in the back. Cris, did you know Dom was on dope?" she asked, her eyes reddened and filled with question. "Did you know?"

One of my best friends was messing with one of the worst drugs on the street. Pedope was a cheap version of heroin and was one of the worst drugs to get clean of. Sadness, helplessness, and guilt washed over me as tears racked my body. "I did not know. I swear, Diane," I whispered, wrapping my arms tightly around my body.

"I didn't raise her to get hooked on that shit," Diane spat angrily.

And my tears stopped for a second as I looked up at her. She did not really raise Dom at all. Smoking weed with your daughter was not a fucking antidrug statement.

Sahad walked up to me, and I turned into his sweet embrace.

First Mo turned Bones in for rape.

Earlier today Rah beat up Alizé and broke her leg in two. She was across town in Beth Israel recovering from surgery.

Now Dom damn near died from overdosing on pedope.

What the hell was going on?

I hated to be selfish, but was I next for tragedy?

I held Sahad closer. "Thank you for being here. I really . . . really needed you, baby," I whispered in his ear, closing my eyes and wishing for better days.

"I'm not going anywhere."

I nodded into his neck, glad that the fact that I believed Mo and he believed Bones did not come between us.

I had not seen or spoken to my friend since the night I dropped her off at home. Her parents truly had her on lockdown. When I went by her house, her father told me it was all my fault Mo was raped and then slammed the door in my face.

As we sat in the ER awaiting word on Dom's condition, I tried to figure out where we had all dropped the ball in our friendship. Dom was using drugs, and as far as I knew, none of us knew it. She pulled away from us after Lex's death. Was that when she turned to drugs?

And Alizé. I told her to leave those damn thugs alone. She was a beautiful, college-educated woman. Why did she fall so easily into the "gotta have a thug" mentality? Had Rah hit her in the past? What drove him to such rage that he broke her leg in two? Would it hurt the dancing she loved so much?

And Mo. Sahad posted bail for Bones against his future royalties. Bones was saying Mo was upset and lying on him because he denied fathering her child. *Shit, so Mo is pregnant?* She would have told us, right? But what about the night Sahad and I found her on the floor of the elevator in Bones's building crying hysterically? What was that about?

Overwhelmed by it all, I dropped my head in

my hands. I was not one to cry easily because my life in foster care made me that way, but at that moment I could not stop the tears from falling. I was not overly religious either, but I had to pray. "Please God, help all my friends. Please."

Sahad hugged me to his side. It did not seem fair for my life to be so perfect when all of my girls were catching pure hell.

My eyes fell on the four-carat Tiffany solitaire on my left ring finger. I had done it. I caught my big fish. I gave him just the image he wanted. I stayed on top of my game. I made sure to be all the things he could ever need when he needed it: supportive, quiet, outspoken, classy, sophisticated, smart, dumb, sexy, trampy, and everything else.

Sahad had proposed tonight on the balcony of his luxurious penthouse apartment.

We stood on the balcony together facing the beautiful New York skyline. A slight wind shifted over our frames. Even on the thirty-second floor the sounds of fast-paced and energetic life reached us.

"I came from nothing," he said suddenly.

I shifted my eyes up to his strong and handsome profile, and I saw the city lights reflected in his eyes.

"People told me I was nothing and that all I was ever going to be was nothing." He shook his head a bit, and his face became cocky as he waved his hand in a sweeping motion before him. "Look at me. How they like me *now.*"

"You have so much to be proud of," I told him,

taking his hand in my own to grasp it tightly. "You worked hard for the life you have, and you deserve these blessings. Do not ever let anyone in your past, present, or future take that from you."

Sahad dropped his head and bit his smooth bottom lip. "You never know how deeply your childhood affects the type of adult you'll become."

"My apartment at The Top is nothing compared to this, but it is a long way from where I came from," I said, in a rare show of honesty. "All I knew was I wanted more and I was willing to work hard to make a better life for myself."

Sahad turned me into his embrace, and I tilted my head back to look up at him framed by the moonlight. "I love the fight I see in you. And how fine and sophisticated you are but you still have the same crazy-ass friends from high school. And your loyalty. Your friendship when I just feel like talking. And the feel of your arms around me when I just want to be held. And your calmness when I'm about to do something I'll regret later. My life is so different with you in it."

I smiled and wrapped my arms around his waist. "Is it?" I asked softly with a smile as I raised up on my toes to nuzzle his neck. I had never wanted him more than I did in that moment.

He reached up to grasp my left hand in his, and a second later I felt the coolness of metal. I leaned back and immediately gasped at the brilliant twinkle of the solitaire ring now on my finger. *Well, I'll be damned.*

Sahad touched my chin with his warm fingers and raised my head a bit so that I looked up into his eyes as my heart pounded. "I'm ready to settle down. I'm ready to slow down," he said, laughing a little. "Marry me."

I fought not to let out a squeal. "Yes, yes, yes."

I smiled a little at the memory as I looked down at my ring. Finally, I was going to be a celebrity wife. My financial worries were over. The man hunt was over.

PART THREE

"That's What Friends Are For"
—Dionne Warwick and Friends

36

Alizé

One Month Later

With extensive physical therapy, maybe you'll dance again like you used to.

Maybe. Maybe? Maybe if I won the lottery, I'd be rich. Maybe if I was a fifth, I'd be drunk. Life wasn't built on fucking maybes.

A shattered thighbone and dislocated knee. Two surgeries. A metal rod through the center of my bone, a leg cast, and no one could promise me I'd be one hundred percent again.

Dancing was *everything* to me.

When my parents split I found my joy in dancing. When my first boyfriend dumped me one week after I gave him my virginity, I tapped his sorry ass out my heart. When my grandmother died, I jazzed away the ache in my soul.

So many times dancing had come to my rescue and served as my savior.

What the fuck was I going to do now?

"Monica?"

I looked up from where I sat propped up on pillows in the middle of my bed at home. My mother was standing in the doorway looking more like me than I wanted to admit.

"Danielle's here to see you. And your daddy called earlier but you were sleeping."

"I'll call him," I told her.

My mom smiled that sweet smile only a mother had for her child before she left my room.

Cristal walked in looking like the celebrity wife she was going to be in just five months. Everything was perfectly in place: her streaked hair long and curly, the faint scent of signature Glamorous perfume surrounded her, her MAC makeup perfectly set, the Burberry silk blouse and tan slacks she wore were all classic Cristal.

The diamond on her finger twinkled almost as bright as her eyes as she smiled down at me. "Hey, lady," she said, setting her crocodile purse on my nightstand.

I eyed it. "Longchamp."

"Nope. Frenchy."

"Oooh, I'm scared of you," I teased. "How's Sahad and the wedding plans?"

"He's fine. Everything is fine," she answered vaguely, diverting her eyes. "But I came here to talk to you about something else."

"What's up?"

"It's about Dom."

My eyes snapped with anger. That treacherous, slick-ass, no-good ex-friend of mine. Fuck that bitch.

"Don't mention her name to me," I said, cold as hell.

That bastard Rah broke my leg, but Dom broke a bond that could never be repaired as far as I was concerned. He was on the run from the police, and her ass was trying to get off dope. Fuck 'em both.

Cris sat down on the foot of the bed, and I could tell she was choosing her next words carefully. "I know Dom—*she*—was wrong for messing with Rah, but "

"But?" I shrieked, looking at my friend like she was crazy.

"Dom overdosed. She is addicted to drugs, and she needs our help to stay clean. We have got to stick together—"

I felt so angry with Cris. How could she even dare ask me to care about Dom? "I'm just supposed to forget that she stabbed me in the back, huh, Cris? Why I gotta be the bigger person?" I shouted. Tears of frustration and hurt filled my eyes. Yes, Dom's betrayal hurt like hell. She had been more than my friend. She was my sistah.

Cris reached out for my hand. "Because—"

"Because hell. Could you—shit—*would* you forgive her if she fucked Sahad?" I challenged her 'cause I felt like" don't judge me 'til you walked in my stilettos."

"Rah is not Sahad," she countered quickly.

I sucked my air between my teeth. "Answer the question."

Cris lowered her head, licking her glossy lips as she tucked her hair behind her ear. "I do not know.

Okay? I do not know," she answered mildly. "But this was not *our* Dom. This was a . . . a . . . a junkie."

"Dom is a nasty-ass, strippin' project ho, and I don't want shit to do with that bitch," I said with venom.

Cris flinched at my words. "Dom is *our* friend," she insisted with emotion. "The four of us have been through a lot together. No man should come between y'all. Especially not a short-dick fool like Rah."

"It's not about Rah."

Cris stood and picked up her purse. There were tears in her eyes that I knew she wouldn't let fall. "You are right. It is about you dancing and walking without a limp again. It is about Mo being raped. It is about Dom getting clean. It is about our *friendship*. To hell with everything else."

I turned my head and looked out the window. "I'm sorry, Cris, but Dom ain't my problem 'cause the trick ain't my friend."

"I am not going to desert her, Alizé," she said with finality.

"That's you," I told her with just as much finality.

"I hope I'm not interrupting."

I turned my head and found Cameron standing in the doorway. The tension in the air was thick as hell, and he looked a little uncomfortable. "Your mother was on the phone and told me to come up."

Cris smiled, the cool facade back in place. "I was just leaving. Cameron, right?"

He smiled broadly and extended his hand. "Yeah. And you're Danielle, a.k.a. Cristal, right?"

She nodded, looking over her shoulder at me with an approving double wink before she faced him again. I could tell from the once-over she gave him that Cris was identifying the designer of his charcoal tailored suit, silk tie, and leather shoes.

"You wear Gucci very well," she told him before leaving the room.

Cam laughed. "I see you described her very well," he said, folding his frame into the chair beside my bed—his usual seat when he visited me.

Not a day had yet to pass that Cam didn't come to visit me, whether for twenty minutes or an hour. My mother adored him, and my father admired him—one of the few things they agreed on.

I watched him as he removed his blazer, loosened his tie, and rolled the sleeves of his shirt up on his strong, muscular arms. He was handsome with his high cheekbones, sensuous mouth, and strong chin. When he smiled his twin dimples became prominent.

I knew he wanted more from me than just a platonic friendship, but we had nothing in common outside of our careers. Cam offered no excitement, no thrill. He just didn't make my pulse race.

So for now he was the William to my Joan like on my favorite show *Girlfriends*.

"Guess what?"

I turned my head to look into his handsome square face. "What?" I asked softly.

"I dreamed you were dancing again." His eyes were smiling as he leaned forward to look at me deeply, taking my hand in both of his. "Promise me a front row seat to your next recital."

Cameron was the kind of man I needed, but I just didn't want him.

Question was, why?

37

Moët

"I'm pregnant, y'all."

I dropped the bomb on them just like that. I was expecting to see surprise on both Cristal and Alizé's faces, but it was the doubt in Cristal's eyes that *surprised* me.

It made me wish like hell that I kept my mouth shut.

"Are we sad, happy . . . or what?" Alizé asked softly from her position on her bed.

My eyes were locked on Cristal, and hers were locked on me.

"What? What's wrong?" Alizé asked, looking between Cristal and me where we sat on opposite sides of her bed.

This was the first time I'd seen her since that night at Bones's. "Why are you looking at me like that, Cris? You got something you want to say to me?"

The doubt on her face increased tenfold, and she shook her head sadly. "I did not say one word."

"What the hell is up?" Alizé asked, her voice louder and more demanding as her head swung from Cristal to me.

"Don't judge me, Cris, until you walk a mile in my fucking shoes!"

Cristal's face became incredulous. "No . . . you . . . did . . . not . . . Mo," she said succinctly.

Alizé banged the bed with her fist in frustration. "Didn't what?" she wailed dramatically.

The room became quiet.

Cristal eyed me in disbelief. "You lied about Bones raping you." Her whispered words echoed in the silence like gunfire.

A single tear raced down my cheek like hot wax.

Alizé winced visibly before she, too, looked at me in disbelief . . . and sadness. "Is that true, Mo?" she asked.

I could tell she was hoping to hear it wasn't true.

"I stood up for you, Mo," Cristal said softly.

I said nothing. I wanted to deny her accusations, but I couldn't. I just couldn't.

"Sahad said that Bones said you were mad because he didn't want the baby, and I stood up for you." Cristal's voice and the look in her eyes was condemning as she rose from the chair to point her finger down at me. "You never told us you were pregnant, so I thought he lied."

"Well, guess what, Cristal? My business is my business," I shouted, rising to knock her hand down.

"Whoa . . . whoa," Alizé yelled out, grabbing one of her crutches to slide between us like an extension of her arm. "Sit down and relax y'all."

"Your ass is wrong, Mo," Cris told her.

I felt guilty and angry and scared and pained and betrayed all at once. My chest burned like it was on fire as one of my best friends judged me. "Why? Why am *I* wrong? Was I supposed to kill another baby?" I screamed, shocked by the anger I felt fill my chest.

"Sit the fuck down, y'all," Alizé yelled out, her face frustrated that she couldn't move.

"I'm not hanging around for this drama," I said, gathering my purse from the floor.

"You started the drama."

"Don't go, Mo," Alizé pleaded.

I walked to the door, ready to run. Before I left them I turned and faced Cristal. "Are you going to tell your man?" I challenged her.

"Are you going to tell the truth?" Cris countered, crossing her arms over her chest.

I left the room and closed the door behind me.

They didn't understand. I did what I had to do.

My parents would've disowned me for being pregnant, so I told them I was raped. When they called the police, I had to follow through with my lie and make a report. They did a rape kit which proved I had sex with Bones. Surprise, surprise.

Now I didn't have to worry about being thrown out of the house: penniless, jobless, and hopeless.

And Bones?

I hadn't heard from him. I didn't know if it was because he never knew where I lived and my cell phone was disconnected, or if he'd rather be called a rapist than step up to the plate and do right by me and this baby.

He deserved whatever he got—plus some. To hell with him.

I hated him. I wanted revenge. I wanted him and every bastard like him—including Reverend DeMark—to pay.

Pay for the lies.

Pay for the hurt.

Pay for my dead baby.

Pay for telling me they loved me when they only loved themselves.

I walked out of the house and down the stairs just as a green-and-white taxi headed up the street toward me. Deciding not to catch the bus, I hailed the cab and was glad to slide inside onto the cracked leather seat. "Five-eighty Eighteenth Street off of Sixteenth Avenue, please," I told the cabbie, letting my head fall back against the seat as I shut my eyes.

My life was a roller coaster, and now I felt drained, tired, and sleepy.

"Are you okay, dear?"

I opened one eye to see the slender, brown-skinned man turn in his seat, looking at me with concerned eyes. "I'm fine, but thanks for asking."

"Okay." He turned back around. "Mind if I play the radio?"

"It's your cab," I said with a yawn, closing my eyes. I wanted to crawl into a ball on my bed and cry myself to sleep.

"I just love this song. How 'bout you?" the cabbie asked as the car came to a complete stop.

I recognized Donnie McClurkin's 2001 gospel hit "We Fall Down." It was my mother's favorite song. That song hit home with me. I listened to the words in silence, surprised by the tears that welled up in my eyes. Quickly, I blinked them away.

I hated my life. The only good thing in it was this baby.

Some emotion rose inside of me, and I felt the tears falling. There was nothing I could do to stop them. I squeezed my eyes shut and wiped them with my fingers.

"Bear ye one another's burdens, and so fulfill the law of Christ."

My eyes shot open at the cabbie's words. I looked through my fingers to find him turned in his seat again and looking at me with concern.

"It must be a heavy load you're carrying, child. Do you want to talk about it? I'm Reverend Hampton."

I stiffened. What was he going to do now, try and get in my panties like the oh-so-great Revered Reverend DeMark? Please. "If you're a minister, why are you driving a cab?" I asked with attitude, not in the mood for another man's lies.

He smiled and laughed at the question. "Our church, the Holiness Church of Christ, is very small, and I don't want to rely on the congregation to pay me a salary. I minister for the Lord not for the wealth."

That surprised me. Was this guy for real?

The light turned green and he faced forward to accelerate ahead.

"Do you want to talk about it?" he asked.

"Why? So you can tell me I'm gonna burn in hell, too?" My tone was sullen as he steered through the busy Newark streets.

Our eyes met in the rearview mirror, and I saw nothing but concern. More concern than I'd ever seen in my own father's eyes. Damn shame when a stranger appeared to care more about you than your own father.

Still. . . .

"I'm pregnant and not married," I told him, being flagrant and cocky, wanting to shock him.

He nodded solemnly. "Do you attend church?"

A fluke of a church led by the devil himself, but a church nonetheless. "Yes."

"That's good. It's during trying times that you need fellowship."

I snorted in derision as I shifted my eyes to look out the window. "These days you can get a whole lot more than just fellowship at church."

I felt his eyes on me.

"You have something troubling you. Share your burden. You can't carry it alone."

That was easy for him to say. I had no one to help me shoulder my burdens. Cristal was mad at me. Ze and Dom had their own problems. My parents were so judgmental. My minister was a fraud. Bones had already fucked me over big-time.

Who did that leave? Just me, myself, and I.

The cab stopped, and I turned my head to the right and looked out at my parents' home. "How much do I owe you?" I asked, opening my purse as I felt myself slipping into an emotional abyss.

"Nothing but a promise that you'll talk to someone."

I looked up at him just as he placed a business card in the money tray of the bulletproof divider.

"If you have no one else to talk to, then you can call on me."

I took the card, not wanting to be rude and planning to throw it away as soon as I was out of his eyesight. "Thanks."

It was a funny thing, though. As I stood on the sidewalk watching his green-and-white taxi pull away, I couldn't bring myself to tear up that card.

38

Dom

"How are you feeling today, Keesha?"

"I'm straight. You?"

"Fine thanks." Dr. Copeland gave me that "let's keep it cool and calm" smile like he was afraid I was gonna flip out and shit.

I wadn't gone lie. I felt like climbin' the fuckin' walls in this m'fer. Rehab was a son of a bitch.

"What do you want to talk about today?" he asked.

"I hate it here, Doc."

It was the truth, and they wanted nuth'n but the truth. So fuck it, there it was.

"Why?"

"I want to go home, Doc."

"Do you feel you're ready to go home, Keesha?"

I eyed him, feelin' hostile as hell as my body craved a bag of dope like it was my savior. My body wanted to get high, but every fuckin' day my brain was fightin' it.

The battle was fuckin' wit me big-time.

"Why do you always answer a question with a question?" I asked, stalling as I fought the urge to scratch.

"I don't recall you asking a question, Keesha."

Sitting forward on the edge of the chair, I made an ugly face and asked, "When can I go home?"

"You can leave anytime you wish, Keesha. This is a center for rehabilitation, not a prison."

I hated this motherfucker's calm, monotone voice. He always sounded like he was tryin' to talk me the fuck down from a ledge.

It was like he could see all the emotions inside of me stirrin' up and makin' me feel like I didn't know if my ass was comin' or fuckin' goin'. I ain't know whether to laugh like I was insane or to cry like I did over Lex's dead body or to scream like Freddy Krueger was standing over my ass.

I hated my life.

I hated myself.

"Why do you want to die, Keesha?"

I locked eyes with his and then dropped mine to avoid the truth. "I didn't want to die. I wanted to forget."

"Forget what?"

Forget that I'm jealous of Alizé's light skin, her relationship with her father, and the support she gets from her mother.

Forget that I put a whack piece of dick before my friend.

Forget that I turned my back on my friends—my sistahs—when they were all the real family I got. The only ones to love me and accept me for me.

Forget that Lex—my love, my soldier, my street warrior—was dead.

Forget that my father chose drugs and the streets over me.

Forget that mother wasn't no kind of mother.

Forget that I wasn't no kind of mother.

Forget that I dreamed of havin' lighter skin and even bleached my face in high school—somethin' that led to even more teasin'. Tar baby. Crispy black. Blue-black. Urple. Black bitch. Dirty self. Ugly self. Jig-a-boo. Monkey. Inkspot.

A wave of sadness washed over me like rain.

"Do you feel you're ready to go home?" he asked again.

I looked at him, and then I looked out the window. I thought about where I would be carrying my ass back to. If I went home, I'd sniff a bag of dope up in a New York minute.

I was a fuckin' junkie.

39

Cristal

Every day of my life since I was fifteen I got up to go to my job. At some points in my life that had meant even Saturdays and Sundays. I did what I had to do to survive.

For the first time in my life, I did not have to rise at seven to shower and dress to be at work by eight. I could lounge around my apartment all day and shop when I pleased. It was the beginning of the life of luxury and leisure I always felt I deserved.

My relationship with Sahad had progressed quite rapidly. With his proposal came his request that I relinquish my position as the receptionist at the offices of Platinum Records. He did not feel it was appropriate for his future wife. He gave me a nice allowance that more than paid my bills and allowed me to shop like a true diva.

And so I was ninety percent of the way to my full dream. The last piece to the puzzle was my wedding, and my future security would be sealed.

And yet, I was anything but happy.

Somewhere along the line love and companionship began to mean something to me. With the "always on the go" lifestyle that my future husband led, I was nearly always alone, and how could I deeply love a man that I did not really know? And how could I know more about him when he was hardly ever in my presence?

Maybe my loneliness would not be so critical if I had my girls around me like we were in the past. In less than a year, our lives were all so different. Sometimes I felt like I didn't know them. Dom on drugs? Mo lying about being raped?

And I was still struggling with what to do about *that* situation. My loyalty should lie with my friend, but wrong was wrong, and there was no way I could let Moët send an innocent man to jail out of revenge.

I had not spoken to her since that day at Alizé's, and I had no plans to speak to her. The stunt Moët was trying to pull was just too scandalous, and quite honestly it showed a side of her that I did not want to even associate with.

So I was mad at Mo.

Alizé was just too through with Dom.

Ding-dong.

I looked over at the front door from where I lounged on the couch, flipping through television shows I was not even watching. I glanced at my watch. It was just five o'clock. Setting the remote onto the coffee table, I rose to make my way over to open the door.

"Mohammed," I said in surprise and pleasure as I looked up into his friendly face.

During the last couple of weeks, Mohammed had become my savior from loneliness and boredom. Our cat-and-mouse game had mellowed into a good friendship, and I looked forward to his platonic company as Sahad left me alone to my own devices.

Mohammed smiled broadly as he pulled a helmet from behind his back. He let it dangle from his finger. "Just bought a motorcycle. Wanna go for a ride?" he asked, smiling and showing off his dimples.

"Me? On a motorcycle?" I asked in doubt. "Please."

"You got anything else going on today besides shopping?"

Mohammed reached out and lightly touched my hand. "Come on, the mall doesn't close until nine-thirty."

I shot him a murderous glare, even as I thought of the call I had gotten from Sahad canceling our dinner plans because he had an emergency meeting with his staff tonight. Why not?

"Just let me change," I said reluctantly, stepping back to let him enter.

"I don't guess your part-time man—"

"Fiancé," I interjected over my shoulder as I headed for my bedroom.

"Excuse me, *fiancé*," he said in a playful, sarcastic tone. "I don't guess he'll call and you'll blow me off again."

I stopped in my bedroom doorway and turned to look at him as he wandered about my living room. "I already apologized for what happened the night of my birthday, and you said we were still cool, right?"

He looked up from a picture of Sahad and me catching some rays on his yacht. When I saw the twinkle in his eyes, I knew he was joking.

I stuck my tongue out at him playfully before I walked into my bedroom and closed the door behind me. Just minutes later I emerged dressed in a pair of Sean Combs Superstar jeans and a white T-shirt with my weave hair pulled back into a tight ponytail.

Mohammed looked up at me, and his face was surprised.

I looked down at myself before looking up at him again. "What?" I asked.

"You look good, that's all."

I cocked a brow. "I *always* look good."

Mohammed walked up to me, looking good and smelling great, his warm eyes locked with mine. "Yes, you do, but it's good to see you in something except those slacks and dresses you wear all de time."

We were a distance apart, but I felt like his fingers brought the bud between my legs to life and teased my nipples to aching hardness. His accent made my whole body tingle. His presence made me weak.

All things Sahad had not made me feel in a while.

Mohammed took one deliberate step toward me, and I took one small step back.

He took a larger step toward me.

I took a smaller step back.

Another large step from Mohammed.

I put my hand out against his chest. "Mohammed . . ."

He nodded with laughter in his eyes. "I want to kiss you. I want to taste you."

My heart nearly leapt from my chest as he lowered his head to mine. His heat. His strength. His prowess. And that damn tantalizing scent of cocoa butter surrounded me until I was breathless and anxious for the feel of those luxurious lips just a few precious inches above my own.

I got lost in his eyes.

"Damn you fine, girl," his words whispered against my lips.

Kiss me, I thought.

His head lowered, and my eyes drifted closed as I waited for the first taste of him.

Moments later I felt a warm kiss pressed to my forehead.

"We better get going, Dani."

What the . . .

I popped one eye open to see Mohammed stepping back from me. I swallowed my puzzling disappointment. "Let's go," I said, turning to open the door, step into the hall, and try to play like my feelings were not hurt that Mohammed passed on kissing me.

40

Moët

I knew better, so I had to do better.

Cristal was mad at me, and I just knew I didn't have long before she dropped a dime on me to Sahad and Bones. I hadn't spoken to her in days.

As much as I defied my religious upbringing, I couldn't deny knowing right from wrong. Lying and accusing an innocent man of rape was just straight crazy—no matter how much I hated him and wanted him to hurt. Plus, it was a crime to falsely accuse someone of rape.

I was scared.

What if they proved I was lying? My ass could go to jail.

What the hell was I going to do? How in the hell did I get myself into this shit?

How would I get myself out of it?

I looked at my reflection in the mirror. I hated the person I had become. Lies and deception, hatred and pain, were my new best friends.

There was only one. Just one thing I could do to reclaim me. To be me. To be freed.

Every step down the stairs felt like rope was tied around my neck and waist and legs and some invisible person was pulling me back, stopping me from what I was about to do.

I pushed on.

I had no choice.

I didn't even know I was crying until I stood in the doorway of the living room. My eyes took in the prim, proper, and almost bland décor. Gospel music played softly from the large wooden 1980s radio sitting next to the television. My mother sat in her rocking chair softly reading aloud from her well-worn Bible. My father sat with his fingers steepled as he listened to her. They were at peace surrounded by the symbols of the religion they loved so much. They were clueless to the pain I felt, the pain I inflicted with my lies, the pain I was about to reveal. My mother looked up at me.

"Latoya, why are you crying? What's wrong?"

"I wasn't raped," I said in a whisper, the words almost running together and sounding like *Iwasn'traped* instead. My poor heart hammered in my chest, and my chest heaved with the tears and snot streaming down my face.

"What did you say, Latoya?" my father asked, his voice so cold.

"I wasn't raped . . . I lied . . . forgive me, please, forgive me."

Their silence was deafening, but the truth was the key to my freedom. At least I wanted it to be. I *needed* it to be.

My mother swooned back against the chair, and my father balled up the newspaper he was reading to fling it across the room. "Lies. A child out of wedlock. Premarital sex. Anything else you want us to be ashamed of?"

I dropped my head, tasting the salt of my tears as I wrapped my arms around my body and wept like a baby. "Daddy, don't," I begged, hating that I felt like a five-year-old being chastised.

He rose and stalked over to stand before me. "We didn't raise you to be a—"

I jerked my head up. "A what, Daddy? What am I? A whore? A slut? A jezebel?"

All of the anger I felt at his neglect swelled inside of me and rushed out like a tidal wave. I saw that he was surprised by my reaction, and it spurred me on.

"Your reaction doesn't surprise me at all." My voice was bitter. "Love and understanding, forgiveness and support—those things from you would've blown me off my feet."

"Honor thy mother and thy father."

I felt so helpless, so overwhelmed with anger, and weak with regrets as my father refused to talk *to* me but quote Bible verses *at* me. "Talk to me, Daddy," I begged.

"Deliver my soul, O Lord, from lying lips, and from a deceitful tongue."

I turned pained eyes to my mother and found her on her knees saying a silent prayer as she rocked.

"She shall be brought to the door of her father's house, and there the men of her town shall stone her to death. She has done a disgraceful thing in Israel by being promiscuous while still in her father's house. You must purge the evil from among you."

"Are you people crazy?" I yelled at the top of my lungs as I backed away from them.

My mother rose. "Maybe we should call Reverend DeMark."

"Call him."

I laughed hysterically at my father's barked command. "Call Reverend DeMark. Y'all don't know nothing 'bout your god."

"Go to your room, Latoya," my father demanded.

"You know what? Call him. That's perfect so that we can get to some more truths."

I was bold and cocky now.

"Let's see if he admits to fucking me when I was just seventeen and then talking me into getting an abortion."

Life paused as soon as the words left my mouth. I was thinking them. I wanted to scream them, but I shocked my damn self when I actually *said* them.

The slap from my father surprised me and sent me down to the floor clutching my cheek. I looked up at him as my mother moved between us.

"Liar. How dare you disrespect my home. How dare you disrespect Reverend DeMark with your lies. I don't even know you, Latoya."

In those heated moments I felt hatred for my own father.

"Beware of false prophets, which come to you in sheep's clothing, but inwardly they are ravening wolves." I gave them what they understood: Bible verses.

"Get out my eyesight, Latoya."

I rose to my feet. "And many false prophets shall rise, and shall deceive many."

"Get out with your lies!"

I gave my parents one last look and turned and fled out of the house.

"Latoya! Latoya! Come back."

I heard my mother calling out for me, but I knew there was no turning back. The time for my freedom had come.

I had balls.

What choice did I have?

I didn't use my key. I knocked and I waited. I needed to know it was okay for me to be there. I needed to know that we were all right again. I needed her help.

I was afraid.

The door opened, and Cristal's face was filled with surprise and then compassion. That made my tears come back full force.

She didn't say a word. She just opened the door wider and stepped back to let me in.

That's what true friends were for.

41

Alizé

Brrrnnnggg.

"Shit," I swore. *All My Children* was just getting good. I put Erica Kane and her madness on mute as I picked up my cordless phone. "Hey."

"You awake?"

"Well, good afternoon to you too, Cristal," I said dryly.

"Girl, hush. We're on our way over there."

"Who—" I started, but Cristal had already disconnected the line. Maybe she had Sahad with her.

Okay, maybe not.

Sahad was busier than a horny fag trying to open a jar of dicks. My friend put on the facade, but I knew the real deal. Cristal was a wine-and-dine chick. Sitting around waiting on Sahad—even while she spent his money—had to be working her nerve.

Brrrnnnggg.

"Damn, just when I was 'bout to get back into my soaps," I said to myself.

I checked out the caller ID before answering. "Hey."

"How's my girl?"

"Your friend is doing good, Cameron. How's Wall Street doing without me?" I settled back against my covers, wishing like hell I had something to get under my cast to handle an itch.

"Wall Street's doing great *with me*. Don't worry. I know we're just friends, Miss Alizé."

"I know that," I said, even though I wasn't sure. A day had yet to pass that he didn't call or come by to see me. "Are you coming to see me today?"

"Actually, no, I can't. I have a date tonight."

I frowned. *A date? A date with who?*

"I'm taking Serena—"

I arched an eyebrow that was ten hairs away from needing a serious waxing. "Is that the broad I saw you with at Neicy's that night?"

"Yes."

"Well, whoop-de-do."

"Something wrong?" he asked.

Yes, something's wrong. It burns my ass to think of you on a date. Humph. He got over my ass quick as hell, didn't he?

"Look, I gotta go. I'll talk to you later."

"Moni—"

I gave him the click-a-lator, hanging the phone up right in his face, hating how pissed I felt. Pissed and hurt. I thought of Cameron sexing his wannabe supermodel, and I felt like throwing something.

"How's my Ladybug?"

I looked up and saw my father strolling into my

bedroom. I smiled, but not even the familiar scent of cigars and Old Spice eased my ruffled feathers.

He kissed the top of my head and handed me the order of crab sticks and lo mein I asked him to bring. "I know you ready to get out that bed."

I set the bag of food on my nightstand. "The doctor said the cast might come off next week, and then he wants me to start aquatherapy. Thank God, because classes start the first week of September, and I refuse to let anything—or anyone—stop me."

"I wish I could get my hands around Rah's neck and his nuts. I'd snatch both in opposite directions."

I smiled, fully believing my daddy would and could handle that punk. "You on lunch?" I asked, purposefully changing the subject before his blood pressure rose.

"Yeah, I gotta get back to work."

My mother strolled into my bedroom in an outfit that was different from the one she'd been strolling around in all morning. And if I wasn't crazy, she had on makeup. I sniffed the air. And perfume.

"Sure your woman didn't warn you to stay from around me, Charles?" she asked, pretending to straighten my covers.

I watched my daddy give my mama a long, leisurely look.

"You know me long enough to know don't no woman tell me where to go or what to do, Elaine." He took his hands from the pockets of his jeans and moved past my mother to the door. "I'll probably swing back through to see you on my way home, Ladybug."

I didn't miss the way my mother winced at the word home. His home wasn't hers anymore.

"See y'all later," he said, walking out the door.

"Charles," my mother called out.

But my daddy was gone.

My heart broke as I watched her move to my bedroom window. I knew she was watching him leave. I was more than just her daughter. I was a woman, too, and I saw the yearning and longing for him on her face.

"Hey, Ma, a *Blackula* marathon will be on TVOne tonight. Wanna watch?"

She turned from the window. "That sounds like fun, Monica," she said, lightly patting my good leg as she walked out of the room.

Seconds later the doorbell echoed through the house.

I was surprised as hell when Cristal and Kimani eventually walked through my bedroom door together. "Hey, Kimani. Don't you look pretty."

"Thank you, Auntie Ze."

She grabbed my remote and started flipping channels like she bought the TV, but I didn't mind. I was glad to see her. I hated her mother, not her. I had nothing but love for Kimani.

"Good to hear that you and Mo came to your senses," I told Cristal as she took the seat next to my bed.

"Yeah, me, too."

"Where's she?"

"Sleeping. She did not want to leave the apartment. I am worried about her."

"After all the shit you told me about Mo last night, I'm worried about her, too. Can you believe she was sleeping with her preacher? And then lied about the rape?"

Cristal shook her head and frowned. "I'm hoping Sahad can help make sure the police don't press charges on her for lying."

Hell, we all have done dumb shit. She was my friend, and I was not leaving her side, especially with her being pregnant and all.

I reached for my new copy of *The Source* magazine, flipping through the pages. I looked up from the Baby Phat ad I was checking out. I cut a sly look at Cristal. "Think the Rev's dick was heaven or hell?"

She shook her head, closed her eyes, and waved her hand like she was testifying in church. "Help her, Lord. That was Alizé by the way and not Cristal."

I laughed a little, even though shit really wasn't funny.

"Once you and Dom work it all out, we can get back to the way we used to be. One for all and all for one. We need each other." Cristal crossed her legs and leaned back in the chair like she'd just stated a sure thing.

I decided to straight ignore her ass; my mind was made up when it came to Dom.

"What's the latest on the wedding?" I asked, wanting a diversion from thoughts about Cameron's date. "I love our bridesmaid's gown. I just hope I can make it down the aisle and not look like I'm cripwalking."

Cristal laughed a little. "Sahad wants me to move in with him before the wedding."

"Goodbye, Livingston. Hello, Park Avenue."

She smiled, but I didn't miss how it didn't quite reach her eyes.

42

Dom

"What's on your mind today, Keesha?"

I looked at Doc, absently scratchin' the back of my hand as thoughts and memories came up. My talks with Doc was slowly openin' up a door to some shit I didn't wanna deal with.

Tears welled up in my eyes.

"Yes. Good. Talk yourself through it. Don't fight it. What are you feeling?"

I closed my eyes. "I feel . . . I feel like I don't deserve to live. Like I ain't good enough. Like I ain't shit. Like I ain't nothin'. Nothin' but trouble," I whispered as my lips trembled.

The tears fell, and my shoulders shook as emotions I couldn't name nearly strangled me.

"Those aren't your words, are they, Keesha?" he asked, his eyes on me.

Images of me just three and four years old huddled in a corner as Diane yelled down at me played in my head like a damn movie.

"You ain't nothin' but trouble."

"I wished I never had your ass."

"Get the fuck out my face before I slap the shit out of you."

"You just like your no-good black-ass daddy."

"Are they?" he asked again.

I covered my face with my hands. "Why?" I asked barely above a whisper.

"Why what, Keesha?"

"Why she treat me like that? Why she have me if she didn't fuckin' want me?"

He handed me tissues.

What's really fucked up is that I said some of that shit to my own daughter.

As soon as I wiped away tears, more filled my eyes and raced down my cheeks.

43

Cristal

New York, NY—Recent rape charges against rap artist Bones have been dropped. An unidentified woman accused the platinum-selling artist of sexually assaulting her in his New York apartment but has since refused to testify at a criminal trial. . . .

I did not need to read anymore. Sahad had already told me about the charges being dropped last night. Plus, it was my third time reading the front page article of the *New York Times*. And the hundredth time I said, "Thank you, Lord," for sparing my friend from criminal charges and public humiliation for her lies.

"Mornin', baby."

I smiled at Sahad as he walked into the brightly lit breakfast room, looking so good in a tailored pinstripe suit that I knew was Todd Smith. "Good morning."

He stood behind me, his warm hand slipping inside my robe to tease and twist my nipple. I let my head fall back against his body. "Uhm, that feels good. Maybe we should go back to bed or give the staff the day off and lounge around naked all day."

He bent to kiss me, but the good feelings were over before they even began as he gave my plump breast one last squeeze and moved to take his seat. "I wish. I have meetings with the producers for this new reality show they want me to do and the photo shoot for the new ad campaigns for Platinum Cologne. You understand, right, baby?"

Disappointment was my newest friend. "Actually, Sahad, baby, I need to—"

"Yeah?" He sat down at the table and looked at me as the butler, Jamison, poured him a cup of his favorite Jamaican coffee.

It was a damn shame that having his undivided attention threw me off. I took a deep breath. "We need to spend more time together. We live together, and I still hardly see you enough."

He stared at me with those liquid eyes I used to dream of. "I know I've been real busy, and you're right, I need to make time for you, for us, and for me—"

His precious Blackberry sounded off, and in the blink of an eye he was back in business mode as he answered the phone. "Sahad Linx."

"Sahad," I tried to interrupt.

"The car should be here any minute, and then I'm coming straight to your office."

I pushed away my bowl of fresh fruit. "Sahad," I said, more sharply this time.

He looked over at me in surprise. "Hold on a sec? Yes, baby?"

I reached across the table and took his hand, squeezing it tightly. "Baby, we need to talk. I am scared you do not have our wedding penciled in."

"Uhm, Roger, let me call you right back. Okay. Good."

He rose and came to kneel beside my chair. "I wouldn't miss our wedding for anything in this world. And I'm so busy now so that we can take our honeymoon to St. Tropez just the way you wanted."

Was I being selfish?

"Listen, I can see you're upset, so uhm, let's go out to dinner tonight and we'll talk. I promise."

I smiled, even though my heart was breaking. He was everything I had wanted and plotted for, but my life with him was nothing like I *thought* I wanted.

Long after he was gone, I sat at the table surrounded by all the luxuries I ever yearned for, feeling alone and lonely. Just like before.

Hours later, I parked my new black-on-black Mercedes Benz CLK500—a gift from Sahad—in the underground parking garage of my old apartment building. I planned on keeping the apartment, although I had no plans to live in it. My life was set up on the Upper East Side of New York, but it was a sorry rat that had only one hole. Okay, all right?

Besides, Mo was living there, and I already planned to invite Dom to bring Kimani and move in. Trying to kick a drug habit while living in the PJs—with a mother like Diane—was just crazy.

I was swamped working with my event planner to finalize the details for the wedding, but I had my mind set on driving to Jersey to check on Moët.

"Ooh, Mohammed, you are *too* funny."

I whirled around at the sound of the ultrafeminine voice to see Mr. Handyman himself lean over and kiss a pretty redbone woman in the front seat of his jalopy. The woman sat in it like it was a Hummer. She looked at Mohammed like he was *her* Sahad.

I turned and pretended to gather items from my backseat when Mohammed looked in my direction as he climbed from his vehicle. I was ashamed to be caught staring at them. Well, staring at him really.

He looked good. Really good. *Damn* good.

I missed him.

I missed our friendship and the things we used to do together. The time we used to spend together. Mohammed had been my distraction from the loneliness of loving Sahad.

A welcomed distraction.

I was closing my car door when my entire body tingled and the fine hairs on the back of my neck rose to attention in the most acute awareness.

"What's the deal, Miss Danielle?"

I loved how his accent made the word deal sound like "deeel." My entire body responded to the scent of cocoa butter as I forced a fake smile and turned to face him. "Hi, Mohammed. How are you doing?"

"Better now that I see your lovely smile, Miss Danielle."

My smile became genuine as I looked into those smoky mocha eyes. "Must you always flirt?" I asked him, unable to keep the softness from my tone.

"I can't seem to help myself around—"

"Mohammed, we're in a rush, sweetie." His date blew the horn briefly twice.

He looked over his shoulder and smiled. "Coming, Yvette."

She blew him a kiss, and I fought the urge to vomit on my new Stuart Weitzman sandals.

"So, where are you two headed?" I asked, purposefully drawing his attention back to me as I fought the jealousy I felt at the way he looked at her.

Mohammed slid his strong hands into the pockets of his jeans as he tilted his head to look down at me. "There's a free reggae concert in Weequahic Park."

"That's the one you mentioned taking me to."

Mohammed shrugged. "Once you moved in with Mr. CEO, I knew it was time for me to move on, Miss Danielle."

I was not crazy, and I knew his words were about more than a date for a concert. I dropped my gaze to keep him from seeing the tears fill my eyes. I would give my new collection of nearly two hundred pairs of shoes to spend the afternoon in the park with Mohammed.

He lifted his hand to lightly touch my cheek and lift my head. Our eyes met, and I shivered from his touch as I inhaled deeply of his scent. "I miss you, Danielle, but I want you to be happy. So I wish you nothing but the best."

His head lowered toward mine, and my heart hammered in my chest as my eyes drifted closed. *Yes, kiss me.*

Just before I got to taste those lips, little Miss Yvette laid on the horn like the devil himself was on her heels.

He pulled back and shook his head regretfully with a smile. "Goodbye, Danielle."

I watched him walk away and climb into his SUV. Yvette immediately entwined her fingers in his locks before pulling him over for a deep kiss. I wondered just what those lips tasted like as they pulled away.

His goodbye sounded so final.

Damn.

44

Alizé

Dear Ze,
Please forgive me. I know I fucked up
and I'm sorry for that. We been
friends for so long, and I miss you. . . .

I balled the letter up in my fist, not wanting to read any more of her words. Not caring about what she had to say.

How could Dom betray me like that?

I closed my eyes as a vision of her and Rah fucking played like a porno before me. I threw the paper like a fastball, and it hit the wall before bouncing back to the floor.

Okay, the real.

Dom hurt me. How long had they been messing around? Who came on to who? Not that who made the first move mattered, but I wanted to know. Did they use rubbers? Was Rah on dope, too? Were they in love? Who else knew about it?

I released a breath heavy with frustration.

The betrayal of a friend.

Tears filled my eyes. Fuck Rah. That wasn't about his crazy ass. Dom was my friend, and she committed the ultimate betrayal. I never would have believed it if I hadn't seen it with my own eyes.

Forgive her? How could I? That's like a man who dogs you out and then says I'll never do it again . . . *after* his ass is caught. All the rules say kick his cheating ass to the curb because he ain't to be trusted. You know, that "fool me once—shame on you; fool me twice—shame on me" kinda thing.

So why are the rules different for friends? Why should someone be able to stab you in the back because their "label" was that of friend?

Knock-knock.

I wiped my eyes and looked up at Cameron standing in the doorway of my bedroom. And looking at him felt like drinking water on a hot and dusty day. It was refreshing and arousing. Exhilarating and titillating.

"Hey, you. What's wrong?" he asked, dropping with ease on the knee of his tailored linen slacks beside the chair where I sat.

Damn, I hated for anyone to see me cry.

"I'm cool, stranger," I lied, trying to joke away the concern I saw in the lines of his handsome face.

"I shouldn't feel this way 'bout you, but I can't help it sometimes," he said suddenly, throwing me completely off base.

My heart stopped, and I was surprised I couldn't look away from his eyes.

"Loving somebody who doesn't love you is hell."

My heart soared and then it flopped. I didn't want his love.

Did I?

Okay, I was assuming. He didn't exactly say he loved me.

"So Serena has stuck her hook in you, huh?" I asked, tilting my head back to free my face of his all too warm hands.

He made a face and then rose, sliding his hands in his slacks as he walked the short distance to the window and then turned. "You know damn well I'm in love with you, Monica, so why play games."

"So why date someone else?" slipped between my lips before I could swallow the words.

"Why wait around for you to deal with your issues," he countered, his face incredulous.

"Issues?" Yes, I said it with all the attitude I could muster.

"Damn right. *Issues.* You're a college-educated woman. You're ambitious. You have goals. Your shit is together in every aspect of your life except when it comes to your relationships."

"Who the fuck are you to tell me about my life?" I gripped the arms of the chair until they could snap off in my hands.

"Somebody needs to tell your behind something," Cameron balked.

"You're not perfect, Cameron," I shouted back.

"I wouldn't ever break your damn leg and screw your best friend! Maybe if I did all that and call out your name—"

I gave him the hand. "Save that drama. You already ran that line by me, remember?"

He eyed my injuries. "Obviously you didn't catch it the first time."

"Get out, Cameron." I pointed to the door, not even sure why I was so angry with him. Guess the truth does hurt.

He stared at me long and hard. His face was made for poker. I held his stare.

Even though we'd just argued, it felt damn good to look into his eyes. Good and so very damn easy.

"I love you, Monica," he said with sincerity. "I love you and I want to be with you. I want to be able to say you're my woman and I'm your man."

I was lost in his eyes and absorbed into his soul.

Cameron knelt before me again and held my face with his hands. My breath caught in my throat as he leaned forward and pressed his mouth to mine.

A jolt of pure awareness and electricity raced through my body and left me shivering as he drew my tongue sweetly into the warmth of his mouth and suckled it like the sweetest fruit.

Damn. He was good.

Shit. Who knew?

"I love you so much, Monica," he whispered against my swollen lips.

I leaned back from his heat and his kisses, raising my hands to lightly touch my lips as I dropped my gaze from his.

"Am I moving too fast for you?" he asked.

"Yes," I admitted, my voice just a whisper.

"I understand—"

"No. No you don't understand."

Cameron remained quiet for a moment, and the

silence was telling. "Will you be able to go to classes this fall?" he said instead.

Okay, the switch in gears confused me, but I played along. I nodded in response to his question. "I started physical therapy last week, and I'm learning how to use crutches."

"I know you'll do well."

"Thanks."

Mindless chatter to cover the real issue. We were crazy.

"I hope you keep Braun, Weber in mind when you graduate."

I smiled at him. "You act like we're never gonna see each other again."

Cameron just shrugged one broad shoulder. "That might be for the best."

That stung like an m'fer which pissed me off. I wasn't even loving him and already he had the power to hurt me. "You might be right."

"Goodbye, Monica."

I bit my lip to keep from telling him not to go. Maybe this was for the best.

With one final look at me he turned and left the room and, I guessed, my life.

As quickly as Cameron left, my mother stepped into my bedroom.

"You really need to get out this room," she said, moving to open the windows.

"Ma, I go to physical therapy twice a week," I protested, using my crutches to rise to my feet and work my way over to my bed.

"What's going on?" she asked suddenly.

I looked up at her as I lowered myself to the bed. "Nothing much, Ma. Why?"

"Cameron didn't look pleased when he left."

"Ma, not now." I had enough on my mind.

"Did you two break up?"

My head jerked up. "He's not my boyfriend."

"It's obvious he loves you, so I don't understand *why* he isn't your boyfriend."

I pinched the bridge of my nose and closed my eyes tightly like I could will her to go away. I loved my mom, but I wasn't up for this right now.

"Nothing wrong with falling in love with a good man and getting married."

"Why? So I can sit around waiting on him for the rest of my life like you," I snapped. Okay, I shocked the shit out of myself.

When my father first left my mother, they didn't sit down together and offer a joint explanation of the reason for the separation. If anything they confused me even more. When my mother wasn't crying and moping around the house in her pajamas, she was busy telling me Daddy would be home soon. When I talked to my father, he only spoke of how much he loved me and that him leaving was for the best because they weren't happy together.

I wasn't a small child, and I had seen the gap widening between them physically and emotionally over the years. I knew there was truth in my father's words, but I also knew my mother wasn't ready to let him and the marriage go. All these years later and she still was grasping for straws. Love had her good and fucked up.

The pain that filled my mother's eyes cut my soul. "Ma, I'm sorry—"

She held up her hand and stopped the rest of

my words. "I'm calling your father," she said before leaving the room.

Poof. Just like that most of the bad feelings I had about flipping off at the mouth disappeared. It was the first time I'd given voice to my subconscious, and it felt like a weight lifted off my shoulders.

45

Dom

The doc said writing in this journal supposed to help me, but he told me writing letters to people I have done wrong would help, too. Well, Alizé ain't answer me or come to see me yet. And Kimani too young to read hers, and Lex is dead. But I got two weeks of writing in this damn journal, and I'm still scared. Still afraid. Still hurting like a bitch. I got so many regrets. Shit I can never change. Things I can only apologize for.

But talking to Doc helps. I hate to admit that shit, but I ain't never cried or let out my anger more than I have since I been in rehab. I look at shit a little different. I try to think before I speak.

Diane and me never gone be Claire Huxtable and one of her daughters, but I know it's a lot of shit between us that we need to work on. But that's hard to do when she laughed about coming to talk to the doc, talking about she ain't the one sniffing dope. Ain't that some fucked-up shit to say? I know I shouldn't feel like this about my own mama, but she make it so hard to love her.

What if Kimani feels the same way about me? I put Lex, and stripping and shopping, and hanging out with my girls over my child. What if she hates me as much as I feel like I hate Diane—and I ain't even gone talk about Doc's face when he first heard me call my mother by her first name. He said we had an uncharacteristic relationship. Surprise, surprise.

So I write in this journal and hope it takes away the shame and the pain and hurt. We'll see.

I'll be getting out tomorrow, and the freedom scares me more than anything else. Thank God Cristal's letting me move into her apartment with Mo. Thank God because I don't know if I can stand to go back to living with my mom and stay clean.

Every day of my life I'm gone have to fight not to get high.

Just like I have to fight to be a better mother to my child.

A better friend to Alizé.

A better woman for my damned self.

46

Moët

After all that drama with Reverend Luke, I didn't know why I decided to trust Reverend Hampton. I don't know why I picked up that phone a week ago and called him. All I know is when I thought of him and how kind he was to me that day in the cab, I wanted to feel that kindness again.

And my instincts this time didn't steer me wrong.

"Come in, Latoya. Come in."

I smiled at him as I slowly walked into his small office that looked more like a storeroom. "Hi, Reverend Hampton."

He rose from behind his plain wooden desk, dressed in a short-sleeved plaid shirt and khakis. "I'm glad you accepted my offer to come down and talk in person."

For a second as he came around his desk toward me, I tensed up, preparing myself for the feel of his hands. He did touch me, but it was a fatherly pat on my shoulder as I took a seat.

"You were very nice to me that day, and I can use some niceness right now." I wasn't surprised by the tears that filled my eyes. Since I ran away from my parents, I haven't done anything but cry.

"Testify, Latoya. You heal through telling your story."

Yes, I'd heard that before, but I never believed . . . 'til now. Still, I was afraid.

"I think the Lord sent me to you to help you heal that broken soul of yours."

I looked up and met his eyes, and I was taken back to that moment when I met Reverend De-Mark's eyes that first day in his office. The day I lost my innocence and my faith.

"Reverend Hampton, the choir would like to see you. Oh, I didn't know you had a visitor."

I turned to look at a young woman about my age standing in the door of his office. She smiled at me like we were old friends.

"Latoya, this is Olana Harris, our Sunday school teacher, church secretary, and organist. Olana, this is Latoya James."

My first thought was, *Are they fucking?*

"Nice to meet you, Latoya."

"You, too."

"Latoya, will you excuse me for a moment?"

I just nodded.

When they left the office I sat for a bit before nervousness hit me. What was I doing here about to tell a preacher my story? Had I lost my damn mind?

I grabbed my purse and quickly made my way to the door. As soon as I opened it, the sweet refrain of an organ reached me, pausing my steps as I walked past the doors to the small inner church.

The choir began singing "We Fall Down," by Donnie McClurkin. Suddenly a man's strong and melodic voice echoed inside the church. His voice was clear. The words to the song emphasized. The testimony in the music unmistakable. The music called to me.

Curious, I walked to the door, my purse tight beneath my arm as I pulled the door open and peered inside.

My mouth shaped in surprise to see Reverend Hampton holding the mic.

It was Saturday, and the choir members were dressed casually for their practice, but the presence of the Lord was there. I could feel it. I couldn't deny Him.

I felt weak and moved forward to clasp the pew to keep myself from falling to my knees.

Tears filled my eyes.

Joy filled my soul.

"Oh, sweet Jesus," I sighed, my eyes closing because I couldn't fight the spirit that filled me.

The choir sang like it was Sunday. Their music surrounded me like a warm blanket. Comforting. Healing.

I had turned my back on the Lord.

I had turned my back on the church and on the blessing of fellowship.

I had lied.

I had killed.

I had cheated.

I had slept with the devil—figuratively and literally.

I had hated. My parents. Reverend DeMark. Bones. Myself.

"For a saint is just a sinner who fell down."

"Forgive me, Lord," I cried, dropping to my knees. "Please, forgive me."

The choir stopped, and the organ ceased playing, and I knew without opening my eyes that they were looking at me. But all I could do was wrap my arms around myself and rock like a baby as I prayed.

Suddenly the music began again, and the choir began to sing. "Get back up again. . . . Get back up again."

"Sometime . . . sometimes we need help getting back up," I heard Reverend Hampton say.

Some of the choir continued to sing.

Some backed him up. "Preach," someone nearly shouted.

"We all fall, but the Lord teaches us not to stay down but to rise and try to walk with him. Never give up!"

"Get back up again. . . . Get back up again."

"Amen!"

"Hallelujah."

"I'm so sorry. Lord, I'm so sorry," I whispered, unable to stop my tears.

I was not surprised to feel Reverend Hampton's hands on me as he helped me to my feet. "It's okay, Latoya. The Lord has nothing but forgiveness for you. He has never turned his back on you, and he never will. Hallelujah."

"Get back up again. . . . Get back up again."

He held me close in his arms, and I welcomed the strength and the love of a man who wanted nothing more than to help me. No man in my life had ever held me just to hold me up when I was weak. Not my father. Not Reverend DeMark. Not Bones.

He continued to whisper prayers in my ear as he rocked me like I was his child.

"I've lied," I whispered in return.

"The Lord forgives you."

"I slept with my minister."

"He forgives, Latoya."

"I'm pregnant."

"A blessing from God."

"I killed my first baby," I whispered, my tears coming back full force.

"Ask him to forgive you."

I nodded, letting my head fall back as I cried like a baby. "Forgive me, Lord. Oh, God, forgive me."

"Now your healing can begin."

"Thank you, Jesus."

47

Cristal

"Mo? You here?" I called out as I walked into my old apartment and kicked off my shoes—out of habit. I closed the door with a push of my hip since my arm was filled with a cake box.

Dom was getting out of rehab today, and I wanted to throw a little welcome home party for her. Nothing big, just me, Kimani, and Mo.

No Diane. She was already pissed that Dom was not moving back in with her, but that was her problem.

No Alizé. I will say one thing for the bitch, she said she did not consider Dom a friend anymore, and she was sticking to that. Now that Dom was out, the split in the friendship was going to cause some strain. Hell, were they going to fight at my damn wedding?

No Sahad. He was still in Atlanta for a big talent search the label was holding. That big old apartment was even bigger without him—or rather without knowing that he would walk through the door no matter how late. It was always worse when he was out of town.

I set the cake box on the dining room table and reached in my crocodile Hermès Birkin bag for my new Blackberry. I hit the #1 speed dial. I was disappointed but not at all surprised when Sahad's phone went to voice mail. "Just felt like hearing your voice, baby. I guess you're busy. Uhm, I'm at my old apartment for Dom's welcome home party. Wish you were here. Call me. Bye."

Dropping the phone back into my bag, I walked back to my old master suite, now Moët's room. It was empty; she was not there.

Maybe it was a good sign she had finally left the house. The first time she moved as far as I knew.

"Hope she gets back before I leave to go pick up Dom," I said to myself as I crossed the hall to the guest room where Dom and Kimani would be staying.

Ding-dong.

My hand froze on the knob, and I made my way back out to the living room. "Mo must have left her key."

Funny how living alone made you talk to yourself.

"Good thing I was here to let . . . you . . ."

The rest of my words trailed off at the sight of Mohammed.

"Hello there, Miss Danielle."

My heart hammered until I was almost deaf. My hands trembled, and I slid them in the pockets of my linen slacks.

This reaction—my reaction—to him was not unexpected. So completely expected.

"Hey, Mohammed. Where's your girlfriend?" I asked, standing on my toes to look over his shoulder.

He just laughed and dropped his head, causing his thin locks to swing down and partially cover his handsome face. He tilted his head up a bit and locked those eyes—those damn sexy eyes—on me.

My knees weakened, and I reached out for the doorknob to steady myself.

"Where ya man?" he asked with that accent.

"Working."

"All work and no play makes Miss Danielle a sad girl."

I took a little breath, but nothing would slow down my pulse.

"I have to give you an invitation to my wedding," I said in a rush, trying to remind myself more than throw him off.

"You think I want to watch you marry another man when I love you so much."

His words were like pushing PAUSE on the DVD. My heart stopped. My body froze. My eyes widened.

"That's right," he said, cocky and self-assured. "I love you, Danielle. And you love me, too."

In an instant the PLAY on the invisible remote got pushed. My heart pounded. My body trembled. My eyes clouded over.

He stepped into the living room, and his heat surrounded me just before his arms did. "Don't you?" he asked, pressing our bodies together.

My hands came up to his chest, but I found myself gripping his shirt instead of pushing him away.

He was not the man of my well thought out plans. He was not my Mr. Right. He did not make enough money. He didn't drive the car. He didn't have the right job.

But . . .

God, I never felt so alive as when I was in his company.

I missed him. Craved him. Wanted him so very much.

I could talk to him. Laugh with him. Just chill with him.

I had to have him. Just once. Just this one time I had to know if he was as good as I thought.

Then I would marry Sahad and live the life I dreamed of.

Just once.

"Fuck me, Mohammed," I begged in a whisper just before his head lowered and his lips crushed against mine.

He growled a little, and I felt the bud between my legs throb and ache. "Fuck you or make love?" he asked against my lips.

It felt so naughty and dirty to talk naughty and dirty. It had been so long since I dropped my shell and got back to the *real* Cristal.

"Right now, I want you to fuck the hell out of me," I told him with every bit of honesty I had in me, leaning back to look up into his hot eyes as my hands undid his belt.

Mohammed used his foot to nudge the front door closed as he picked me up easily with one strong arm around my waist. "My pleasure," he whispered back.

I tangled my slender fingers in his locks, making fists as I lowered my head and traced the outline of his full lips with my quivering tongue while he carried me to the couch. His lips shifted down to nuzzle my neck with his lips, suckling soft tender spots from my collarbone as he whispered patois against my moist flesh. As he laid me down and knelt between my open thighs, I unbuttoned the white shirt I wore, exposing my breasts—firm and high—as they filled the delicate cups of my black lace bra. He used his strong hands to pull his T-shirt over his head, revealing his rigid six-pack abs and broad shoulders. I let my fingers play in the soft hairs on his chest and enjoyed the slight tremor I felt race across his body.

As his hands moved up the soft silk of my body to warmly grasp my breasts, I didn't care about anything but enjoying being with him. Not my white furniture. Not his girlfriend. Not Sahad. Not my wedding and my good life. Not a damn thing.

He stood long enough to kick off his sneakers and finish unbuttoning his pants. They dropped to his feet as he massaged the thick, throbbing length of his dick.

I pressed my legs together and groaned with a little lick of my lips at the muscular eleven inches with a curve that made that dick sure to please.

"Stand up and put that pussy in my face, woman." He sat down on the sofa, his legs wide open as he stroked his dick and squeezed the tip.

I rose to my feet and stepped between his open legs, presenting him my ass as I hitched my precious four-hundred-dollar skirt up around my waist like it came from Wal-Mart. I looked over my shoulder, working my clinging panties down my hips as I made my ass jiggle like I was the ex-stripper and not Dom!

Mohammed bit his bottom lip lightly and reached out with one hand to lightly slap my ass as I slowly bent over and put the pussy in his face just like he asked.

"Damn," I heard him whisper as he sat on the edge of the couch and grabbed both of my ass cheeks with his hands.

I shivered as he sucked small hickies onto each one before he spread my cheeks and licked a freaknasty trail from my swollen clit and fat pussy lips up to circle my asshole before he blew cool air against it.

Back and forth he went like he was on a fuckin' mission. From pussy to ass. Blow. Pussy to ass. Blow. Pussy to ass. Blow. And all over again and again.

"I knew this pussy would taste good."

I smiled. "It's good, ain't it?"

"Uhm, uhm." He sucked my pussy whole.

"Best you ever tasted?" I asked brazenly as I wrapped my hands around my ankles and gave him a little ass shake.

"Damn right," he said, slapping my ass like he was trying to jumpstart me. "Now let me give *you* the best you ever had."

"Oh, yeah?" I asked as the juices of my core lightly dampened the top of my inner thighs.

"*Hell,* yeah."

He rose, lightly tapping my ass cheeks with his dick, making solid "thuds" before he bent his knees to work the thick, smooth tip inside me.

I gasped as each delicious inch filled me 'til I felt nothing but sweet pressure as his hands grasped my ass. I cried out, sweat coating my body as my clit jumped and throbbed and pulsated.

"The pussy so hot," he moaned just as he pushed in the last final inch until I felt the soft curly hairs of his groin scratch my buttocks as he wiggled his hips.

I winced as I tried to adjust to his size, but I didn't want one bit of that dick out of me. I tweaked and teased and pinched my own pebble-hard nipples with my quivering fingers as I worked my pussy walls like I was trying to give that dick CPR.

Slowly, like he had nothing else in the world he wanted to do, Mohammed began to ease that dick in and out of me. I felt every pulsating vein and every strong muscle slide against my tight walls until the sound of my juices and the slapping of our flesh echoed in the room with our moans of pleasure.

I began to circle my hips, and a jolt shot through me as I felt his dick harden even more. It felt like a cement rod stirring in my flesh.

"You should see this dick going in and out this good pussy," he said thickly.

"Uhhhmmm," I hummed in pleasure, reveling in the flow of electricity between our bodies as we connected.

"Uhm, uhm," he answered in return, fucking me a bit harder so that my breasts slapped against my chest.

I reached behind me to put a restraining hand to his abdomen. I bent my legs and worked my hips up and down so that my slickly wet pussy walls pulled downward on his snakelike dick like a vise grip.

His grip tightened on my waist until I almost hollered out in pain, but the pleasure of our sex overrode any other feeling.

"Danielle," he moaned.

I could visualize him flinging his head back

until his dreads nearly touched the top of his hard, square buttocks.

"Damn right, you big dick motherfucker, say *my* damned name," I demanded, feeling free and sexy and powerful.

"Make me say it," he teased sexily.

I moved my hands up to grip the edge of the coffee table and began to pop my hips and pussy like I was trying to save my life. "Say it."

He shifted his hands to grip my ass.

"Say—" Pop. "It!" Pop-pop.

"Danielle."

"Louder!" I shouted as my heart thundered like a storm.

Pop-pop-pop-pop.

"Danielle."

"Aw, hell no. Lou-der."

Pop-pop-pop-pop-pop-pop-pop-pop.

"Danielle," he cried out hoarsely at the top of his lungs.

I laughed huskily as I slowed the pace and circled my hips.

Suddenly Mohammed bent his weight down on me and took control, fucking me like he was a madman. I cried out in pleasure, my face twisted as each jolt made my pussy wetter. He fucked me down to my knees until I was bent over the coffee table. My titties and the side of my face were pressed flat against the cool wood.

"Gracious," I cried out as each stroke made his heavy balls swing and hit against my clit as he softly kissed the smoothness of my shoulder while fucking me like a machine.

"Now say *my* fucking name," he ordered huskily in that sexy accent of his.

"Mohammed."

"Again."

"Mohammed. Mohammed. Mohammed!"

"Hold still, baby. Don't move."

We were both still. So very still as he held me close, his dreads surrounded my upper body like a shield.

I felt his dick throb. Once. Twice. Three times.

"You feel that," he asked thickly as he sucked my earlobe.

I closed my eyes and nodded. "You came?" I asked, disappointed it was over.

"Just a little bit."

I felt the hard muscles of his body pressed into my back as the pounding of his heart echoed my own.

I felt him lean up a bit, and I knew he was looking down at me.

"I love you, Danielle."

Tears welled up in my chest at his words and the raw emotion evident in them.

"I love you, too," I whispered back, unable to deny the truth. "So very much."

He kissed my tears and held me closer as he began to slow-grind his hips against mine, causing little tiny thrusts of his dick deeper inside of me. It was just as lethal as the pussy pounding.

In a voice barely above a whisper, he began to talk to me as he made love to me.

"I love the way your eyes light up when you smile.

"I love the smell of your perfume on your skin.

"I love the way you laugh.

"I love the way you say my name.

"I love the way your body feels when you ride on my bike.

"I love how smart you are."

On and on and on he worshiped my soul with his words and my body with his dick until I let the tears flow and gave in to him completely.

So completely that I didn't hear the front door unlock and swing open.

"What the fuck?"

My eyes popped open at the intrusion, and I turned my head to look at Sahad storming toward us.

Mohammed and I sprang apart, and I clutched a pillow to hide my nakedness as Sahad and Mohammed began to tussle, falling backward on the coffee table and sending it crashing to the floor as the legs broke.

"Stop it! Stop it," I cried, dropping the pillow to pull at Sahad's neck as he landed atop Mohammed and began to strangle him.

He flung me off him like a fly, and I landed a bit away, almost hitting the bar.

"You motherfucker you," Sahad shouted as he raised up to deliver Mohammed a blow.

Mohammed reached up first and gave Sahad a vicious uppercut that sent him backward onto the sofa.

I dashed between them, forgetting my nudeness as they both jumped to their feet, and I put a restraining hand on both their chests.

"Stop . . . it!"

Sahad looked down at me, and I forced myself not to look away. "This the motherfucker you want?" he asked in a cold, hard voice.

"I'm sorry," I told him. "I really am."

"No good trick." He reached for my hand, wrestling the engagement ring from my finger before he turned and walked out of the apartment. "I come home early to surprise your ass to find *this* shit? Stay the fuck away from me, Danielle."

He slammed the door behind him.

Leaving that voice mail on his phone had sent Sahad right to the scene of my betrayal.

Mohammed gathered me into his arms, and although I knew I hurt Sahad, I knew that nothing felt more right in the world than being held by the man I loved.

Fate was a no-good bitch.

48

Alizé

Five months later

I got something in the mail from Cameron. I felt excitement and curiosity. I studied it, turning it this way and that. I sniffed for a hint of his cologne. There was none.

I hadn't seen him since that last time in my bedroom. Funny, but I thought he would call or come see me, but he didn't.

I started to call him so many times.

When I got the cast off my leg.

When I finished physical therapy.

When one of my graduate classes started kicking my ass.

When Dana offered to let me teach dance class to little girls who were six to eight years old.

When I missed him so much I could cry.

But I didn't.

I was chilling out for the first time in my life, enjoying me, myself, and I. No Lionel with the tantalizingly terrific dick. No more thugs catching my eye and sending a shiver of pure excitement through my body.

See, a motherfucker like Rah—them thugs that come and go—would never have me sitting around with my head up my ass waiting on them to love me or come back to me. It was men like Cameron and my father—reliable, loving, trustworthy and lasting—that broke a woman's heart, like my mother's, every damn time.

Dangerous, thuggish men made it so easy to keep my distance when it came to my heart. They were everything my father wasn't, and so my heart was safe. Being with them I made sure—without even knowing it—that I would never become my mother. I was so busy protecting my heart that I lost sight of possibly being physically hurt by one of those dangerous men—bad boys—that my ass loved so much.

I loved my parents, but their shit—or me trying not to repeat it—had me good and fucked up. I was afraid of a normal, healthy adult relationship. I avoided them like the plague because I was afraid of being hurt. I sought only relationships where I maintained control of my heart.

To discover and dig into the realness behind my "thug love" was hard to swallow at first. My shit went deeper than loving a hard brotha in a wifebeater and a pair of Timbs. Deeper than loving the street cred. Deeper than fast money. Designer clothes. Bling.

So I took my ass to a therapist, although most Black folks like to lay their problems at the altar. Some sistahs took it to their friends, but this was bigger than the advice of the sistah-girl circle. I needed a professional. Period. Sometimes God blesses you with resolution right here on earth.

Yes, that's right, laying up on someone's couch twice a week and giving them hundreds per hour to get my mind right. I'm working through my issues. I'm working on closure about my parents' divorce. I'm getting out my anger at Dom. I'm focusing on why I drew men like Rah to me like flies to shit. I'm coping with my loss of dancing and admitting to my love for Cameron.

Once I admitted to my feelings, I wanted call him or go and tell him, but I paused because I had to get myself together before I could welcome a man into my life. And my life now was all about school. Teaching dance classes and hanging out with my girls without Dom. Okay. Therapy was good, but it wasn't *that* good. Yet.

I opened the flap and pulled out the card to read it.

As my eyes took in each word that felt like a blow to my body, tears filled my eyes, blurring the words. Thank God, because I couldn't stand to read them again.

Glenda and Frank Lemons
request the honor of your presence
at the marriage of their daughter
Serena Evonne Lemons
to
Cameron Lance Steele
on Saturday,
the Sixteenth of December,
at three o'clock

Damn. Damn. Damn. Diggity damn damn!

49

Dom

Was I crazy?
I *had* to be.

I parked my car on the corner of Springfield Avenue and Seventeenth Street just like he told me. I glanced at my watch: 12:00 P.M. I looked up and down the street through my rearview mirror.

I was so nervous. I felt like I had to shit, and my stomach was bubblin' like crazy. My heart pounded in my chest, and my hands were shakin' like an m'fer.

I wished he would hurry the fuck up 'cause I had to get back to work.

I looked down at the colorful smock I wore over my T-shirt and jeans. I couldn't do shit but shake my head. Me workin' at my daughter's day care center as an aide. Hollerin' kids. Snacks. Nap time. ABCs and fuckin' 123s.

It was a long way from workin' the pole.

And the $8.50 an hour was a long way from the loot I used to make. It took me two weeks to make the same money I used to make in a night. On the real? Sometimes I missed the motherfuckin' stage and the money, especially having to pay my share of the rent on the apartment and tryin' to hold on to my Lexus.

My life was so different, and I was proud of my damn self. Five months clean. No booze. No weed. No dope. Nothin'. It wasn't easy. Every day was a struggle, and my journals was filled with my fight to stay clean.

I was even thinkin' 'bout writin' a book. Me? Shit, I remember when I used to frown up when somebody mentioned readin' some shit besides a magazine. Now I read to Kimani every night.

My eyes shifted to the wallet-sized photo of her I kept on my dashboard.

I wasn't a perfect mama or nothin', but I was tryin', and she loved me. She *loved* me.

All the love I was looking for up on that stage butt naked with a smile or in a bag a dope or weed, I had in her eyes the whole fuckin' time.

I loved the hell out of her little ass, too.

My cell phone vibrated, and I picked it up from the seat. My mother's number showed up. I dropped it back on the seat.

I had nothin' but distance for Di—*my mother* right now.

For one she didn't want me and Kimani to move out, and she threatened to use DYFS to take my daughter from me. I called the bitch's bluff, and we moved right out. On top of that she kept callin' me beggin' my ass to bring Kimani for a visit. Now peep *this* shit.

How 'bout Diane smoked weed in front of me and then offered me a hit.

What the fuck?

It hurt me more than anything, so I grabbed Kimani and bounced. I ain't spoke to her since.

A knock on my passenger side window shook me. I turned to look through the window into Rah's face. My heart hit my chest so hard I thought I was 'bout to have a f'ing heart attack.

Am I crazy?

He'd called my cell phone out of the blue and begged me to help him. He said the police raided a house where he staying with friends and he needed somewhere to run to. Somewhere to hide.

"Open the door, Dom."

Our eyes locked, and I made myself not look away.

A second later the shrill cry of sirens and the rough cries of police officers surrounded my car and Rah with their guns drawn.

"Put your hands up!"

"Don't move!"

"Move away from the car!"

My car door was snatched open, and I felt myself being pulled out. I looked over my shoulder as Rah tried to make a run for it and was wrestled to the ground just a few feet away from my car.

It felt like everything was moving in slow motion.

Everything but my fuckin' pulse.

"Are you okay, Miss Lands?"

I looked up at the male officer still holding my arm. "Yes. Thank you. I'm fine."

"No, thank you. Your tip helped us catch him."

I nodded and wrapped my arms around my chest, turning to watch as the police roughly pushed Rah into the back of one of the police cars.

50

Moët

I was *so* ready to have this baby. I wanted to hold him—yes, it's a boy—and play with him and nuzzle my face in his neck, but mostly I wanted my body back. I felt like a water balloon about to pop. I could hardly see the television if I lay flat on my back, and I had to pee all the time.

I had just gotten off from my job as a caseworker for DYFS and was lying across my bed flipping through television stations when I caught a flash of Bones's face on the screen.

My heart felt like it flew up to my throat as I watched him surrounded by a group of ass-jiggling video vixens.

I shook my head. "There's your daddy."

Bones stood in the center of the club as a stripper-like woman danced around him like he was the pole, and I frowned, then winced, and finally gasped in shock.

I quickly turned the channel.

I wouldn't say I loved Bones anymore—if I ever really did— but I knew that video made me hot and not in the sexy way.

God, if I could turn back time, I would do so many things different. So many, many things.

Thank the heavens I didn't wind up in jail for my lies.

Finally, I made peace with God and myself. Maybe one day I would make peace with Bones. Ask him to forgive me for lying. Encourage him to be a part of this child's life and not just for money.

That was hard to do when he was still denying paternity.

His attorneys contacted me requesting a paternity test, but since I was too far along for those that could be given prenatally—which were unsafe for the baby—the tests would be done as soon as he was born.

That was fine with me. I was one hundred percent sure Bones was the father. Trust me this was not going to be one of those "Oh, no she didn't, I know she shame" Maury moments.

Other than Bones my life was good. Thank God. Yes, I thank *Him*.

I'm still living at Cristal's and have been with DYFS for the last three months. I was determined to do my job right. There would be no children left in abusive situations on my watch. Not just because I was a good person and all that, but because it was my job. Period.

The Lord and I were back on good terms. I wasn't saved and half out my mind with Bible verses, but I went to church every Sunday and even helped Olana out with Sunday school. I didn't know if my parents would be proud of my version of faith, but I was proud of myself, and that was important to me.

My parents.

I closed my eyes at the familiar dart of pain at our estrangement. I missed them. I even missed my father because some of him was better than none of him. I missed my sisters—although we spoke on the phone as often as we could and whenever my parents weren't around. I wasn't proud of the example I set for them, and although they, too, complained about our parents, I encouraged them to continue respecting and honoring our parents. I didn't want them to do some of the crazy things I did, so I told them the truth, hoping they learned from my lessons.

Bzzzzzzzzzzz.

I reached for my vibrating cell phone sitting on the coffee table. The caller ID said Cris.

"Hey, you."

"How are you, Mommy?" she asked.

"Ready to push." I used the remote to put the TV on mute.

"Well, I am at the store. Do you want me to bring you anything?"

"An IV drip to induce labor would be sweet," I joked.

Cristal laughed. "How about a gallon of double mocha walnut ice cream."

"That, too."

"Dom and Kimani home yet?"

"No, not yet, but something's up with Dom. She was acting real distracted this morning."

"You would have shit on your mind, too, if you helped the cops catch a fugitive today."

I sat up straight. "What!"

"Rah's cornball behind called her for help, and Dom called the police."

I held my hand to my belly. "And she didn't tell me?"

"Hell, I just found out this afternoon when I called her after lunch."

"Wow. Then good. I'm glad he's in jail where he belongs."

"Yeah, me, too."

We both fell silent, and the question hung between us, so I gave voice to it. "Does Alizé know?"

"I did not tell her. I am so tired of trying to get Alizé and Dom back cool again."

Yes, Cristal had tried everything including begging, and Alizé wouldn't budge. I could see why she would give up, but I wasn't ready to lose our foursome forever.

"I'll call her." I winced as a pain radiated across my back.

"Call me back and tell me what she said."

I ended the call and quickly dialed Alizé's cell phone number. I wished Ze would just beat Dom's butt—or at least try—and get it out of her system.

As the phone rang, I glanced back at the sight of a burning building on the television.

"Hey, Al—"

"I'm glad you called, Mo. Guess who's getting married? Just guess. You won't believe it."

"Your mother."

Ze sucked her teeth. "Yeah, *o-kay.*"

"Your father?"

"No."

"Your aunt with the six toes and a mustache?"

"*Hell* no."

I shifted on the bed, looking for comfort and pressing a throw pillow behind me. "Okay, this game is so old right now," I said around another wince.

"Okay. Cameron. Cameron is getting married."

Ouch. Ze liked to front like she and Cameron *used to be* nothing but friends. Yeah, okay.

"You okay?"

"I'm cool. Why wouldn't I be cool? I'm so cool, I'm icy. I'm so straight, I'm a ruler. I am *so*—"

"Okay, I get it," I said dryly. "Are you going?"

"If I have nothing else to do."

"Well, since you're so cool and so straight, let's play guess who went to jail?"

"No," Ze said, drawing it out. "Who?"

"Rah. Dom helped the police catch him."

The line went quiet just like I knew it would.

I gave her time to process that, reaching behind me to massage my lower back as my eyes caught sight of television. The police were leading someone out of a church. *Wait a minute that's my parents' church.*

I sat up straighter. *And that's . . . Reverend DeMark.*

"Ooooh, shit," I said, my first cuss word in ages.

"What's wrong, Mo?"

I picked up the remote and turned up the volume. "Hold on one sec."

". . . the identity of the fifteen-year-old minor Reverend DeMark is accused of having a sexual relationship with is not being revealed, but she is reported to be the daughter of one of his longtime parishioners."

My jaw nearly hit my chest as one police officer pushed the Rev's head down to assist him into the back of the police car.

"Mo, what happened."

"I'll have to tell you later."

"Why?"

I looked down at my lap. "My water just broke."

51

Cristal

Okay, that is way more of Mo than I wanted to see. I turned my head as the OB/GYN checked Mo to see how far she was dilated. I glanced at Alizé and saw she had her head turned as well.

And I have got to remind Mo that a bikini wax is not at all a bad thing. Jesus, it looks like she is trying to hide Buckwheat's afro under her gown.

I felt my cell phone vibrate. When I flipped it open, a text message read: COME DOWNSTAIRS.

"Ladies, I'll be right back." I left my purse by Alizé and gently squeezed Mo's foot on my way out the door.

The scent of hospital and sickness was never as strong in the Labor and Delivery unit as elsewhere. Thank God, because my stomach couldn't take it.

I felt nervous like something was about to happen . . . like enough was not going down right now. Mo having the baby. Dom playing bounty hunter.

Al looking sad, fronting like Cameron getting married didn't hurt her.

Getting married.

Six months ago I thought I would be getting married now. Everything I thought I wanted had been in the palm of my hand, and I held that hand up and blew those dreams into the wind like dust. I had not seen Sahad—in person anyway. That same day two of his burly security guards brought all my belongings to me in plastic trash bags.

And that was my belongings pre-Sahad.

He kept everything he ever bought me. And I mean *everything*. The seven-piece Louis Vuitton luggage, all of the jewelry except what I had on, the clothes, the shoes—oh, God, the shoes, even the expensive lacy lingerie. All of it. Later I found out my new Benz was gone as well. Maybe he did a male version of the Angela Bassett scene from *Waiting to Exhale*.

No more wifey living the high society life I longed for.

Having a man take back everything he ever gave you—including your underwear—was one helluva wake-up call on being independent.

I was back working as a receptionist for a law firm downtown. Thank God I had kept my apartment for Dom and Mo or I would have been homeless right now. With us splitting the expenses three ways, my life was not about struggling financially to keep up appearances. Plus, my appearances had downgraded a bit. More GAP and Baby Phat over Escada, Cavalli, Armani, and Norma Kamali. Nine West and Etienne Aigner shoes over Manolo Blahnik.

It was hard, but I was trying my best not to put myself in a situation where I needed a man to bail me out. So very damn hard.

But my life was good. Different, but good. Damn good.

The elevator stopped on the first floor. Dom and I nearly walked into each other. "Hey, girl. Good, you made it."

"Mo ain't dropped yet?" she asked, shifting her shades up to the top of her head. She held her car keys in her hand.

"Not yet, but she is taking the pain like a soldier."

"Shit, that real pain just ain't hit her ass yet." Dom laughed.

"Where's Kimani?"

"Spending the night with her friend."

I reached out and grabbed her hand. Dom did not like mushiness, but I held on to that hand even when I felt her pull away. "Hey, I am so proud of you. For everything. Kimani. Your job. Staying clean. Handling you mother. Helping catch Rah. All of it."

Dom's hand went from being slack to clasping mine just as tightly as I squeezed hers. That was her way of saying thank you, and I understood that. Dom was just being Dom.

"Ze's upstairs."

"I know." Dom reached behind me to hit the button for the elevator. "She hates my guts. I'm the worst bitch alive and all that good shit, but I *ain't* missin' Mo havin' this baby."

Uh-oh.

"Wait on me in case I have to play referee."

I caught a movement out of the corner of my eye. I turned and was pulled into a warm, strong, and oh so *familiar* embrace. I buried my face in his neck and inhaled deeply of the scent of cocoa butter in his locks. My heart pounded. My pulse raced. My stomach fluttered. "Hey, baby."

"Whaddup, Miss Danielle."

Okay, I was in love. For the first time in my life I was truly and completely in love. He was nothing I ever thought I would want but everything I discovered I needed.

Girl Talk

When Dom and Cristal went back up to Mo's room, it was bustling with activity. She was being prepped for the delivery.

"You can have up to three in the room during delivery. Are they all staying?" the nurse asked Mo.

"Yes," Mo snapped. Her eyes closed as she winced and then bit her bottom lip. She opened one eye and looked at each of them. *"Everybody."*

"Get them some gowns," the nurse told the nursing assistant as she reached in a drawer for other supplies.

Mo released the bed rail she was gripping tightly to hold out her hand.

Cristal immediately stepped to the side of the bed and entwined her fingers with Mo's. "I am here for you. You know that."

Dom stepped up next and moved to the head of the bed. She took Cristal's free hand in one of hers and lightly grasped Mo's shoulder with the other. "I got you, Mo."

There was no denying the apprehension on Alizé's face.

Dom licked her lips and focused her eyes on Mo.

Cristal gave Alizé a meaningful stare.

Time seemed to tick by slowly in those awkward moments.

Ze stepped up to the other side of the bed and took Mo's free hand in one of hers. "I'm not going anywhere either."

Cristal smiled. "Okay y'all, let's have this baby."

Niobia Bryant delivers a sexy, unforgettable novel about love, infidelity, and the importance of keeping your friends close and your enemies closer . . .
Message from a Mistress

Coming in March 2010 from Dafina Books

Jessa's Prelude

Where do I begin? How do I tell the story? Our story. His and mine.

He was my lover and her husband. You would think that wasn't possible—like saying dry rain or cold heat—but it was true. She had the ring and the certificate . . . but I had him. From that first heated moment in their kitchen when his strong hands reached beneath my skirt to grab my soft, bare ass, I knew I had him.

I don't recall the specific moment when our lust turned to love. When our time spent together became about more than just fucking, more than just rushing through electrifying sex that left us both panting, sweaty, and in various stages of undress. We shifted so easily from sharing clandestine and wonderfully sneaky moments—even in their house while she was there—to him sneaking out of their home to be in my arms and in my bed.

I hated to lay alone at night surrounded by nothing but cool cotton sheets and plush down pillows, while she had his hard and warm body to hold close.

I knew the time would come when I would want more from him than just his dick. I wanted his love, his time, his all . . . for me and only me.

She was my friend—true, but he was my lover, my love, and in this game there could only be one winner as far as I was concerned.

Me.

1

Jaime Hall enjoyed the feel of the steam surrounding her body as she sat in the glass shower of their bedroom suite. The thick swirling vapors felt like a lover's gentle touch against her skin and those intimate parts of her body. Her breasts. Her nipples. Her thighs. Her lips—both sets.

She relished it. She needed it.

Sadness weighed her shoulders down and soon she felt tears fill her oval shaped eyes and race down her cheeks. Jaime brought her shaking hands up to hug herself close. "God, I can't take much more of my life," she whispered into the steam as her head dropped so low that her chin nearly touched her chest.

She heard a sudden noise in the bathroom. Her head jerked up and she immediately swallowed back the rest of her tears and frantically wiped any traces of them from her face. The last thing she wanted was for him to see or hear her crying.

"Eric," Jaime called out to her husband of the last seven years.

No answer. Nothing to acknowledge her. Seconds later the bathroom door opened and then closed. Disappointment nudged the door to her heart shut as well. The body's automatic defense mechanisms were amazing.

Jaime rose from the bench and stepped out of the shower. She grabbed a towel and wrapped it around her frame as she raced out of her bathroom suite and through the master bedroom and out to the hall.

"Eric!" she called out, striding down the staircase and through the circular foyer to the kitchen.

The house was quiet. As she looked out the kitchen windows over the driveway, the sun was just starting to rise. Sure enough, Eric's new Ford F150 was gone from its parking spot, leaving just her older but still reliable convertible Volvo.

He left to go deep-sea fishing and didn't even bother to tell her good-bye. She turned and let her body slide down to the polished hardwood floor as tears wracked her body. She wrapped her arms around her knees and rocked to make herself feel a little better.

"Shit!" Renee Jackson swore as the gray acrid smoke rose from the frying pan with fury. She hurried to turn off the lit eye of the Viking stove before shifting the pan to one of the remaining five burners.

"Damn, damn, damn it all to hell."

Renee could only shake her head at the blackness of the bacon she'd been frying. It was *beyond* crispy.

"Is something on fire, Ma?"

Renee looked over her shoulder as her thirteen-year-old daughter, Leila, walked into the kitchen on dragging feet in her oversized fuzzy pajamas. "Just breakfast," Renee said.

"*You* were cooking?" Leila asked in disbelief as she leaned her hip against the island in the center of the kitchen.

"I wanted to fix your father breakfast before he left to go fishing." Renee slid the halfway decent looking slices of bacon onto a clear glass plate.

"You never cook." Leila moved across the kitchen to the pantry.

"I know *how* to cook," Renee protested as she ran a hand through her wavy hair. "It's remembering that I have food on the stove that I have a problem with."

Leila stepped out of the pantry and approached her mother, her hand digging into a box of cereal. She threw handfuls of the sugary sweet cereal into her mouth and frowned at the bacon-filled plate in her mother's hand. "Good thing Daddy loves you," she joked before turning to walk out of the kitchen.

"Yeah, good thing," Renee said with hesitance as she cracked eggs into a large red Le Creuset ceramic bowl and whisked them with extra ferocity.

She poured the eggs into the stainless steel pan and left them so that they would set before she scrambled them. She moved back to the end of the island where her briefcase was open and instantly became absorbed in the facts and figures of the report she'd brought home to review.

At thirty-three, Renee was the vice president of marketing for the CancerCure Foundation, one of the largest nonprofits serving cancer research and awareness in the country. It was her job and her passion to develop partnerships with major corporations for invaluable donations and increasing the national visibility of the foundation. She took her work seriously—not just for the six-figure income she received—but because it intrigued and challenged her every day. It was easy for her to get deeply absorbed into her work.

Renee picked up the oversized cup of gourmet coffee with one hand and the open report with the other.

"What the hell is burning?"

The words on the report disappeared as Renee closed her eyes and frowned as she thought, "damn," at the sound of her husband Jackson's voice from behind her.

She dropped the report and snatched the burning pan from the stove in one continuous motion. "This just isn't my morning, Jackson," she told him, looking over her shoulder at her tall, solid husband of the last thirteen years.

His square, handsome face shaped into a frown as he took in the papers and files on the island. There was no mistaking the immediate look of disapproval.

Renee hated the guilt she felt at that one look that spoke volumes about their marriage. "I thought I would cook—"

"*And* work?" he asked, moving past her to fill the thermos he held with coffee.

Renee swallowed her irritation. She looked down at the burnt bacon on the plate and the brown eggs in the pan and scraped them both into the garbage disposal. "I'm trying, Jackson," she stressed, her eyes angry and hurt.

He just snorted in derision.

Renee felt tension across her shoulders. She jumped a little as he moved close to her to press a cool kiss to her cheek. She closed her eyes, absorbing his scent as she raised a hand to stroke his bearded cheek. He felt familiar and strange all at once. It had been so long since they had shown each other simple affection.

She tilted her head back to look up into those eyes that had intrigued her from the first time she saw him on the campus of Rutgers University. "I love you, Jackson," Renee whispered, hating the urgency in her voice as her eyes searched his.

For what seemed like forever, his eyes searched hers as well. "We need to talk. We *have* to talk," he said, his voice husky and barely above a whisper.

A soft press of his lips down upon hers silenced any of her words or questions.

Moments later, he was gone and Renee felt chilled to the bone.

"You didn't have to get up so early with me, baby."

Aria Livewell shrugged as she followed her broad-shouldered husband, Jamal, down the stairs of their three-thousand-square-foot home in the family-oriented subdivision of Richmond Hills. A home they planned to fill with children. "It's no problem. You know me and the girls are hanging out today and I wanted to get some housework done before they picked me up."

Jamal set his fishing equipment by the wooden double doors. "Think you four will be back on time? You know we're supposed to meet at the Jacksons' tonight to fry up all the fish we'll catch today."

"Just three, actually. Jessa said she had *something else* to do today." Aria made a playful face and waved her hand dismissively.

Jamal put his broad hands beneath her short cotton robe and pulled his beautiful, mocha-skinned wife close to him. "If we whup our friends in bid whist tonight, I have one helluva surprise for you."

Jamal was *so* competitive.

Aria tilted her head up to lightly lick his dimpled chin as she pushed her hand into the back pocket of his vintage jeans to grasp his firm buttocks. "Can I get a hint?" she asked huskily with a teasing smile, the beat of her heart already quickening with anticipation.

"Damn, I love you," he said roughly, his eyes smoldering as he slid one hand up to her nape.

Aria moaned softly in pleasure at the first heated feel of her husband's lips. As she gasped slightly, he slid his tongue inside her mouth with well-practiced ease. She shivered. Her clit swelled to life. Her nipples hardened in a rush.

"Do we have time?" she asked in a heated whisper, barely hearing herself over her own furious heart beat as Jamal undid her robe and planted moist and tantalizing kisses along her collarbone.

"We'll make time," he breathed across her flesh.

As her robe slipped open and his familiar hands caressed her silky skin, Aria enjoyed their passion and wondered if a time would come when she didn't cherish and yearn for her husband's touch. His dick. His kisses. His love.

With his mouth, Jamal made a path to the deep valley of her breasts, bending his knees to take one swollen and taut dark nipple into his mouth. He sucked it deeply and then circled it with the tip of his clever tongue.

"Yes," Aria whimpered, flinging her head back.

Jamal turned them and pressed Aria's back to the towering front doors as he quickly undid his belt and zipper. His own hands shook as he placed them on her lush hips and lifted her with ease until her pulsing and moist pussy lips lightly kissed the thick tip of his dick. "Why is your pussy so good?" he whispered against the pounding pulse of her throat.

Aria didn't answer. She just smiled wickedly as she caused the swollen lips of her vagina to lightly kiss the smooth, round head of his dick . . . twice.

Jamal dropped Aria down onto his erection, her pussy tightly surrounding and gripping him like a vise. "Damn," he swore, his buttocks tensing as he froze. He didn't want to come. Not yet.

Aria pressed the small of her back to the door and began to work her hips in small circles, anxious not just to have his dick pressed against her walls but to feel his delicious strokes.

Jamal's jaw clenched. "Don't make me nut, baby." His voice was strained.

Aria raised her hands to tease her own nipples with her slender fingers as she enjoyed the tight in-and-out motion as Jamal began to work his hips. She felt wild and free, uninhibited and sexy. "Umph. I'm gon' come, baby. Please make me come," she whispered with fevered urgency as each of his deep thrusts caused her pussy to smack and echo in the foyer like applause.

Jamal's chest and loins exploded with heat as he felt a primal need to feel as much of Aria's pussy as he could. He pushed deeper up inside her, drawing quick and uneven breaths as his heart thundered. His buttocks clenched and then relaxed as he touched every bit of her ridged walls with his solid inches. "Damn, Aria," he swore, planting adoring kisses along her collarbone as his dick filled her with several warm shots of cum.

2

For Jaime, image was everything. And in her world, the image was all about perfection. It was a must. The right look. The right hairstyle. The right clothes. The right associates and friends—love them or hate them. The right business contacts. The right thing to say. The right place to be. The right husband, house, and finances. This was all she knew. It was her comfort zone and in her life she *had to* find comfort wherever she could.

Jaime pulled her silver convertible Volvo C70 in front of the valet stand of the renovated 1930s Georgian cottage that served as the day spa Serenity. She double-checked her appearance in her Chanel compact. Her bone-straight jet-black hair— the best complement to her cinnamon-bronzed skin—was evenly part down the middle and lying better than Pocahontas' ass could've ever dreamed thanks to a celebrity hairstylist who catered to East Coast celebrities. She had to save up for six months to afford the hefty two-thousand-dollar fee, but no one knew that. She damn sure felt worthy. She was a beautiful woman and she knew it.

Her MAC makeup was perfectly in place on high cheekbones that screamed of her father's African heritage and deep-set feline eyes that were all about her mother's Asian legacy. It was that mixed exotic look that first drew her husband to her. Once upon a time, she thought he would never be able to deny her anything because of her beauty. She thought her seat on his pedestal was unshakable. A constant. Till death.

She focused her vision on her reflection and tried to suppress the sadness filling her eyes. *I was so wrong.* She snapped the compact closed and dropped it into her oversized woven-straw Coach tote. The diamonds of her two-carat wedding band twinkled brighter than the summer sun, but they were mocking her and so she quickly shifted her gaze away from it.

Literally shaking it off, Jaime slid on her Bottega Veneta shades and climbed from the vehicle dressed in a bright lemon Nanette Lepore silk scoop neck tank and matching flowing pants. If she felt as good as she looked, her walk of confidence into the building would've been more than just a front.

"Hello, Mrs. Hall. The ladies are waiting for you in the Heaven Room," Hannah, the tall and thin receptionist, told Jaime as soon as she stepped in front of the solid mahogany desk of Serenity's foyer. "I have you all set up in changing room number one."

"Thank you, Hannah," she told the well-tanned and toned redhead as she passed the desk on the right to reach the changing rooms. Sure enough, a white robe and slippers sat folded and awaiting her on the suede chair. The warm décor, plush carpeting, and soft lighting certainly made her feel serene.

A spa day with her friends was just what she needed to forget that the shambles of her marriage was all her own doing. Guilt was a damn hard pill to swallow. Some drinks, pampering, and gossip with her friends would make her forget . . . hopefully.

Jaime hung up her clothes and slid her undergarments into one of the net bags supplied in the small closet. She sighed at the feel of the plush robe against her nude skin. Her nipples tingled and goosebumps raced across her flesh. Eric's little sabbatical from sex had her horny as hell. She tried to ignore that steady pulsing of her clit as she left the room and walked down the wide private hall in search of her friends.

"Hello, Mrs. Hall."

She smiled at the male attendant standing outside the double doors in his all-white attire. He was there to service any of their requests for the day. She gave him a nod and a fake smile as he opened the double doors leading into the private room. Her smile became genuine as she eyed Aria and Renee already comfortably seated in two of the four plush leather massage chairs situated in the center of the all-white room. Jaime knew without asking that they were having chocolate pedicures. She couldn't wait to join them.

Aria was young and pretty with the kind of laidback, no-fuss/no-muss style that Jaime had long ago lost and sometimes yearned for. There was no denying that Aria and Jamal were in love. Jaime always fought hard not to let her jealousy of their marriage taunt her. She made the bed of her marriage and now she was lying in it.

Renee was the senior of their group but her looks would never reveal it. The woman was thick and solid, with more curves than a roller coaster ride. Forty looked damn good on her and that eighty-hours-a-week corporate job wasn't hurting her either. *Just too bad Clinton doesn't appreciate her,* Jaime thought as she set her purse on the floor and slid onto her leather club chair.

"Girl, your ass is gonna be late to your own funeral," Aria teased before taking a sip from some frosty red concoction in her crystal goblet.

"And looking good as ever, baby. Believe that," Jaime teased back, stepping up on the platform to take a seat beside Aria.

Renee snuggled down deeper into her chair and closed her eyes. "Better late than never."

Aria cocked a well shaped brow. "We talkin' 'bout Jaime or a period?"

"Shee-it . . . *both.*" Renee opened one eye to peer at them as she laughed and reached on the side for her BlackBerry.

"I know that's right," Jaime added as she accepted the slender, suede-covered menu the attendant offered her on a small silver tray. "I was hoping Jessa would show today because I had to ask her about Olivia's husband getting caught in the wine cellar . . . *with* a man . . . *without* a stitch of clothes."

"What?" Aria and Renee gasped in unison as they both leaned in close.

Jaime nodded. "Yup, yup."

"Confirmed?" Aria asked, her bright eyes wide.

Jaime shook her head and studied her hands. "Can't confirm it. That's why I was hoping to see Jessa. She knows everything about everything."

Aria nodded in agreement. "That's true. Jessa always has the best gossip. Our girl does not play. Humph. Wendy Williams don't have shit on her."

"Who?" Renee and Jaime asked in unison with confusion on their faces.

"Never mind," Aria muttered, reaching for her drink.

Jaime just shrugged and waved her hand dismissively. She was sure they had missed one of Aria's ghetto colloquialisms. "You have to admit that Jessa is easy to talk to, and that puts her ear to a lot of mouths telling their business in Richmond Hills."

"Call her," Renee suggested as she sat her PDA down on her lap.

"I tried and she didn't answer." Jaime paused as the tall and muscular attendant came to quietly stand by them. Briefly, she eyed him, and she couldn't help but notice that his lean but athletic frame was similar to that of Eric. And that made her remember just how long it had been since she enjoyed the sexual comforts of her man. *Way too damn long,* she thought as she pressed her thighs together just to get *any* type of feeling in her pussy. Even more than the wicked strokes of his dick, she would take more than a one- or two-word response from her constant attempts to talk to him. She was so sick of wondering if he would ever forgive her.

Jaime quickly placed her order for a mimosa,

anxious to get right back to the juice. Anyone's business but her own was always interesting and . . . distracting. "I feel for Olivia. Can you imagine not only the embarrassment of your husband screwing a man but walking in on them? Thank God I'm not her."

Renee placed her right elbow on the arm of the chair and held her chin in her hand. "I don't know what I would do if . . . if it were me. I mean, Jackson and I have problems but I never figured infidelity was one of them."

Aria leaned forward, a don't-fuck-with-me expression on her face. "Well, if I walked in on Jamal cheating on me, I would walk right on outta there and come back with nine reasons why both of they ass shoulda been more careful."

Jaime and Renee both laughed at their young friend as she used her hand to mimic a gun. Aria was a chameleon and could change her demeanor to meet the situation. It was mostly the dignified wife of a doctor, but at times the little girl raised in Newark who didn't take any shit came out with much too much ease.

Jaime waved her hand dismissively again as the manicurist quietly entered the room and stooped to prepare the chocolate concoction for her feet. "Well, things couldn't be better between Eric and me. Marriage is tough, but thankfully we have a strong one, and I feel blessed. I really do," she lied, hiding the truth behind a bright and continually fake smile as she slid her feet into the marble bowl.

* * *

Aria looked down to study her freshly polished toes as they walked down the short hall to their private room for coconut massages. As soon as the three women stepped inside, the sweet but subtle scent of the coconut milk that would be drizzled over their bodies was intoxicating. She allowed herself a deep inhale as they all removed their robes and laid their naked bodies down on their individual massage tables. The feel of the crisp cotton pressed against her skin made her sigh as her masseuse covered her to the waist with another sheet.

Aria bit her bottom lip as she thought of Jaime's declaration of her terrific marriage during their mani-pedis. Something about it irked her. Something about their constant perfection always irked her. "Jaime. Question. If a marriage is good, does that mean a wife should sit and act like the other shoe might not fall?"

"Where's the trust in that?" Jaime asked.

Aria lifted her head from the table and looked over at Jaime on her left. "There's a thin line between trust and stupidity," she said, as the masseuse gently guided her head back down with one hand.

"Well, without trust, the line between being married and being divorced is even thinner," Jaime shot back in a holier-than-thou tone.

"I think you're both right," Renee joined in from Aria's other side.

Aria rolled her eyes. "I am married to a prominent wealthy black doctor who is fine . . . matter of fact, fine as hell. Single women stay on the prowl for those endangered species," she said matter-of-factly, her eyes closed as she fought to find the relaxation of the massage. "God forbid the wrong bitch with tits and ass for days puts him in a corner, his ass *just* might come out. Y'all feel me?"

"So you don't trust your husband around *any* single woman?"

That came floating over from her right.

Aria cocked an eyebrow. "I don't trust him around *anything* that pees sitting down."

Jaime coughed as if to clear her throat. "What about Jessa?" she asks slyly.

Aria tensed at the question. "What about her?"

"She's got tits and ass for days. How you know she's not fucking your man?" Jaime asked calmly.

Now watch me fix her ass, Aria thought as the hot stones were pressed deep into her lower back with just the right amount of firmness. "I guess the same way you know she ain't fucking yours," she said with equal calm.

Renee moaned in disapproval. "Ladies, Jessa Bell is our friend—our best friend—and she's not sleeping with *any* of our men."

Aria opened her eyes and playfully turned her nose up at Jaime who in turn winked. "Jessa knows better."

Jaime nodded. "I was just playing."

"Aaaaah . . ." Renee let out a long drawn out sigh of pleasure that was more erotic than therapeutic.

Aria whipped her head over to eye her friend. "You all right over there?" she asked with a teasing tone.

The masseuse's face remained stoic even as Renee began to giggle. "Girl, I'm *good*," she stressed with another soft smile.

Aria closed her eyes and tried to get focused on

the goodness of her massage. This spa day—which she knew would cost her close to a thousand dollars—was a long way from her days back in Newark. That was a time when shit like a manicure wasn't on the radar of things to spend money on. Food, rent, light bills, bus fare were the first, the last, and the only priorities.

The big-time career as a freelance writer, the big car, and the husband with the big bank and a big dick were all good, but sometimes she missed the heat and the unique beat of the hood. Sometimes, if she kept it real, Jaime and Renee were too white picket fence for her.

Aria felt out of place with the ladies' upper-middle-class upbringing and private-school educations. The same background as Jamal's. Sometimes, Aria felt like she wasn't good enough for her husband, his life, or his family and friends. Still, she made it her business not to embarrass him or remind him that she was just a poor kid on a full scholarship at Princeton with a caseload of Salvation Army clothes when they met. Aria knew that he loved her—or at least he loved what all he knew about her.

Once the massage drew to an end thirty minutes later and she rose from the table to don her robe, Aria caught a glimpse of her reflection in one of the mirrors on the wall. Her eyes were filled with the secrecy of her past.

"I am so ready for my coconut and sugar body scrub," Jaime said, as she swung her hair behind her back.

"Me too," Renee joined in as she stretched and then pulled her PDA from the pocket of her robe.

Aria barely heard them as she studied her reflection.

The thick and smooth texture of her trendy Rihanna asymmetrical cut.

The slender, almost African beauty of her dark-skinned face with its just-barely-there makeup.

She thought of the clothes awaiting her in the changing room. The hip and stylish dark Rock and Republic jeans paired with a bright red Biba ruffled shirt of sheer silk—an outfit that retailed for more than one year's rent in the low-income projects where she was raised.

She wondered how much of the woman she was today was Aria Livewell, the doctor's wife living up to her surname, or Aria Johnson, who was just a ghetto girl at heart?

Their spa treatments were over. They had been massaged, exfoliated, and bathed to perfection. The scent of the coconut milk used throughout each treatment still clung to their soft and supple skin. Now it was time for a light lunch at their favorite restaurant, the Terrace Room, to cap off their relaxing morning. Nothing went better with good friends and good food then damn good conversation. Renee was more than game.

"I'm worried about my marriage," she admitted softly into the silence surrounding their table. She checked her BlackBerry for the hundredth time. Her job meant being accessible at all times. A day off—even the weekend—was never really a day off for her . . . it was just a day out of the office.

As she slid the device back inside the leather case snapped to her crisp Ralph Lauren black linen pants, she looked up and felt pitied at the look in her friends' eyes. The truth was the truth and if she couldn't be honest with her friends, than who?

Renee had long since lost her mother to a massive heart attack. Her father now lived in Beverly Hills with his third wife and their ties were invisible. She would never lay her marital problems on her children and, well, Jackson was a part of the problem. So who did that leave? Her friends.

"He gave me that 'we need to talk' bullshit before he left this morning," she admitted.

Aria reached over and squeezed her hand, leaving the faint scent of Armani's Diamond perfume. "Maybe it's a talk to improve things. You always think the worst."

Renee raked her manicured fingers through her curls. "And you always see the glass half full."

Jaime flung her weave over her left shoulder as she settled back in her chair to eye them. "We've been saying for years that you should encourage Jackson to go to counseling with you to deal with his issues."

Renee ignored the PDA vibrating against her hip . . . again. For the first time in a long time, her focus was on her marriage. "I love him," she admitted fiercely. "I just don't understand the whole Ward Cleaver shit he's caught up in because I'm not June in the least. Well . . . not anymore."

As soon as she said the words, her eyes shifted to Jaime. "No offense to you and Jessa. I just love working."

Jaime just shrugged and waved her hand glibly. The diamonds on her bracelets flashed. "None taken."

Jaime was a diva and loved it.

Renee finally pulled her constantly vibrating BlackBerry from its case and looked down at the screen. "I have to take this call," she said, already rising to her full five-foot-ten height.

She made a striking picture as she weaved her way through the tables to reach the privacy of the restroom.

Renee actually sent the call from her assistant to her voice mail as she opened the mahogany wooden door of the ladies' room. It swung close behind her and she barely took in the warm plaid and floral French Country décor as she leaned her hip against the counter and crossed her arms over her chest.

Fuck it, she needed a moment. Facing the end of a marriage—*her* marriage—wasn't easy . . . especially when both of her friends had the picture-perfect life she used to have.

Renee wanted her marriage.

She wanted her husband.

But she also wanted her career and she couldn't have both. Period.

She gripped the edge of the counter. Her stomach felt like she swallowed sharpened nails.

"I love you, Jackson."

*"We need to talk. We **have** to talk."*

She tilted her head up and looked at herself in the mirror just as one lone tear raced down her cheek. She closed her eyes and released a breath heavy with her frustrations and fears.

Jackson wouldn't leave her. He'd better not.

She swiped away her tears and straightened her back while she studied her reflection in the mirror. The soft and curly tendrils of her inch-long hair fit her oval-shaped face, wide eyes, and full, pouty mouth. She never felt sexier . . . especially with her signature smoky eye makeup, extended lashes, and glossy lips.

Jackson didn't speak to her for a week after she first cut her long "good" hair. He used to love to play in it as she laid her head on his chest after steamy sex. But once she went back to work she caught all kinds of hell trying to manage it.

It had taken one hell of a freaky fuck fest to get him past the haircut drama.

She smiled naughtily at her reflection even as her eyes burned. A blow job and some handcuffs helped him right on down the road to forgiveness.

Would that type of "screw me 'til I'm sore" sex fix their problems now?

Renee walked into one of the wooden bathroom stalls. She made sure to flush the commode and then carefully wrap the seat with tissue before she dropped her pants and took a seat.

Her PDA vibrated and she remembered the call she had to return to her assistant, Kiena. She took the BlackBerry from its case. She frowned at the text message icon.

She was a grown-ass woman with teenagers and several e-mail accounts. She didn't mess around with the text message trend. To hell with trying to keep up with all those abbreviations. LOL. KIT. BFF. How about LMTFAWT—leave me the fuck alone with text.

Renee opened the message with her elbows braced on her thighs.

Life has many forks in the road and I've decided to travel down the path leading straight to your husband waiting on me with open arms—

"What the fuck?" Renee gasped. She continued to scroll down and read some more as her heart slammed against her chest.

I can't lie and say I have regrets. I love him more than you and I need him more so he is my man now. Trust, I will give him everything he needs and wants . . . only full time now. Thanks for not being woman enough 4 him.
    Smooches
    XOXOXO

Renee jumped to her feet and some of her pee ran down her thigh, wetting the rim of her pants. Her stomach felt like someone had gut-punched her. She clutched the BlackBerry with both hands as she read the message again.

And again.

And again.

And again.

"Oh . . . hell . . . no!" she shrieked, sounding more like Aria than herself.

She damn near dropped the BlackBerry into the commode as she snatched up her silk panties and her pants. She barely registered that she didn't wipe.

Jackson was cheating on her?

Couldn't be.

Shouldn't be.

"Motherfucker . . . it *better* not be." She left the stall even as she dialed Jackson's cell phone number. She knew it was a waste with the fishing boat deep in the middle of the sea, but she tried anyway.

It went straight to voice mail.

She took a deep breath as she willed herself not to fall to the floor and cry like a baby. Somehow she found the strength to open the door and make her way back to her girls. With each step, the text message seemed to mock her.

Leading straight to your husband's arms.

Boom.

I love him more than you.

Boom.

I need him more than you.

Boom.

He is my man.

Well, right now she needed her friends more than she needed Jackson. She nearly dropped into her seat as she roughly pushed her BlackBerry toward them atop the table. It hit against one of their glasses with a *ding*.

"How about some bitch just texted me that she's running away with Jackson?" Renee snapped as she drummed her neatly manicured fingers on top of the wooden table.

"Well, I'll be damned," Aria said in disbelief as she twirled Renee's phone to look down at the screen.

Renee looked from Aria to Jaime in question. Both women held up their own cell phones with the same exact message displayed.

"What?!" they cried in unison.

"Oh that's not the cherry on top of the sundae yet, baby," Jaime said with much attitude. "Check your message again to see who it's from. You're not going to believe this shit."

Renee swooped up the BlackBerry and worked her thumb to scroll to the top of the message. She gasped as she felt an angry fire begin to burn in her stomach.

Jessa Bell.

Best friends Alizé, Dom, Moët, and Cristal
encounter more ups and downs in
Show and Tell

Available now wherever books are sold

Prologue

Ladies

2000

The four teenage girls walked through the double doors of University High's cafeteria like they owned the school. They knew without looking that all eyes were on them. Hating them and hating on them. They were used to it and maybe even thrived on it a bit. Popularity. Envy. High school fame.

Even as they settled at "their" table and began munching on the sandwiches they purchased from the store up the street—of course the cafeteria food was a no-no—people watched them. Wanted to be them. Wanted to be with them. But it was just the four.

Friends since freshman year, they weren't looking to enlarge their clique. It was them and only them. One for all and all for one. Even though they all were as different as night and day, they clicked. They had each other's backs. They knew their friendship would last past their high school years.

"Did y'all see the new Biggie video last night?" Keesha Lands asked, in the Tommy Hilfiger tank she wore with tight-fitting jeans. Her gold herringbone chain and bamboo earrings gleamed against her smooth dark skin and seemed to glisten in her cat-shaped eyes.

"Not me," Latoya James said, looking prim and proper as always in her white collared shirt and ankle-length navy blue skirt with her shoulder-length hair pulled back into a tight ponytail that seemed to make her caramel complexion stretch.

Danielle Johnson rolled her deep-set eyes heavenward as she applied pale pink lip gloss that perfectly matched her fair complexion and pretty features. "My new foster family let their sickening sons watch *Nickelodeon* last night," she said, putting the gloss into her Esprit purse before taking a bite of food. She made sure not to spill a drop on her dark denim dress.

"Well, I'm an only child and my parents ain't churchy, so you know I was right there in front of the TV," Monica Winters said, flipping her thick shoulder-length jet black hair over her shoulder as she flashed them a sassy smile on her cinnamon face. She did a little dance in her seat and winked at Keesha.

Keesha started rapping the words to "Juicy" and the girls all joined in with her. Even Latoya knew the words, although her parents ran a secular music-free zone. Ever since pulling the shy church girl into their fold, the girls were sure to bring Latoya up to speed on everything fun and fly.

They all laughed and gave each other high fives after they finished.

"Well, I've decided to call myself Dom," Keesha stated with confidence.

"Dom?" the other girls all asked in unison.

"Yup, Dom as in Dom Perignon," she explained with attitude. She pointed to Latoya. "You're Moët . . . Danielle, you're Cristal—"

"What about me?" Monica asked, feeling left out.

"I don't know any more champagnes," Keesha said with a helpless shrug. "But Biggie's always talking about Alizé. I heard it's a real sweet drink with liquor in it."

"Then that's me to a tee," Monica said with satisfaction.

The four girls all raised their cans of soda and toasted their new names.

1

Cristal

*"Hello, this is Cristal again. I have my mind
on money and money on my mind."*

2008

Okay. Let me explain how I feel in my man's
arms—if it is at all explainable. I feel secure.
Loved. Cherished. Pampered. Needed. Perhaps most
important of all . . . I feel wanted. Growing up as a
foster kid and not knowing if my parents were dead,
alive, or indifferent, feeling wanted is important as
hell to me.

I am Cristal, or Danielle Johnson, and my man
is Mohammed Ahmed. He is tall, handsome, and
strong with cocoa-scented dreads that reach to his
waist. He is everything I ever needed and nothing
that I ever wanted.

Just *try* to make me leave him.

"Danielle," he whispers in my ear with that sexy
Jamaican lilt.

I shiver as he presses his warm naked body above
mine. My legs spread with ease as I wrap them

around his waist. His body and the bed sandwich me. The feel of his hard dick against my belly makes me anxious. Ready. Waiting.

As he bends his strong muscled back to lower his mouth—that delicious and skillful mouth—to my breast, he circles his tongue around my nipple. Clockwise. Counterclockwise. He uses his strong hips to prod the tip of his dick between my lips. We both gasp hotly. He circles his hips, pressing his hardness against my walls. Clockwise. Counterclockwise.

Jesus.

These moments in his arms and his bed are worth it all. Worth every damn thing I gave up for him. For this. Each stroke delivers my point home.

The money.

Pop.

The fame.

Pop-pop.

The fancy houses and cars.

Pop-pop-pop.

The glamorous life.

Pop-pop-pop-pop.

Mrs. Sahad Linx.

Pop-pop-pop-pop-pop-pop-pop.

All of it. Gone.

We are in tune with one another. United. Joined. He knows he is making me cum and that makes his dick harder than jail time. And that makes me cum even harder until I am panting. Sweating. Clutching him with my pussy walls and my limbs as he strokes harder and faster inside of me.

"Yes," I cry out as he leans up a bit to look down at me with those silky brown eyes I love.

His sweat drips down onto my titties as each of

his pumps makes them bounce up and down. "Dick good ain't it?" he asks roughly as his face gets intense. "Huh? Huh?"

"Yes, baby, yes," I whisper as I reach up to caress his handsome face with my quivering hands.

His head whips to the right to capture my fingers in his mouth. He sucks them deeply as he slows down his strokes to a lethal grind that brings the base of that dick against my clit.

Damn. Goddamn. Damn. Damn.

"Watch this, Miss Danielle," he says thickly around my fingers.

I already know what time it is.

His entire body freezes as he looks hotly down into my eyes. I feel the jolt of his dick against my clit as he fills me with his cum. He smiles as he licks my fingers like the freak that he is. Each pluck of my clit pushes me further over the edge until I am working my hips up and down off the bed to pull downward on *my* dick. His mouth forms a circle as he closes his eyes and pushes down deeper into me.

I reach up to snatch off the leather strap holding his hair and his dreads surround our heads like a curtain. "Who the best? Huh? Who?" I whisper up to him.

"Danielle . . . Danielle . . . Danielle," he chants as I drain that dick until it is empty.

With one final kiss to my lips, he rolls over onto his back and then pulls my weak body to his side. I gladly snuggle my face against his chest and take a deep breath of his scent like I can absorb it into me. With his free arm, he reaches over to turn off the lamp.

"Damn, that was good," he whispers into the darkness before he slaps my butt cheek playfully.

"I aim to please," I whisper back with a smile.

He laughs a little but soon his snores fill the air. Damn, I love him.

"Good morning, Miss Danielle."

I open my eyes and stretch. There he is just as constant as time looking down at me as he lays on his side on the bed. Okay, I love him but I do not do morning breath. Okay? All right.

I pull the thin sheet up over my nose. "Good morning."

Mohammed just laughs at me before he flings back the covers and rolls out of bed. "You have time for breakfast?" he asks over his broad shoulder.

I hardly hear him. I am too busy letting my eyes skim over the hard details of his back and buttocks. "No, I did not bring a change of clothes," I finally answer once he turns fully to look at me.

Mohammed reaches down to open a drawer. "What do we have here?" he says mockingly. "An empty drawer. What should we fill it with? Any suggestions, Danielle?"

I give him a sarcastic smile. First a drawer and then some of the closet and then pack up all your things and move in. Nothing doing. The last time I lived with a man he threw me out of his penthouse apartment. Well, he caught me cheating (ahem, *with* Mohammed) but that did not excuse the fact that if I had not kept my apartment for my friends, Dom and Moët, to live in, then my pretty high-yellow behind would have been homeless. To make matters worse, he kept mostly everything he ever bought me, even down to my lacy La Perla underwear.

No. I am nicely settled back in my beautiful apartment in The Top in Livingston. I have my best friends to help me keep up the hefty rent. Sure, I had to get used to the lack of quiet or privacy but it is *mine* and no one can throw me out.

Plus . . . Mohammed's house left *a lot* to be desired.

"One day, baby. One day," I promise as I roll out of bed.

I look at him and I know from the look on his face that he did not believe me. Truth. He is smart not to. I begin to climb back in the Gap charcoal gray turtleneck and pencil skirt I wore to our dinner date to IHOP last night. I wish I had a pair of sneakers to throw on instead of my suede high-heeled boots. As soon as I pull on my black leather trench, I walk over to where Mohammed is lounging across the foot of the bed watching a recap of some football game.

"Enjoy your day off," I tell him as I bend down to snuggle his cheek.

Mohammed is the repair man at The Top. My friends, Dom, Alizé, and Moët, still cannot believe I am with him. Not when my life used to be about men who helped keep me from my life of robbing Peter to pay Paul. Athletes. Celebrities. Wealthy businessmen. I had been on the hunt to be the ultimate celebrity wife. My ex-fiancé Sahad Linx is the CEO of Platinum Records. His money, his fame, and his lifestyle had almost been mine. I let it slip through my fingers like sand so that my hands were free to grab Mohammed.

He reaches across to lightly touch my face and I get chills. Fuck the money and the fame. I got love and lots of it.

"See you later?" he asks in that Jamaican accent that has the power to make me wet.

"Yes," I whisper against his lips.

Walking out of that bedroom and leaving my man in the bed naked, willing, and with his dick rising is almost as hard as he is. I try not to judge his house as I grab my hobo from the kitchen table. I can fit half of Mohammed's entire three-bedroom house inside my living room. It is furnished just like the bachelor he is. Mismatched this. Tore-up that. Wal-Mart this. Target that. Mohammed likes to say his house has character. Whatever.

I look inside my Gucci purse (a purchase from my more glamorous days) for my keys and my hand rubs across my "bible." Forgetting the keys, I pick up the address book. Inside is each and every man I have ever dated or slept with. For each man there is a brief bio and a photo, if I had one. I used dollar signs to rate how free giving they were with their money, and stars to rate how good they were in bed. The more dollar signs and stars the better.

But this book isn't me anymore. Since I have been with Mohammed I have not made an entry. I have not called one number. I have good friends. A good man. A good life.

I am happy. I am.

Then why do I still have it?

Ignoring the answer to that million-dollar question, I shove the address book down deep in my bag. I finally close my fingers around the keys before I rush out of the house.

ABOUT THE AUTHOR

Niobia Simone Bryant is the national best-selling and award-winning author of eight works of romance fiction. She splits her time between South Carolina and New Jersey and is busy on several upcoming projects including *Hot Like Fire*, the follow-up to *Heated; Show and Prove*, the follow-up to *Live and Learn*; and *Desperate Hood-wives*, her debut writing, gritty and sexy urban fiction as Meesha Mink (book cowritten with Christian Williams). She is also coediting two up-coming short story anthologies. For more on this author who "Can't stop, won't stop," check out her online presences:

E-mail: niobia_bryant@yahoo.com
The New Niobia Bryant Online:
www.niobiabryant.com
Niobia Bryant MySpace:
www.myspace.com/NiobiaWrites
Meesha Mink MySpace:
www.myspace.com/MeeshaMink